HER RUTHLESS DUKE

ROGUE'S GUILD
BOOK ONE

SCARLETT SCOTT

HEA
Happily Ever After Books

Her Ruthless Duke

Rogue's Guild Book One

All rights reserved.

Copyright © 2023 by Scarlett Scott

Published by Happily Ever After Books, LLC

Edited by Grace Bradley

Developmental Editing by Emerald Edits

Cover Design by EDH Professionals

This book or any portion thereof may not be reproduced or used in any manner whatsoever without the express written permission of the publisher except for the use of brief quotations in a book review.

The unauthorized reproduction or distribution of this copyrighted work is illegal. No part of this book may be scanned, uploaded, or distributed via the Internet or any other means, electronic or print, without the publisher's permission. Criminal copyright infringement, including infringement without monetary gain, is punishable by law.

This book is a work of fiction and any resemblance to persons, living or dead, or places, events, or locales, is purely coincidental. The characters are productions of the author's imagination and used fictitiously.

For more information, contact author Scarlett Scott.

https://scarlettscottauthor.com

For my family, with much love

CHAPTER 1

Trevor William Hunt, sixth Duke of Ridgely, Marquess of Northrop, Baron Grantworth, glared at the menace who had invaded his home, doing his utmost not to take note of the tempting ankles peeping from beneath the hems of her gown and petticoats. A damned difficult task indeed when the menace in question loomed above him from the top rung of the ladder in his library. There was nowhere to look but up her skirts.

In his time as a spy working for the Guild, reporting directly to Whitehall, he'd faced fearsome enemies and would-be assassins. He'd been shot at, stabbed, and nearly trampled by a carriage. But all that rather paled in comparison to the full force of Lady Virtue Walcot, daughter of his late friend the Marquess of Pemberton, Trevor's unexpected and unwanted ward, and minion of Beelzebub sent fresh from Hades to destroy him.

"Come down before you break your neck, infant," he ordered her.

He hadn't a conscience, but he had no intention of beginning his day by witnessing the chit tumbling to her doom. He had yet to take his breakfast, after all.

"I am not an infant," she announced, defiance making her tone sharp as a whip from her lofty perch.

The minx hadn't even bothered to cast a glance in his direction for her response.

No, indeed. Instead, she continued thumbing through the dusty tomes lining the shelves overhead, relics from the fifth Duke of Ridgely. Likely, the duke had wanted to impress his mistress of the moment. Trevor strongly doubted his sire had ever read a word on their pages. *Hmm.* When he had an opportunity, he'd do away with the lot of them. He'd quite forgotten they were there.

"Child, then," he allowed, crossing his arms over his chest and keeping his gaze studiously trained on the shelves instead of the tempting curve of her rump overhead. "For a woman fully grown would never go climbing about in her guardian's library, putting her welfare in peril."

"She would if she were looking for something to occupy her mind, aside from the tedium her guardian has arranged for her."

Lady Virtue was, no doubt, referring to the social whirlwind he had arranged with the help of his sister, all in the name of seeing the vexing chit wedded, etcetera, and blessedly out of his life.

"Ladies love balls," he countered, uncrossing his arms and settling his hands on his hips instead.

Lady Virtue made him itchy. Whenever she was within arm's reach, he found himself wanting to touch her, which made absolutely no sense, given that she was an innocent, and he didn't bloody well *like* the chit.

"Not this lady," she called from above.

Trevor was certain she was disagreeing with him merely

for the sport of quarreling. "Ladies adore those terribly boring affairs with musicians."

"Musicales, you mean?" She sniffed. "I despise them."

"A tragedy, that," he quipped. "In order for you to find yourself happily married, you need to attend society events."

Another disdainful sniff floated down from above. "I have no wish to be married, happily or otherwise."

So she had claimed on numerous occasions. Lady Virtue Walcot was as outspoken as she was maddening. But she remained his burden for the year until she reached her majority and was no longer his ward. Those twelve months loomed before him like a bloody eternity. The only respite would be in finding her a husband, which he intended for his sister to do. Clearly, Pamela was going to have to work harder at her task.

When Lady Virtue married, she would still remain his ward, but her unsuspecting spouse could at least be burdened with keeping her out of trouble, and Trevor could carry on with life as he wished.

He caught another glimpse of Lady Virtue's ankles and then cursed himself as his cock leapt to attention. He'd always had a weakness for a woman's legs. Too damned bad these delicious limbs belonged to *her*.

He cleared his throat. "You'll change your mind."

"I won't." She pulled a book from the shelf. "*The Tale of Love.*"

Oh, Christ. He knew the title. Knew the contents within. Despicably bawdy, that book. Decidedly not the sort of tome she ought to be reading. If anyone corrupted her, it wasn't going to be Trevor.

Unfortunately.

"That's not for the eyes of innocent lambs," he said. "Put it back on the shelf."

"I never claimed to be an innocent lamb." The unmistakable sound of her turning the pages reached him. "Why, it's an epistolary. There can hardly be any harm in that, can there?"

He ground his molars and glared at the spines of books before him, surrendering to the need to touch something and settling on the ladder. At least it wouldn't go tumbling over with him acting as anchor.

"Don't read it, infant," he called curtly. "That is a command."

"I'm not that much younger than you are, you know." More page turning sounded above. "*Oh*! Good heavens…"

"Saint's teeth, I told you not to read the book." He gripped the ladder so tightly, he feared it would snap in two. "If you don't get down here this moment, I'll have no choice but to come after you and bring you down myself."

"Don't be silly. The two of us will never fit on this ladder, and your head would be nearly up my skirts."

Yes, precisely.

And he wouldn't hate it, either.

"Down, or I go up," he countered grimly. "You have until the count of five. One, two, three—"

"You are not going to climb this ladder, Ridgely," she interrupted.

"Four," he continued grimly. Because he bloody well *was*. She couldn't read that damned book. And not just because the notion of Lady Virtue consuming the indecorous smut within its pages made him hard. "Five."

Gripping the ladder in both hands, he settled his right foot on the lowest rung and commenced his ascent.

A gasp sounded from above. "Stay where you are!"

Another rung, and the hem of her gown brushed the top of his head.

Don't look up, you scoundrel, he warned himself. *Do not look up.*

He swallowed against a rush of forbidden desire. "I don't take orders from babes."

"You'll send us both crashing to the floor."

The ordinarily unruffled Lady Virtue sounded a bit worried. Not without reason. Trevor advanced another rung and the ladder shifted precariously. Ah, the irony. Years of facing dangerous villains yet surviving, and mere weeks of having her as his ward would prove his untimely end.

To his inner sinner's disappointment, his head didn't land up her petticoats. Instead, he gripped the ladder on either side of her knees, a frothy confection of jaconet muslin and scalloped flounce keeping him from the previous, glorious view of luscious ankles and pink kid slippers on dainty feet.

"We haven't crashed yet, have we?" Trevor asked triumphantly, even as he felt the ladder shift a bit more. "Now give me the blasted book."

She partially turned on the ladder, twisting about so that she faced him. The movement didn't do anything to enhance their stability.

He jerked his gaze upward, past the tempting curve of her breasts, lovingly delineated beneath the clinging, pale fabric. Up the creamy hint of her throat visible above her gown's demure neckline. All the way to her face. And, as always when he looked upon her, the full effect of her beauty hit him like a blow to the bread-basket.

Lady Virtue was despicably lovely. Lustrous mahogany hair, warm brown eyes sparkling with intelligence and fringed with long lashes. A dainty nose, aristocratic cheekbones, a defiant tilt to her chin, and a mouth that was full, lush, and just begging to be kissed. But it was the way she carried herself that made her irresistible—proud, stubborn, and utterly saucy.

If she'd been a widow or an unhappy wife or any other female with whom a dalliance was possible, he'd have bedded her in an instant. But she was his ward, and she was also the bane of his existence, so he had to make a daily effort to restrain his inconvenient lust.

Whenever her lips were moving, he found it aided him greatly in this task.

Such as now.

"If you don't go back down the ladder, I'll have no choice but to kick you," the minx declared, holding the book in her hand aloft and beyond his reach.

He moved up another rung, bringing his face in line with her waist. Which meant that if she followed through with her threat, one of those delicate pink slippers would land directly in the fall of his trousers. It would undoubtedly go a long way toward quelling his unwanted desire, but he wasn't in the mood to be made a eunuch today.

"If you kick me, there will be consequences," he growled. "Such as no books."

Lady Virtue perpetually had a book in hand everywhere she went. Sometimes two. He found them everywhere, scattered about like little crumbs showing him where she'd been. His carriage, his drawing room, the breakfast table, the library divan, the garden.

There was no greater punishment than denying her reading fodder.

Her gaze narrowed. "That would be cruel of you."

He raised a brow. "Have I ever claimed to be a kind man?"

They both knew he hadn't. Because he wasn't. He was bad. Unlikable. Irredeemable. A rogue, through and through.

The ladder shifted again.

"Ridgely!" Her eyes went wide.

He extended a hand, palm up, and wiggled his fingers. "The book."

She pressed it to her heart, as if protecting the tome from him. "No."

The chit's tenacity was most vexing.

He could easily pluck *The Tale of Love* from her. However, a quick motion and a resulting struggle would likely end with the both of them on the floor. And not in the fashion he'd caught himself contemplating on numerous occasions since she had made her first appearance in his life, either. It was too early in the morning for broken bones.

It was time to exercise the cunning that had rendered him such an efficient spy.

Nonchalantly, Trevor flicked his gaze past her to the wall of books beyond and heaved a feigned sigh. "Well, if you must, I reckon there's no stopping you from reading it. At least you didn't find the volume of *Love Letters from a Courtesan*."

As he predicted, her curiosity got the better of her. When she followed his gaze to where the bawdy book he'd just invented was presumably housed, he struck with the agility of a snake, snatching *The Tale of Love* from her loosened grasp with ease. He slid it safely inside his coat and made great haste with his descent, triumphant.

"You wretch," she accused from above. "You distracted me so that you could steal the book."

"A man cannot steal his own property, my dear." Feeling uncharacteristically gentlemanly, he held the ladder for her as she stormed down.

"The book is yours, then? I ought to have known."

He made the mistake of glancing up in time to catch a glimpse of beauteous thighs above pink garters. Lord above, her underpinnings matched her slippers and the ribbon embellishment on her gown. A perfect pale rose, like her lips.

He jerked his gaze away.

This particular copy of *The Tale of Love* wasn't his. He had his own copy. Which meant that it had either belonged to his inglorious predecessor or one of Father's many mistresses.

Certainly, it hadn't belonged to his late brothers, Bartholomew and Matthew, who had both been as meek and mild as a pair of mice. Regardless, Trevor didn't care to contemplate the volume's origin.

"Everything in this house is mine," he told her instead of answering her question directly.

Or his responsibility. Being a duke came with a great deal of that, much to his everlasting dismay. And a ward atop it all. Bartholomew, or even Matthew, would have been far more suited to the role of duke and guardian. Christ knew his brothers would never have dreamed of daring a glimpse up anyone's gown, let alone a ward's.

But then, Bartholomew and Matthew had both been good chaps. He missed his brothers. Couldn't always shake the feeling he was an usurper. Trevor had been the scoundrel to counterweight so much decency. It had always been Father's favorite sons versus the reviled third son, who had never proven himself to possess any talent worthy of the duke's note. *A vile disappointment*, so the duke had told him, and often. Until Trevor had simply ceased speaking with the old blackguard. He'd never wanted the title, it was true, nor the dreaded weight of responsibilities accompanying it. Life had been so much less complex when he had been the third son, no expectations made of him.

"How thrilling it must be to be in possession of one's own home," Lady Virtue said as she alighted on the Axminster, taking a step closer to Trevor, finger pointing in the air as if to punctuate her point. "And one's own library of books." Another step. "And one's own funds." Another, until her finger landed on his chest, giving him a sturdy poke. "And one's own *future*."

Her tone was quite scathing as she reached the last portion of her diatribe. She stood so close, slippers toe to toe with him. He suddenly became aware of all the tiny flecks of color in her rich, brown gaze and a hint of freckles dappling the bridge of her nose.

He couldn't blame her for resenting her precarious position as a young lady alone in the world, with an as-yet unsettled dowry to recommend her and no true means of making her own decisions until she reached her majority or married.

And after she found herself wedded, she'd still have no decision-making power of her own. But Trevor wasn't going to allow that notion to haunt him or foster even a modicum of regret. Because he needed to be rid of the troublesome baggage.

Yesterday.

He hadn't asked for a ward. *Jesus*, hadn't Pemberton realized the old devil-you-know proverb was nothing more than a lot of rot?

It would seem not, for the marquess's lovely daughter was standing within Trevor's reach in his library. An innocent entrusted to his dubious care. And he was living proof that the devil you know is still just a devil, in the end.

Trevor took a much-needed step in retreat, putting a safer distance between them.

"The world isn't fair, infant," he told her, gentling his tone to take the sting from his words. The endearment was one he used with her often, a verbal reminder to himself that she was his ward. *Forbidden.* Ten years younger than he was. Far more innocent. "The sooner you realize that, the better off you shall be."

"I don't need a man to tell me that," she snapped. "Especially not a duke who hasn't a care in the world and who insists upon forcing me into a marriage I do not want."

Her barbs had found their mark, but he ignored them. He didn't want the encumbrance of this pink-bedecked virgin with the tempting mouth and body of a seductress. His fingers were itching to touch her again, and his vexing cock refused to stand down. He *couldn't* touch her. She was Pemberton's daughter. His ward.

"I've been tasked with seeing you happy as your father wished," he reminded her, clasping his hands behind his back to keep them occupied. "To that end, have you breakfasted? Lady Deering is taking you shopping today, I believe."

He had no notion of what his sister had planned for Lady Virtue, other than that she was taking the chit away for the day. He strived his utmost to keep from knowing what was happening or when or where. The less he knew, the less his ward invaded his thoughts. Which was how he preferred it.

"I breakfasted long ago," Lady Virtue informed him.

And that was another irritating quality she possessed— the innate ability to rise early. She was up and roaming the halls of Hunt House long before him every morning. Hence her current foray into his library. It was akin to harboring a band of enemy soldiers in his midst.

Only worse, because he wouldn't be tempted to shag the enemy soldiers.

"Lovely, then." He forced a smile. "Why don't you go about doing something more constructive than pilfering my library before my sister relieves me of my unfortunate duties?"

Lady Virtue breezed past him, her seductive floral scent trailing after her. "Perhaps I'll go for a ride on Rotten Row," she called over her shoulder, apparently having decided he was dismissed.

Gritting his teeth, he stalked after her as she crossed the library. "It isn't the fashionable hour. Only grooms will be about at this time of the morning, and that decidedly isn't the place for a lady trying to ensnare a husband."

"Fortunately, I have no intention of *ensnaring* a husband." She stopped and whirled about, facing him once more. She wasn't wearing a cap, and the sight of her tresses loosely pinned in a chignon was its own temptation. "Good heavens, Ridgely. You make the process sound like a hunter capturing a hare for his dinner."

He raised a brow. "And how is it not? A husband, when caught, is often spit-roasted over the miserable flame that is otherwise known as marriage, much like his counterpart the rabbit. The hare rather has the better bargain, if you ask me. One is eaten for dinner whilst the other is slowly tortured, over the period of his lifetime."

She pursed her lips. "Quite a grim sentiment from a man determined to see me unwillingly imprisoned in such a situation."

"You possess the dramatics of an actress," he drawled, keeping his expression a mask of indifference.

"I reckon if anyone should know, it would be you," she returned saucily. "Likely having bedded half the actresses in London."

The daring of Lady Virtue Walcot never failed to astound him.

"Ladies do not refer to such indelicate matters," he scolded sharply.

Good God, if the minx went about speaking so brazenly in conversations, she would never secure a husband. And quite likely that was her intention.

She shrugged. "Perhaps I'm not a lady."

Curse Pemberton for dying and saddling Trevor with his spawn.

"You *are* a lady, and you'll conduct yourself as one," he gritted, "or I will see all the books hauled from this bloody house and burned."

Her nostrils flared. "You wouldn't dare!"

"You didn't think I'd climb the ladder either. Try me, my dear."

They glared at each other in silence, waging a battle of obstinacy.

Whatever she saw in his eyes apparently persuaded her to relent, because she sighed, some of the fight fleeing her figure. "Very well. I shan't go riding. I'll find something else to occupy me until Lady Deering is ready."

With a curtsy that somehow felt like a rebuke, Lady Virtue turned and swept from the library with the majesty to rival any queen. Trevor watched her departing form, too afraid to wonder just what that *something* could be. The less he knew, the better.

Pamela couldn't see the girl married off soon enough. His duties would not be entirely absolved, but at least she would be beneath her husband's roof where she belonged instead of tempting him here. He'd have to speak with his sister. Frowning, Ridgely went off in search of his breakfast.

CHAPTER 2

Virtue pressed her head against the cool floor-to-ceiling window which overlooked Grosvenor Square and heaved a frustrated sigh, clouding the pane before her. The stately street in the distance below was obscured for a moment, which was just as well, for she had no wish to see the passing barouches and curricles conveying the *beau monde's* most fashionable lords and ladies to their destinations. Not any more than she wished to be here, awaiting an audience with the Duke of Ridgely.

Nor any more than she had wanted to be in London itself.

Ever since the discovery she was to be packed up like a piece of unused furniture and bundled off to the city and her new guardian, the Duke of Ridgely, her every day had been awash with dread and the fear that the life she had intended for herself might be forever beyond her reach.

A whirlwind had inevitably followed that bleak news. There had been the onerous travel from her haven at Greycote Abbey after a suitable period of mourning. Then meeting the duke for the first time—how startled she'd been to find him young and almost disturbingly handsome. Notoriously wicked too, as she'd quickly learn.

Then the subsequent and, she now reckoned, obligatory parade to a sea of society soirees, chaperoned by his sister. All the better to marry her off. Her fate in life, it seemed, was to be wanted by nobody, forgotten or ignored, passed along from one person's care to the next. At every moment, Virtue was reminded that she must choose a husband, as it was what her father would have wished for her.

"Lord Pemberton would want to see you settled," Ridgely had claimed at their first meeting.

As if her father had cared what she had done with her past or present when he'd been alive, let alone her future now that he was gone.

Indeed, the Marquess of Pemberton may have engaged in the requisite bedding to beget her, but he had thereafter done his utmost to forget her existence. Virtue's mother had died of childbed fever. Virtue's father had chosen to pretend she had never been born. Until he had inexplicably made the decision to entrust her future to the whims of the Duke of Ridgely.

"But of course you must find a husband," Lady Deering insisted over every objection Virtue issued to the contrary.

It was often accompanied by a raised brow and stern expression of disapproval as her ladyship proclaimed, *"Every unmarried lady wishes to wed."*

"Not every unmarried lady," Virtue muttered to herself, her breath dancing over the window and creating more fog.

Quite likely, it was not well done of her to smear His Grace's otherwise spotless windows. She had no doubt she'd leave a mark. But she was rather in a dismal mood, for Ridgely had discovered the day before that she had been sneaking into the mews and indulging in early-morning rides without a groom when he had expressly forbidden it.

Virtue's chaperone possessed an indefatigable constitution when it came to spending her brother's coin. The lady had been entirely unwearied by hours spent in the finest shops, ordering gowns and millinery and slippers. Lady Deering had taken her to task as they had gone on another dizzying shopping trip that had left Virtue with an aching head and acute longing to return to her garden at Greycote Abbey. A warning had been issued. *"His Grace will have an interview with you on the morrow,"* Lady Deering had pronounced.

Apparently, one of His Grace's grooms had seen Virtue yesterday morning when she had returned with Hera, and the enterprising fellow had gone directly to the duke. The duke's pressing engagements—more than likely a romp with one of his ladybirds, Virtue thought grimly—had meant that he could not take her to task until a full day later. And which also had meant that she'd spent the night in a fitful state, tossing and turning in her bed, unable to sleep for wondering what punishment Ridgely would mete out.

He had threatened her before. They had matched wits before. But she had never previously defied him so brazenly. She'd been more than aware of the risk she'd taken. However, it had been worth it for the exercise, the chill air, the blissful solitude of Hyde Park devoid of its preening lords and ladies, the chance to ride such an excellent horse.

Still, she had no notion of what to expect. The duke had certainly never summoned her to him before, then forced her to wait in the hall until he was ready to see her. She had no mantel clock to consult for the time, but Virtue would wager that at least half an hour had passed whilst she had paced the hall before finally surrendering and crossing to the temptation of the massive windows. The cool of the glass was calming in much the same sense that taking the air and defying Ridgely was.

She would continue to circumvent his plans for her at every turn.

Anything to escape the future he intended for her.

The click of a door and the sound of footsteps approaching told her that her ruminations were at an end.

She turned away from the window to find Mr. Spencer, Ridgely's secretary, with his customary stern expression. He was all sharp angles and weathered planes, his hair powdered in a fashion even Virtue recognized as outmoded. Quite a wonder how a man as serious as he could find himself at the behest of an unscrupulous rake such as the duke.

"Lady Virtue." Mr. Spencer offered a solemn bow. "His Grace will see you now."

She inclined her head in acknowledgment. "Thank you, Mr. Spencer."

Virtue crossed the hall to the door which had been left ajar in anticipation of her entry. She had a moment to collect herself in preparation—being alone with Ridgely never failed to affect her, despite her dislike of him—and then she was over the threshold, in the lair of the devil himself.

Ridgely stood at the fireplace, his back to her, his attention centered upon something on the mantel which was obscured by his broad shoulders. She found herself grateful for the additional respite from the force of his magnetism. He may have been a cynical ne'er-do-well who didn't have a care what happened to her or what she wanted for her own future, and she may dislike him strongly, but not even Virtue could deny his stark masculine beauty. Looking upon him always created an initial shock, quite as if she had inadvertently touched a hot surface, her breath arresting in her lungs, until the ferocity of her reaction subsided.

He was tall, broad, and strong, with a body that belied the profligate lifestyle he was rumored to lead. Since she had first learned Ridgely, a man previously unknown to her, was to be her guardian, she had read every scrap of gossip about him. His exploits were well-known and widely written about, particularly in the pages of *Tales About Town*.

And yet, curse her wandering gaze, for it traveled down his firm posterior. In the absence of a coat, his bottom was on full display in his well-fitted buff trousers, as were his long legs and muscled horseman's thighs. There was something sinfully intimate about his informal dress, his arms encased in a white shirt beneath a striped piqué waistcoat.

Cease gawking at him, she ordered herself firmly. *You do not even like the man.*

Virtue cleared her throat to indicate her presence. "You required an audience with me, Your Grace."

"Mmm," he said, his voice a low, pleasant rumble that sent awareness sliding over her like warm honey. "I did indeed, infant."

Infant.

How she loathed his casual insistence upon reminding her that she was younger than he. A mere babe of only twenty to his superior and advanced thirty. Ten years was not a vast chasm of time in her estimation.

And still, he had not deigned to face her in the customary fashion, toying with whatever it was upon the mantel that so distracted him, his hands out of view.

She chose to ignore his rudeness and the unwanted sobriquet both, straightening her shoulders and preparing for yet another clash. "If you intend to punish me, you needn't delay."

"Punish you, yes." Again, the timbre of his voice, coupled with the innuendo laced through those words, filled her with heat. "I do intend to do so, but the question remains how?"

Virtue pressed her lips together, telling herself it mattered not what he chose. For there would be no fate worse than marriage.

"I eagerly await your decision, Your Grace," she told him dryly.

"Eagerly, do you?"

There was amusement in his voice now, but it was dark levity.

The Duke of Ridgely's sense of humor was perverse, his words and actions often cryptic. After all this time in his home, she should have unraveled some of the mystery enshrouding him, and yet she had not.

"Quite," she responded, not afraid to battle him however she must. "Will you tell me, or am I left to wonder?"

Preserving Greycote Abbey was her primary objective. The estate and its people were the only family she had ever known. But because of the provisions in her father's will, the property, which her mother had brought to the marriage long ago, was to be sold at the discretion of her guardian, the funds to be used for her dowry.

The answer to her troubles was quite simple: if she did not marry, she had no need of a dowry. And if she did not require a dowry, neither was there cause for her to wed. Hence, there was absolutely no need to sell her family's estate. She had reasons aplenty why she wished to remain unmarried, but Greycote Abbey was chief among them. All she needed to do was persuade the stubborn duke that it was in her best interest to allow her to keep the estate and remain unmarried until she reached one-and-twenty, at which time he would be absolved of his guardian's duties. She could have the future she had always wanted for herself, happily continue running the estate and tending to her people, and collecting the books and papers which brought her happiness.

How better to persuade him that allowing her to return to the countryside rather than enduring a year of her as his ward was in the best interest of them both, aside from causing Ridgely as much trouble as possible? In Virtue's estimation, there was none.

"Perhaps there is something *you* might tell *me* instead," he drawled, pulling her from her thoughts as he finally turned about to face her.

Virtue could not contain her gasp as she took in the swollen, red-purple bruise marring his forehead. "Good heavens, what has happened to you?"

He flashed her an ironic half grin. "What, no clever quips about irate husbands this morning?"

Yes, she had often needled him with the worst of his reputation, it was true. All as part of her carefully constructed plan to force him to allow her return to Greycote Abbey. Not that her taunts were undeserved. However, she did not relish the sight of such an egregious injury to his person.

"None." She drew nearer, inexplicable worry tightening her stomach into a knot. "Have you seen a doctor?"

He raised a brow and then winced, as the old habit must have caused him pain. "Concerned for my welfare, o ye sharp-tongued ward?"

Yes, not that he deserved it. Particularly if it had been an angry cuckolded husband who had delivered the blow. And yet, it did not sit well with her.

She stopped near the hearth, settling her hands on the back of a chair. "I do not take pleasure in someone having done you violence."

It occurred to her then, the reason he had taken his time in facing her. He had been reluctant to show her the extent of his injury. Why? Was he embarrassed? Was it vanity, perhaps?

He pressed a hand to his heart. "I am singularly uplifted by your tender feelings."

His sardonic expression suggested the opposite.

They stared at one another in charged silence. His scent—the delightful blend of leather and musk with a hint of citrus—reached her. Despite the ugliness of the lump on his head, he was as alluring as ever. Little wonder he was rumored to have bedded half the women in London.

She forced a pleasant smile. "And I am happy to have been the source of your uplifting."

"You often are," he said.

A rather confusing remark, and she didn't know what to make of it. For certainly, there was no double entendre. Was there?

Her smile felt suddenly tight and uncomfortable. "How pleased I am to know it."

His lips quirked. "I shouldn't think you would be if you understood the full implications, my dear. But that is neither here nor there, is it? I haven't brought you here to discuss my unfortunate collision with a footpad last night. Rather, I've brought you here to discuss your insolence."

At last, the reason for their audience.

"Forgive me, Your Grace," she began with a gusty sigh. "You see, I am not familiar with London life. At Greycote Abbey, we may take the air whenever we wish."

He waved a hand at their sumptuous surroundings. "If you have failed to take note, you are no longer at that moldering pile of rocks but are instead here in the bastion of polite society."

The room in which they stood was, quite undeniably, a great deal more elegantly appointed than all of Greycote Abbey combined. However, it was not handsome furniture that made a home.

"I am disastrously bereft of Town bronze," she said. "If you wish to send me back to Nottinghamshire, I understand. My actions have not been a credit to either yourself or to

Lady Deering. I would hate to further soil your reputation or to negatively affect your sister."

The last was true. Lady Deering was kindhearted, despite her affinity for shopping and insistence that every lady must certainly yearn for a husband.

"There is nothing for you in Nottinghamshire now," the duke said smoothly.

Nothing for her in Nottinghamshire? Everything and everyone she loved was there.

Virtue gripped the chair's back so tightly that her knuckles ached with the strain. "Greycote Abbey is there."

"A failing estate," he countered. "And a failing estate which is being sold, in accordance with your father's will."

She had argued with the duke before, always careful to keep from revealing the full extent of her interest. Ridgely was cunning and shrewd, and she had no notion of whether he would use the intensity of her feelings against her.

"Is not the intent of its sale to provide me with a dowry?" she probed. "As I have no intention of marrying, there is no need for a dowry, and therefore the sale of Greycote Abbey is not required."

"I am obliged to follow your father's will," Ridgely said, frowning. "We've discussed this before. The estate's income is hardly what it should be, given its size."

"Mr. Leonard has been mismanaging it badly for the last decade or more," she defended. "Lord Pemberton chose to ignore every letter I sent him imploring change, and my hands were tied. However, if I am allowed to oversee the estate, I am reasonably certain I can produce an increase—"

"You'll not be allowed to oversee it," Ridgely interrupted, "as it is being sold forthwith."

Sold.

The landscape of her youth, forever lost to her in

exchange for a small sum that could not possibly hold a candle to the people and place she loved. Gone. Forever.

The very notion made something inside her, some part of her she had not realized was hopelessly fragile and delicate, crack open. It felt like a death, a loss beyond compare. And to think she had no control over it, that her home should be sold at the behest of the father who had never loved her, carried out by a man she scarcely knew… It was devastating.

She longed to throw something at the Duke of Ridgely's head.

"It need not be sold," she tried again, trying to maintain her calm. "My father's will stipulates that the estate be sold to fund my dowry. However, there is no need for a dowry as I shan't be marrying."

"You *shall* be marrying, and soon." He stalked toward her, hands clasped behind his back, cutting a fearsome figure with the bold way he carried himself. Rather in the fashion of a great general guiding his troops to victory. "If you think I'll endure playing guardian to a spoiled lamb for the next year, you're as featherheaded as your recent behavior suggests."

"If you truly wish to be rid of me, why not send me to Nottinghamshire now as punishment?" she offered with feigned meekness.

His eyes narrowed. "Ah, that's your game then, is it not?"

"Game?" She pretended confusion. "I am afraid I haven't one. I am merely seeking to atone for my rash actions yesterday morning."

He had paused before the chair, which stood between them as sole barrier, his dark, glittering gaze far too intelligent for her liking as it searched hers for answers she didn't want to give. "Do you truly expect me to believe you only went riding on your own yesterday morning?"

Far too intelligent indeed. She wondered what hidden

depths lay behind his rake's façade. Was it possible that there was more to him than the conscienceless seducer he portrayed to the world?

For some reason, Virtue did not like the thought. It was far easier—and preferable—to think him despicable. After all, this was the man who was insistent upon stealing her independence from her.

"I have been riding each morning whenever the weather has permitted," she allowed, hoping the revelation would serve to heighten his frustration with her.

You see, she wanted to shout. *I am trouble! Return me to my home and in a year's time, you shall be freed of me, and I shall be equally freed of you.*

"No more riding alone at six o'clock in the morning, infant," he said sternly.

"I am sorry for the potential scandal I could have caused," she offered. "However, surely you must see I am not at home here. I do not belong in London."

"It isn't the scandal that concerns me. It's your wellbeing. The city is dangerous. Christ, when I think of what could have happened to a babe like you, wandering about without protection…"

Ridgely allowed his words to trail away, shaking his head, his jaw tensed.

Impossible to believe that he cared if anything ill should befall her.

"I'm not a babe," she countered. "Nor am I a missish society lady who cannot tend to herself."

She could outride anyone, especially on a mare such as Hera. Of that, she had no doubt. And in a particularly difficult circumstance, she knew how to punch, kick, and bite, and where best to land a blow on a man to cause maximum injury.

"No more riding alone in the morning," he repeated,

ignoring her protestation quite as if it had never been spoken. "I'll have your promise."

"Ridgely, please listen to reason—"

"Your promise," he bit out, interrupting her. "Now."

"No more riding alone in the morning," she offered, frowning at him before adding, "in London."

"Anywhere," he growled. "At least until you are married, because thereafter, you'll be your husband's problem, and good luck to his sorry hide."

"Very well," she allowed, for she had no intention of either honoring her promise or marrying. "Anywhere."

He nodded. "Good girl. As for your punishment, I'm afraid it must be the books."

Books? Not books. Surely Ridgely was not mad enough to go through with the threat he had issued in the library when he had denied her *The Book of Love*. Her books were all she had in London. All she had left of herself, now that she'd been torn from Greycote Abbey.

"You'll not burn them," she said.

"Not yet, but neither shall you be reading them," he returned, a note of triumph in his voice. "You are to gather all the books you've pilfered from my library, along with any others in your possession, and deliver them to me here in one hour's time. If you can behave yourself for a fortnight, they'll be returned to you. You are also barred from entering my library for the next two weeks."

"*All* the books," Virtue repeated, aghast. "For a fortnight? But I have some rare and important volumes in my possession."

The sole benefit of being in London, it was true. Lady Deering had been willing to take her to some fine book shops, the likes of which Virtue had never previously dreamt of, let alone seen. Oh, the knowledge waiting at her fingertips. It had been astounding. She'd spent all her pin money at once. But with the nonsensical balls and suppers and calls, she hadn't had sufficient time to consume them as she would have preferred. And now the duke meant to *take* them?

"Especially the rare and important ones," Ridgely said, his tone absolutely diabolical.

It was as if he were enjoying himself at her expense. Immensely so.

She released the chair at last and crossed her arms, not caring if the gesture was unladylike or argumentative. "They are mine, and you cannot have them."

He smiled, so handsome and vexing and *horrid* that it almost hurt to look at him. "*You* are mine until you turn one-and-twenty or marry some blockheaded fool mad enough to have you as his wife. And it is my duty to keep you safe for said blockhead, a feat which cannot be achieved if you persist in gadding about London unchaperoned in the midst of the night."

The early-morning hours had hardly been the midst of the night. Also, she resented his intimation that only a blockheaded lunatic would want to marry her. But the books—*her books*—concerned her chiefly in that moment.

"What does keeping me safe have to do with stealing my books?" she demanded, outraged and aghast and frustrated all at once.

He cocked his head at her, giving her a pitying look. "That's the punishment, my dear. Unless it hurts, you'll keep doing stupid things. Now, run along like a good little ward and gather up those books."

She struggled to maintain her composure at his condescension, gritting her teeth in restraint as she swallowed down her anger. That settled the matter quite firmly, if there had ever been the slightest hint of question in Virtue's mind. The Duke of Ridgely was utterly, irredeemably, despicable.

She dipped into as mocking a curtsy as she could manage.

"As you wish, Your Grace," she said, her words brittle.

But she intended to make him pay richly for his chosen punishment.

To make him pay until he surrendered and sent her back home to Greycote Abbey where she belonged.

CHAPTER 3

His termagant ward hadn't given him all the books in her possession.

Trevor knew it like he knew some bastard had hit him with a bludgeon the evening before when he had been leaving The Velvet Slipper. The very notion of falling prey to an aspirant thief, *him*. A man who had faced the deadliest foes without flinching, and who had never been bested. Former spy and pride of Whitehall.

Yes, him. Robbed and left for dead in a darkened alley.

Thank Christ his coachman had dragged him into the landau and brought him home before he'd been run over by a carriage or some equally terrible fate. The fault for his predicament was, of course, his preoccupation with Lady Virtue.

He'd been thinking of *her* when the villain had struck. Thinking of how he might solve the problem of her sneaking about before he was out of bed and running off with his prized mare to Rotten Row when Hyde Park opened. The throbbing lump on his head and the ten pounds which had been filched from him were stains upon her soul.

Piqued, he glared at the neatly stacked books lining the right edge of his mahogany-and-rosewood desk, placed there by her hand the day before. He tried not to think of how she had paled at his proclamation that all her books would be confiscated. Nor of the sheen of what could have been suppressed tears in her expressive eyes. She wouldn't make him feel remorse for her own foolishness. She *deserved* this punishment.

And by his estimation, there weren't nearly enough books present on his desk. Even so, he knew Lady Virtue well enough to suspect she would never be willing to part with every tome she had.

There was no hope for it.

He was going to have to investigate her chamber. The very notion made his cravat tighten, heat prickling down his spine. Her room, where she dressed, where she slept. Good God, he'd have to rummage through her belongings like a Visigoth raiding the Romans. He'd have to be in her space, which somehow felt as intimate and delicious and wrong as a touch. Where would a cunning minx like Lady Virtue hide her books from him? Beneath her bed? Under a pillow? Secreted in her wardrobe?

"Blast," he cursed, picking up the first book atop the pile and flipping it open to the frontispiece.

Transactions of the Royal Society of Edinburgh, Volume 1.

Ah, the scientific. He had no doubt this one had not been pilfered from his library. The former Duke of Ridgely would never have consulted something so deadly dull. Trevor turned a few pages, finding some notes neatly penned in the margins, the penmanship distinctly feminine. Not only had she read this tedious treatise, Lady Virtue had mulled over its contents enough to offer her own commentary.

He stopped on a page which discussed the powers operating the globe. She had underlined a passage, which he read to himself. *This subject is important to the human race, to the possessor of this world, to the intelligent being Man, who foresees events to come...*

In the margin, her tiny scrawl asked *What of the intelligent being Woman?*

A knock sounded at his study door, happily intruding upon the moment. What the devil was he doing, reading such tripe, mooning over her words like a lovesick swain? It hardly mattered what she thought. She could take her inquisitive mind and her undisciplined rebelliousness to her husband where it belonged, and Trevor would happily forget her existence.

"Come," he called, snapping the book closed and returning it to its pile.

The door opened to reveal his sister, wearing her customary expression of disapproval as she entered his study. Her blonde tresses were swept into an unforgiving chignon, and she wore a pale, afternoon muslin with a triple layer of embroidered flounces at the hem and a blue satin spencer. The picture of English womanhood. Little wonder she had firmly established her position as one of the arbiters of polite society—Pamela always dressed the part. And judging from the exorbitant bills he had received from the *modiste*, he had paid for the entire affair.

"Pamela," he greeted her, rising and offering a bow.

"Ridgely." She curtsied, the epitome of elegance and flawless manners.

Quite the opposite from himself.

"To what do I owe the pleasant surprise of your sisterly presence?" he asked, skirting his desk and gesturing for her to take her seat in one of the armchairs flanking the hearth.

"Surprise?" Her tone dripped with sarcasm. "You told me to meet with you at this time."

Christ. He had?

Trevor waited for Pamela to settle on her chosen chair, arranging her gown daintily around her before he sank into one opposite her. "Of course. Remind me precisely why I did such a thing, won't you?"

She frowned at him, her gaze flicking to the ugly lump on his head. "Dear heavens, what have you done now?"

Naturally, she assumed the fault was his for the damage which had been done to his poor, unsuspecting cranium. He tried not to allow her conjecture to needle him, and yet it poked at his skin like a burr under a saddle nonetheless.

"This?" He gestured wryly to the offending evidence of the attack. "Oh, I was merely suffering from *ennui* and decided to alleviate it by knocking myself silly with a fire iron."

Her expression turned cross. "Must you jest?"

"It is either that or pitch myself from the nearest window," he returned, undeterred by her vexation.

Pamela was far too serious. She always had been, but her husband's untimely death had not helped matters.

"You were not fighting a duel, were you?" Pamela demanded.

Trevor couldn't resist the opportunity to further annoy her. "Oh yes, did you not hear the new fashion of fighting a duel? Pistols at dawn are quite old news, I'm afraid. Sneaking up behind one's opponent in an alley and giving him a sound beating to the head is just the thing."

Her golden brows arched. "Is that what happened to you? Who was it, an angry husband?"

Why the devil did his reputation always precede him?

Trevor sighed. "I haven't an inkling who it was. A footpad."

Pamela gasped. "You could have been killed!"

"And Cousin Cluttermuck would have rejoiced," he said wryly. "I dare say Ferdinand would be here even now, stealing all the family silver and Sèvres like the conscienceless weasel he is."

"You know his surname is Clutterbuck, not Cluttermuck," his sister chided gently.

He took note that she did not otherwise argue with his assessment of their avaricious toad of a cousin, next in line to inherit.

"Cluttermuck is more suiting," he said. "He ought to have it changed by royal license."

"You are obfuscating the point," Pamela countered, "which is that you could have been grievously injured. Whatever were you doing skulking in an alley, giving some criminal the opportunity for attack?"

"I do not skulk, sister," he said smoothly. "I move with great deliberation and intent. As it happens, I was leaving my establishment and returning home for the evening when the incident occurred. I take my responsibilities seriously, you see. A business must be looked after."

"I do not wish to speak of that dreadful place," she said primly, folding her hands in her lap as she made her disdain for The Velvet Slipper abundantly clear—and not for the first time. "However, I am quite pleased to hear that you take your responsibilities seriously, for surely that means your reason for requesting this interview was not so that you could once more cry off attending a ball with myself and Lady Virtue."

Ah, yes. That had, indeed, been the reason. He recalled it now.

He cleared his throat and shifted in his chair, an unusual surge of guilt hitting him. "I do have a great deal of correspondence awaiting me that I must attend."

"Ridgely," she snapped, sounding so much like their mother that he experienced a visceral reaction. "The Montrose ball is quite likely one of Lady Virtue's greatest opportunities for setting her cap at a husband. You promised you would attend."

So he had. Blast Past Trevor for being so daft.

"I cannot think my presence would prove a boon for my ward," he pointed out carefully. "As you said, my reputation is hardly pristine."

"You are, nonetheless, a duke." Pamela's tone was crisp and cool, much like her blue gaze so like their father's. "The girl is gauche. There is no gentler way to phrase it. Whilst you may be something of a heartless scoundrel, I cannot help but to think your attendance as her guardian—perhaps even a dance with her—would help to enhance her appeal. At the very least, it would show that you are actively supporting her search for a husband."

A dance with Lady Virtue? Never. Trevor did not dance. Not because he wasn't adept at it. But rather because he didn't bloody well like it. Colossal waste of time, jumping about and whirling and smiling. Unless it was a waltz. That was a different matter entirely, although he wasn't about to waltz with her either. The very thought of holding her so close, having her in his arms, was enough to make every part of him go uncomfortably hot.

"I'll not dance with the chit," he decided.

"Then attend," Pamela beseeched. "I am begging you to aid my cause."

"Your cause is hardly a munificent one," he could not resist reminding her. "If I hadn't agreed to funding your wardrobe for the next year, you'd never have agreed."

"Yes, but that is only because you are dreadful," his sister said without heat.

He couldn't argue the point. He *was* dreadful. He made rather a habit of it. There was no easier means of keeping everyone at a polite distance.

Trevor sighed. "When is the ball?"

"Tomorrow evening."

Bloody hell.

"Tomorrow?" He scowled. "I cannot possibly. I have previous engagements, to say nothing of the matter of my injury. Tongues shall wag, making all manner of assumptions as even my own beloved sister did."

She waved a hand at him. "Have your valet arrange your hair in an artful fashion to cover the lump. It is certainly long enough."

Her voice was tart, and he heard the unspoken disapproval in her assessment of his hair.

"I prefer to wear it as it is," he groused, just to nettle her.

"For one night only, it shall suffice."

"Pamela."

She huffed a sigh. "You desire to be rid of your duties as Lady Virtue's guardian with as much haste as possible, yes? If so, you must act in her best interest and attend the Montrose ball. I have no doubt that your sponsorship will prove beneficial. If nothing else, it will garner her some notice."

That caught his attention.

His frown deepened. "No one has noticed her thus far?"

The notion beggared the imagination. When the chit was in a room, Trevor could see nothing and no one else, and only partially because she was the most vexing female alive. Hell, when she *wasn't* in a room, she was still on his mind. Particularly when he was alone at night.

No need to linger on that unworthy thought whilst seated across from his sister, however.

"No one she will have," Pamela said, rising. "There now, it's been decided. You must admit it's in your best interest, and unless I'm mistaken, that's what has always concerned you most."

He ignored the taunt, not far from the mark. It was what

he *wanted* the world to believe was his chief concern. Keeping secrets had been easier that way.

Trevor stood as well in deference. "You are certain it's necessary?"

"Certain. The sooner you see her wed, the sooner you'll no longer have to fret over her stealing your horses and riding Rotten Row at such an ungodly hour of the morning."

Ah yes, there was that.

He winced. "Excellent point."

Pamela moved past him, preparing to take her leave, but paused at his desk. "So many books, Ridgely? I didn't think you were such a voracious reader."

He followed his sister. "They're not mine. They're hers. I've taken them as punishment for her waywardness."

"I am certain she will be telling me all about it." Pamela chuckled and offered him an arch look over her shoulder. "Until later, dearest brother. If you will excuse me, I need to collect your ward and take her for a trip to the milliner's."

Yet another one? This, too, would cost him dearly, he had no doubt.

"Until later," he agreed with great reluctance.

⁓

SOMEONE HAD BEEN in her bedchamber.

Virtue knew it the moment she crossed the threshold after returning from a visit to the milliner with Lady Deering. Just as she knew *whom* it had been. The scent of him lingered, undeniable and treacherously alluring.

Ridgely.

But why would he have ventured into her private rooms? Despite the fact that he was her guardian, such an act was terribly scandalous. And she could think of no reason why...

Understanding dawned.

The books she had hidden!

Virtue rushed to her wardrobe and threw open the doors, frantically feeling about for the philosophical treatise she had been reading. Its hiding place, amongst the layers of her freshly laundered petticoats and chemises, was empty. He had been here, touching her undergarments, and curse the man if the realization didn't send a little thrill down her spine.

"Blast," she muttered, turning to her bed. The coverlet appeared distinctly rumpled. "Oh, no."

Not the book she had planned to begin reading before retiring this evening, *Sir Isaac Newton's Theory of Light and Colors*, as translated by Elizabeth Carter. She threw back her counterpane and pulled aside a pillow to find her bed empty. The shrewd scoundrel had located and absconded with that book as well. But surely, he would not have lowered himself by peering beneath her bed to find the other book she had secreted?

Virtue dropped to her knees, eyes searching the darkness, but could find nothing. Stuffing her arm beneath the carved mahogany bedstead, she performed a perfunctory sweep, her fingertips meeting with nothing save the pile of the Axminster.

He had found all four volumes of *The Orphan of the Rhine*.

"Curse him," she said, disbelief and frustration warring with outrage.

How dare he steal into her chamber when she had been away? And not only to trespass in such a highhanded manner, but to go searching for the books she had failed to provide him and then take those as well? What did he expect her to *do* at night before falling asleep?

She *needed* those books.

On a mission, Virtue rose to her feet. She didn't even bother to smooth her gown before stalking across her chamber, inwardly fuming. She would find the duke and demand the return of her books. Bad enough that he had forced her to surrender the others. She'd thought to retain just a few for her edification and enjoyment until he decided her punishment was at an end or he allowed her to return to Greycote Abbey, whichever came first.

But now, he had invaded her privacy and her chamber both. Worse, he had thieved the few remaining books she had taken care to hide away. She strode down the hall, ignoring the watchful eyes from the portraits of Hunt family ancestors, which seemed to mock. Grumbling to herself, she reached the commanding staircase that lent Hunt House its true air of elegance and wealth and descended.

Her feet flew, her ire growing with each step until she reached his study, only to find the door open and the room deserted. No hint of Ridgely within. She moved carefully about, ascertaining that her books were nowhere to be found.

Disappointment sent her into the hall, where the housekeeper, Mrs. Bell, was bustling.

"Good afternoon, my lady," Mrs. Bell greeted, offering a curtsy. "May I help you with anything?"

"Yes," Virtue answered. "I am looking for His Grace."

"I expect the duke is not currently at home," the housekeeper replied. "Between twelve and three o'clock on a Wednesday, it is customary for His Grace to visit Angelo's School of Arms."

Ah yes, it was Wednesday, was it not? Ridgely's routines were what the household revolved around, after all. She ought to have remembered. He fenced once a week, which was no doubt partially where his admirable physique hailed from. Not that Virtue wanted to notice. If he was gone, however, that meant that she had ample opportunity to search for where he had taken her books.

She beamed at Mrs. Bell. "Thank you. I shall seek him out upon his return."

"Of course, my lady." The housekeeper offered a nod and then departed, carrying on with her undoubtedly endless tasks and leaving Virtue alone to stew upon the location of her missing books.

If I were a dreadful duke, where would I hide my ward's stolen books? she wondered to herself.

Where was the one place he would suppose she'd never dare to look?

The answer was instant. His bedchamber, of course. Just as she had never truly reckoned he would encroach upon her personal territory, let alone discover each of her hiding places, he likely would not dream she would summon the boldness to so trespass in return.

But she was more intrepid than he could ever know.

Gathering her gown in her hands to facilitate faster movement, Virtue hastened back up the stairs to Ridgely's apartments. She hesitated outside the door, with a careful glance in both directions to ensure no other servants were hovering about. It most certainly wouldn't do to be seen entering the duke's private room. Not a soul was about, so she knocked.

No answer.

Excellent.

With a deep breath, she slowly opened the door, peering within. The curtains were open, permitting sunlight to stream through a bank of windows and illuminate the space. There, on a writing desk at the far end of the room, sat two stacks of books. Hers? She could not recognize them from so far. The ducal chamber was cavernous and, well, *ducal*.

Her whirling mind accepted details in hasty bursts—carved rosewood furniture, a tremendous bed swathed in drapery, rich carpets, pale walls. Neat, so very neat. The chamber was decidedly spare of the superfluous, quite unlike hers, where books and writing implements and journals and combs were frequently strewn about. But then, his manservant and a host of others likely tended to him with the diligence of an acolyte to the king.

Never mind all that. The time to inspect his room was decidedly not now. Or ever. Closing the door gently behind her, she ventured inside, half-expecting Ridgely to appear at any moment and chastise her for her impossible audacity. When he did not, her feet hastened over the sumptuous Axminster—new and elegant and thick, decorated with acanthus and scrolls—to the desk.

She snatched a book from the top of the pile, confirming it was indeed one of hers. Success bubbled up, until she realized that she could not simply take the entire collection away. Ridgely would notice. One book would have to do. Surely he had not counted them. A lone, missing tome would be quite unnoticed, she was certain of it. The first volume of *The Orphan of the Rhine* would do quite nicely.

She moved through the first stack in search of it and was examining the second when an unmistakable, low masculine voice sounded somewhere in the hall.

Her heart leapt into her throat. Not the duke! Mrs. Bell had assured her he was not at home, that he was fencing. But there it was again, that voice. Coming closer now.

Heavens, what to do? She could not linger and face discovery, but neither could she escape. There was but one entrance and exit. Horrified, she cast a wild glance around the chamber, looking for a place where she might hide. In her distress, she accidentally knocked against the books, sending a few of them tumbling to the escritoire's polished surface.

Footsteps sounded in the hall. She was running perilously low on time to do something, *anything*, to keep Ridgely from finding her. Her gaze caught on the massive bed, its four posters carved and glorious. It was high, draped in fabric. Leaving the books abandoned for now—she would have to hope Ridgely wouldn't take note of their state—she raced across the chamber and dove beneath the bed. Using her forearms as leverage, she pulled herself into the darkness, cheek pressed to the wool pile, as the door opened and a familiar pair of boots crossed the threshold in Ridgely's typical, long-limbed style.

He walked as if he owned not just this impressive Mayfair manse, but all London. It was the confident stride of a man accustomed to his power. And as a man and a duke, oh what power he possessed and wielded over all. Especially her, she thought grimly.

There was a second pair of shoes then, not the expensive, well-shined footwear of a lord but the practical black leather of a servant, traveling at a respectful distance. The duke's valet, she realized, when she heard him speak.

"Forgive me, Your Grace, for my lack of preparation."

The boots paused. She held her breath, praying Ridgely was not looking at the disheveled stack of books.

"Think nothing of it, Soames. I arrived earlier than expected." His deep baritone had its customary effect on her, even wedged as she was beneath his bed, the Axminster tickling her cheek.

Heat unfurled in her belly. Unwanted, vexing heat.

"Ames had a question on the matter of the library, sir," Soames began.

The library? Virtue held her breath, straining to hear more. Surely the duke didn't intend to burn the books after all?

The rustle of clothing suggested Ridgely had moved his upper body. "Later, if you please, Soames. That will be all for now, I should think."

"You have no further need of me, Your Grace?" the valet asked.

"Not presently." Ridgely's tone was light. He was moving again, turning to face his valet, his boots moving a few paces. "Thank you, Soames."

More of the duke's body had come into view once more. Buff trousers tucked into those high, gleaming boots. He wore a waistcoat only, putting his backside on display. She told herself not to look, but then she reasoned that there really was no other means of distraction, save closing her eyes. Any movement on her part risked discovery.

The valet was gone now, the door shut.

Ridgely crossed the chamber to the hearth, and there was another unmistakable rustle of cloth. She could see almost all of him now, those long legs, well-muscled thighs, his rump —*heavens*. She had never bothered to take note of the male form often, for there had been none near enough in age to her at Greycote Abbey, but Ridgely's was a thing of beauty. More of that deuced infuriating heat swept over her, like warm honey being poured all over. Sticky and messy. That was how she felt, how Ridgely made her feel.

Angry, too. Irritated beyond redemption.

She had never expected to be shuffled into the care of a guardian, and particularly not one like *him*. Her awareness of Ridgely as a man was an unending source of disappointment.

But Virtue was trapped here, and the duke was moving with calm, efficient motions. Unbuttoning his waistcoat, she realized as he shrugged the garment from broad shoulders and laid it across the back of a chair. He was not *disrobing*, was he? He remained a mystery, an enigma, halfway across the room, only a portion of his fine figure visible to her. An intriguing one.

Her wicked eyes would not close. He had a lean waist, his shirt tucked into those trousers with perfect care, delineating the effect of the hours he spent at Angelo's each week. The hushed glide of more fabric denoted the removal of his cravat, which he draped atop the discarded waistcoat.

Oh no. Oh *dear*. He truly was removing his garments, one piece at a time.

Now.

Here.

Whilst she watched.

His movements indicated more buttons being undone. She knew precisely how many there were—three—sliding from their moorings. Virtue held her breath, waiting for him to grasp twin handfuls of that shirt and haul it over his head.

Sinful excitement trilled down her spine. She was about to see the Duke of Ridgely's naked back. Or a portion of it. Half. Three-quarters if she were to press her face deeper into the pile...

No. Virtue ought to announce her presence. Honor demanded it. Yes, she must. It was wrong to allow him to conduct such an intimate act as she watched without his consent. She would have to slide from beneath the bed in ignominy, admit to her trespass, and face the consequences for her actions. But then, he could hardly punish her more than he had. He'd taken her books, curse him, and her access to the library as well. She had nothing left of value to lose.

She was about to shift, to slide from under the bed and reveal herself, but then his shoulders flexed beneath the brilliant white muslin, and up the shirt went. Over his head. And beneath was nothing but skin. Sleek, male skin. The Duke of Ridgely's skin.

She hadn't supposed a man's back would be so glorious to behold. Perhaps not every man's was. But Ridgely's back was masculine and strong and endlessly fascinating. There went that inconvenient warmth again, this time pooling between her thighs and making her feel restless and breathless all at once. Her avid gaze drank in every detail. His flesh was smooth—how soft it looked. And yet, beneath was the evidence of his power: the long line of his spine, his ribcage delineated as he stretched, his shoulder blades protruding delightfully, and all those muscles tensing and moving in a miracle of motion.

What a marvel man was, hiding beneath the trappings of society. Her fingers longed to touch. To trace the planes and curves and hollows, all the sharp parts of him. To learn the landscape of his body and know the feel of his bare skin against hers.

It was a foolish yearning, a dangerous one.

She tamped it down as he draped his shirt over the chair and spoke, shattering the stillness of the chamber and the illusion that she was hidden.

"You may as well come out from beneath my bed now."

CHAPTER 4

Trevor turned to face his ward's hiding place, willing the strong tide of desire that had been rising within, almost out of control, to abate. Silence reigned from beneath his bed, but he knew she was there. He could *feel* it. His body was ridiculously aware of hers. There had been a tingling down his spine when he'd crossed the threshold, then the faint floral scent of her. The stack of books which had been recently trifled with had been the final, telling clue.

He had dismissed Soames, deciding to carry on with this little game, initiated by her. To see how far she would take it. And she'd taken it quite far. Farther than he had suspected, it was true.

Yes, she was here, Lady Virtue.

Beneath his bed. Hiding. *Watching*. Trevor liked that knowledge. Liked it too much. Liked her eyes on him. Devouring him. Had felt it like a touch.

And that was why he had to stop. Why of the two of them, it was he, the practiced seducer, who was surrendering. He'd never been so hard without touching a woman. From her mere presence alone.

Fuck.

Still, no movement from beneath the bed.

He clung to his amusement, hoping it would make some of his longing recede. "I know you're there, Lady Virtue. No sense in pretending you are not."

He knew she was there because his prick was like a divining rod in her presence, pointing to the source of what it wanted most. What it couldn't have. *Ever.*

His body and head ached from the bout of fencing at Angelo's. He'd been forced to admit that the strenuous nature of a match against his skillful friend, Archer Tierney, had been ill-advised so soon after the blow he had taken to the head. He had cried off and returned home early, only to find that his chamber had been invaded.

Unfortunately, it would seem that his cockstand didn't give a damn if wanting his ward was wrong, or if he'd recently nearly been knocked into the next century by a bloodthirsty footpad. He moved away from the hearth, stalking toward the bed, annoyed by her silence and refusal to emerge every bit as much as his inconvenient desire for her.

A city full of lovely women, many of whom would be quite easily persuaded to go to bed with him, and all he wanted was a willful, book-loving bluestocking. He hadn't bedded anyone since the day she'd arrived at Hunt House. Perhaps another beating about the head would force some sense into his bloody mind.

Trevor stopped just short of the bed, crossing his arms over his chest. He was half-naked. It was quite barbaric of him. Certainly, scandalous. Truly, he ought to have a care and put his shirt back on, but that did not mean he was going to.

"Out, Lady Virtue," he commanded.

"I am not a dog," came her muffled grumble of indignation from beneath the bed.

He might have known that ordering her about would produce the desired result. Stubborn chit.

"Believe me, my dear," he drawled wryly. "No one would ever mistake you for a hound."

"Is that an insult?" she asked.

He was still talking to a bed.

Trevor scowled down at the offending piece of furniture. "Come out from under there, curse you."

There was a moment of hesitation, then some rustling, and a quiet *oof*, followed by a sigh.

"I fear that I'm stuck," Lady Virtue said, her voice unusually quiet and devoid of impudence.

Stuck? Beneath his bed? If he'd required additional proof that she had been sent from the bowels of hell to plague him, surely this was it.

"What do you mean by *stuck*? My bed is relatively large, whilst you are, in comparison, sufficiently small."

Not too small. In fact, she was, by his estimation, just wonderfully right. Well-curved in all the proper places, particularly her rump and breasts. Best not to think upon it now, however. Indeed, best to think upon it *never*.

"My dress seems to be caught on something," came her hushed answer.

It was damned disconcerting, knowing she was under there, somewhere, and he could not see her as he wished. Toying with her had been wickedly entertaining. But half the sport of crossing verbal swords with Lady Virtue was watching her as he did so. Her countenance was animated in the most entrancing way. He'd never seen another woman so brimming with enthusiasm and audacity. The combination was ridiculously compelling to him.

"Your dress is caught," he repeated grimly, wondering if he would have to go under the bed himself to rescue her.

Surely not?

"I cannot seem to free it."

Blast.

He lowered himself to his knees and leaned forward, peering into the darkness. "Where the devil *are* you?"

As his eyes adjusted he could make out the womanly silhouette of her enough to detect that she was lying on her belly. Ah, yes. There was her bottom, delightfully rounded.

"You're not wearing a shirt."

Her observation stole a chuckle from him. "You've only just noticed now? Silly me, for I thought you were under here watching me undress."

"I wasn't watching," she denied, the tone of her voice giving her away.

"You were," he said softly, amused. "You're a dreadful liar, my dear."

She wriggled about, then made a frustrated sound. "Do you intend to keep me trapped here for eternity, or will you help me?"

Oh, ho. He was not about to allow her such an easy escape. No, indeed. His wicked little ward was going to have to suffer for her sins.

"What a curious minx you are," he said, ignoring her. "I never would have guessed. You needn't have hidden yourself away beneath my bed to catch a glimpse of the male form. Though you *did* choose an excellent specimen when you decided to play the spy. If you'd have asked nicely, I would have shown you whatever you liked."

"You... I never would have... I didn't wish to... You utterly insufferable..."

Her furious sputtering trailed away.

"No need to rush, my dear." He flashed a grin into the shadows. "Doesn't look as if you'll be going anywhere any time soon."

Her bottom moved some more, quite suggestively this time, followed by the sound of rending fabric. "Oh good heavens, now I've ripped it!"

"Never fear," he drawled. "My sister will be more than happy to take you on a shopping excursion to find one replacement for you and ten for herself."

He really did have to speak with Pamela about her expenditures, now that he thought upon it. *Frivolous* didn't begin to describe her. And yes, he was bribing her to keep Lady Virtue occupied and well away from him. But look at how that bribery was faring now, with the chit stuffed beneath his bloody bed.

Not that he was particularly displeased to find her at his mercy, in his chamber. Nor was it a chore to watch her squirming with such delectable frustration, having been caught in her nonsense.

"You've had your laugh at my expense, Ridgely," she muttered.

This was the most delightful diversion he'd experienced in years.

His grin deepened. "Oh, but I've only just begun."

"Can you reach my gown? I can't seem to find the place where it is caught, and I'd hate to cause further damage."

Her discomfiture was heightening by the moment. He didn't think he'd ever heard Lady Virtue so ill at ease. Little wonder. He poked his head a bit deeper into the shadows, her sweet floral scent taunting him. It was a ghastly little space, and quite warm. Still, she had to pay for her misadventure.

"Hmm," he hummed, sliding his right arm across the

carpet, the wool of the Axminster lightly abrading his bare skin and reminding him he remained without a shirt. This could get decidedly dangerous if he didn't take care. His cock was still mercilessly hard, but that was likely due to all the writhing of her luscious bum. "First, I'm afraid you must tell me what it is you are doing under my bed."

"Is it not plain, you scoundrel? I was hiding from you."

He clucked his tongue in chastising fashion. "It's hardly properly done of you to call me names, when I am the injured party, my dear."

"You?"

"Yes, me." He felt about in the darkness and his hand connected with the warm give of feminine flesh beneath layers of gown and petticoat.

Her thigh, he thought, giving it a tender squeeze to investigate. And that was a mistake, for he liked it too much, that touch. In the darkness, the eroticism of her watching him disrobe leaving him in a rather rude state, he could not deny that it was far easier to forget why he ought not to touch her.

His fingers flexed of their own accord. God, so much sweet softness. So much lush femininity. And she had been watching him quietly from her hiding place as he stripped off his garments one by one. At any moment, she might have called out and stopped him. Yet, she hadn't. He suspected he knew the reason why.

"What are you doing?" she demanded.

"Seeking the place where your dress is caught," he said, sweeping his hand lower, following the line of her limb, the dip behind her knee, the curve of her calf. He leveraged himself on the carpet, partially wedging himself deeper into the abyss so that he could find her ankle.

It was every bit as wonderful a fit in his palm as he had imagined when he'd admired it from below on his library ladder. Saving her from this latest scrape was utter torture.

"That…that is my ankle," she said, sounding curiously breathless.

His lips twitched, for again, he imagined he knew the reason why. He should make haste with plucking her gown free—rip the thing to shreds if necessary—withdraw from the madness of the moment, haul her from under the bed, and demand she leave his room and never dare encroach upon it again. That would be the honorable thing to do. The sane thing to do.

"Is it?" he asked mildly instead, his fingertips traveling over silken stockings, learning the firmness of her Achilles, a vulnerable place on so fierce an opponent.

Temptation broke him. There was perspiration on his brow now. He had permission to touch. She'd asked him for help, had she not?

Trevor stroked once with his forefinger, then again with his thumb, the hitch of her breath and the sensation of this forbidden part of her making him almost giddy. Who would have thought, that of all the occasions upon which he had caressed a woman, the most erotic would be in the shadows beneath his own bed, his touch skating over a place as uninspiring as the back of an ankle?

"Yes," she said, a hiss of sound breaking the spell touching her had cast upon him, but not entirely. "Ridgely, my bare ankle is not where my dress is caught."

He might have told her that her ankle was not truly bare. The stockings were an unwanted impediment to the seduction of her skin. And he almost asked her to call him Trevor. But that would have been stupid. Easily as buffle-headed as lingering here, caressing the ankle of his very forbidden, very innocent ward. Truly, he should be ashamed of himself.

"I was merely eliminating the possibility," he said, allowing his investigation to travel higher again, then extending his reach, sliding until both his shoulders were wedged beneath the bed. What a dilemma it would be if the two of them managed to trap themselves here at once, he thought wryly before treating her to some queries of his own. "Why were you hiding from me in my own room? Or perhaps the true question is why were you in my room at all?"

Muslin and linen were no match for his hand. He felt all of her, every exquisite curve, and he was certain, as he caressed his way to her other leg, that the sensation of Lady Virtue Walcot's limbs would forever be impressed upon his palm. It would be a memory that lasted all his days. A sensual taunt of what perfection truly felt like.

"What were you doing in *my* room?" she demanded, some of her sauciness returning.

Regrettably, he found the place where her gown was indeed caught on a rough, wooden slat beneath his mattress. His fingers began to work her muslin free.

"I was discovering that you lied to me," he told her, forcing some sternness into his words as he reluctantly remembered their disparate roles.

He was not here to corrupt her. Rather, his task was to see her estate sold off and to wed her to a suitable gentleman as hastily as possible. Then he could bed someone far more suitable. He could bed two someones if he wished. Ten, even, though not all at once. One for each night. A sennight and a half of wickedness. Better yet, a full fortnight. Oh, the possibilities.

Pity the only female who interested him was the very vexing one who had entrapped herself in this most compromising scenario. Time to get out from underneath the bed. The position was doing strange things to his bewildered mind. Perhaps there was a lack of air. Yes, that explained it quite nicely.

He slid away in retreat. "You are freed now."

Trevor rose to his feet, rubbing idly at his chest where the woolen rug had chafed him. He opened and closed the hand that had touched her, bemused by the lingering sensation of her tempting curves.

With a rustle and a groan, Lady Virtue's hands appeared first, then the tempting mahogany tresses, gathered in a now-terribly-untidy chignon. She tilted her head, gazing up at him, and the effect of her brown eyes was akin to a lightning bolt crackling into the deepest, darkest part of him. Her cheeks were pink from her exertion, and he could not resist wondering if she also would look as delightfully flushed and rumpled if she were under him in bed.

"Will you not help me?" she demanded.

Quite rudely for the woman who had invaded his chamber and then so thoroughly intruded upon his privacy. But then, he supposed that the sooner he had her out, the sooner she could be on her way as well. And she would be far beyond his reach, no longer a temptation.

He caught her hands and pulled in one strong motion, bringing her gliding across the Axminster like a fish through water. It would have been amusing, the scene they presented, had he not been half-naked and were it not entirely, despicably wrong for her to be here alone with him in his chamber. She was his ward, damn it all.

His maddening, vexing, infuriating ward.

She was the minion of Beelzebub who refused to marry and leave him in peace.

She was *delicious*.

And she had to get out of his chamber at once.

He tugged her to her feet, the sudden motion sending her swaying and pitching directly into his chest. God, what a mistake, for he had no choice but to catch her there and hold her against him, to absorb how pleasant it felt, all her softness pressing into his hardness. How wickedly, inexplicably *right*. To feel the fullness of her bountiful breasts crushing into him, her hands splayed on his chest.

Yes, she bloody well had to get out of here before he did something foolish.

~

VIRTUE WAS in Ridgely's arms.

His *bare* arms.

And her palms were on Ridgely's chest.

On his *bare*, well-muscled, impossibly hot chest.

One of his hands flattened to the small of her back where it curved just above her bottom. The other grasped her waist in a possessive hold, his fingers gripping lightly enough that it was not painful and yet firmly, keeping her where she was, trapped as surely as she had been under that dratted bed of his. Except, the confining darkness there had been stifling and unpleasant whereas being held in place by Ridgely was neither of those.

No, indeed, it was heady. Decadent. *Potent*. It made her heart pound and awareness unlike any which she had previously known blossom in the lowest part of her belly. It made her breasts, where they pressed into him, ache, her nipples tightening beneath her stays. It made her body feel languorous and heavy, and it made an impossible longing—a desperate need—pulse between her thighs.

There was a name for this wickedness the Duke of Ridgely made her feel.

Desire.

Yes, as impossible and stupid as it was, she desired him. She was conscious of him as a woman was aware of a man. And she was aware of every part of him, from the satiny-smooth skin of his chest, lightly dusted with dark hair beneath her fingertips, to his masculine strength. From his wickedly seductive lips, still curled in a knowing half smile, to the defining slash of his jaw shaded by the prickle of whiskers. From his scent, man and musk and the freshness of citrus, to his clever gaze as it hovered on her mouth.

Some dim part of her befuddled mind told Virtue this was wrong, the way she felt, her body's reaction to his. Because she could not possibly long for the Duke of Ridgely with such skin-tingling furor, as if his touch, his presence, the man himself, were essential for her continued existence. As if her next breath depended upon his hands cleverly caressing as they had done in the shadows under the bed, touching her where no one had dared, lighting a fire inside her she hadn't previously dreamed existed.

She didn't even like him.

He had stolen her books.

He was intent upon selling her home.

He had foisted her off onto his sister as if she were an unwanted chore.

He was a known rakehell.

Yes, he was deplorable.

And she was appalled to realize that none of that mattered. Common sense could not prevail, and nor could it mollify the ache. She wanted to rub herself against him like a cat. Wanted to rise on her toes and claim those smirking lips with hers. She wanted things she wasn't certain existed. Wanted dark whispers and decadent caresses. But only from *him*.

She shocked herself.

"Steady?" he asked.

Even the low timbre of his voice made something inside her turn molten. Liquid. Her insides were jumbled. Her heart was pounding.

She should push away from him. Should stop touching his chest.

But she didn't want to, and he didn't show any inclination of releasing her either.

"Yes," Virtue said instead, staying right where she was, in the maddening circle of his embrace. And then she remembered something, forced her sluggish mind to work. "You knew I was there, under the bed."

There was a slight inclination of his head, his wicked gaze burning into hers. "Of course."

There was a quickening in her belly, an acknowledgment of what that meant. But she needed him to say it. Needed *him* to say it, even though she knew that when he did, everything would change. But then, perhaps it had already changed.

"For how long?" she asked.

Had he known when he had undone his cravat? When he had stripped away his shirt and waistcoat?

The customary arrogance Ridgely exuded faded, an uncharacteristic seriousness settling on his countenance as his gaze burned into hers. "From the moment I crossed the threshold."

"You...*oh*."

She was breathless. Shocked at the implication, although it came as no surprise.

"You aren't nearly as clever as you think yourself, my dear."

"But you disrobed," she pointed out needlessly, as if they were both unaware of his state of dishabille.

He was half-naked before her.

"Partially," he admitted, his expression inscrutable.

What did it mean? Surely it could not mean what she thought, what her foolish, quickening heart and traitorous body yearned to believe, that he was attracted to her. That he desired her, even.

That this man, this duke, so unfairly handsome and longed after by so many women, would want her...

Impossible to believe.

"Why?" she asked anyway. "Why did you do it?"

She had to know. Somehow, a part of her which had long been dormant had been awakened. She, who had spent the entirety of her stay in London attempting to keep men at bay so she could remain unmarried and return to the haven of her home, suddenly wanted a gentleman to take note of her.

But not just any gentleman. It was the least suitable, the most forbidden, a man she did not trust, who infuriated her at every turn. One who held her very future in the palm of the hand that had caressed her so knowingly, turning her own body against her.

"Perhaps I wanted to shock you," he said mildly, as if they were not still holding each other in a disastrously scandalous embrace in his bedroom. "To punish you for invading my territory without my consent. To teach you a lesson."

It was hardly a punishment, his beautiful male body partially on display for her delectation. Indeed, quite the opposite. He had to know that. And the only lesson he had taught her was that her own body was unforgivably weak where his was concerned. That all it had required was the pass of his hand over her backside for her to turn as mindless for him as his legion of female admirers undoubtedly were.

She made none of those revelations.

Because also, she had seen the intensity in his expression when she had emerged from beneath the bed. And she did not think she mistook the masculine interest in the hands which had so tenderly passed over her form. He had not merely been searching for the place where her gown was snagged. She would wager every stitch of clothing she currently wore upon it. He had touched her and looked at her with wickedly erotic sensual intent.

But how to force him to admit it? And moreover, for

what purpose? Surely, such confessions could bring nothing but ruin upon them both.

"You cannot shock me," she said, finding her flagging bravado and clinging to it the way she was currently clinging to his beautiful chest. "I could look upon you all day thusly, and it would not affect me in the slightest."

A terrible, towering lie, that. But it was hardly his concern, the way he made her feel, feverish and flushed and confused and wanting something sinful and mysterious.

His lips—far too lush for a man's—curved again, into a smile laden with wicked intent. It was the smile of a man who was well aware of the effect he had, not just upon her, but most every other woman of his acquaintance.

"How amusing. Perhaps we should put it to the test."

She laughed at the notion, so utterly nonsensical. "You wouldn't dare."

His eyes glittered in the late-afternoon light. "I've certainly done far worse than taking off my shirt, cravat, and waistcoat in the presence of an innocent lamb."

"I've no doubt you have."

The curtains were open. Did he always divest himself of his clothing with them thrust wide, so that anyone passing in the street below might glimpse him nude? Knowing Ridgely, it was likely. But then, she supposed Hunt House was set too far from the street for any curious onlookers to spy him or—worse—the both of them as they stood now, entwined with such indecent intimacy.

She must extricate herself from his embrace. From this conversation. From his chamber.

And yet, she remained reluctant. His arms were warm and strong and reassuring. She'd never been held this way, caressed as if she were someone worthy of worship, worthy of notice. Their bodies were perfectly aligned, melting into each other. She couldn't shake the feeling that when she did finally go, this moment would never happen again.

What a pity and a blessing that would be, all in one.

The hand on her lower back suddenly moved again. Slowly. As if he had all day to conduct his task, sweeping up her spine. Melting her, one tantalizing touch at a time.

"Are you certain you're unaffected by me?" he asked softly, his tone self-assured and redolent with disbelief.

She forced a smile, attempting to mimic the smug arrogance he so easily emitted. "Have I bruised your vanity? You must forgive me."

"I've never yet held a woman in my arms who *wasn't* affected." His hand glided with delicious torpor between her shoulder blades, the one on her waist remaining planted like an anchor, holding her there.

Not that she would have fled, despite reason telling her to do so. There was nowhere else she would rather be, to her everlasting shame.

"There is a first for every occasion," she mocked.

"Truly, my dear?" Now his touch had reached the back of her neck, and it was the startling familiarity of his bare fingers grazing her nape that caused her to inhale sharply.

It was as if she had burst into flame.

His tone was lazy, suggesting that for Ridgely, this attempt at seduction was minor and commonplace. She knew him for a scandalous, wicked rake. But this was the first time he had exerted his wiles upon her. She hadn't supposed he would. Until today, their interactions had been, whilst steeped in enmity, more comprised of bickering than aught else. This was different, a heaviness between them, and she could not think she was the only one suffering from such an unbearable ache, deep inside. Surely, experienced though he was, Ridgely was similarly moved.

"Truly," she forced herself to repeat, holding very still as his fingertips found the tensed muscles of her neck and gently massaged. "Quite unaffected."

His head lowered, just a fraction. The duke was a tall man. He bent forward enough so that his breath coasted over her lips. Tea had never before possessed the scent of an invitation to sin.

But it did now. And she'd remember that scent, the sweet promise of it on the air, remember the heated whisper of his exhalation, the way he surrounded her, consumed her, and all with but a look and the slightest of touches.

And still, closer his face came to hers, his head angled, the magnificence of his dark eyes burning into hers, stealing the air from her lungs, it seemed. So close that he was all she could see. There was nothing but Ridgely, silhouetted by the sunlight, handsome and cunning and dissolute.

His lips were almost grazing hers. A nod of her head, and she would bring their mouths into wondrous alignment, just like their bodies.

"You're lying," he murmured, no accusation there. Only a knowing air.

She was. She was deceiving them both. Telling him she felt nothing, whilst telling herself she could step away at any moment. The truth was, she couldn't. It was as if he had cast some manner of spell over her. A carnal one.

This show was likely yet another display of Ridgely's power. Bored, handsome, powerful scoundrels were no different than cats who liked to toy with their prey before ultimately devouring them. But she would not be devoured.

Even if she wanted to be.

"I feel nothing," she repeated lightly. "You could be a lady's maid for all the passion you inspire within me. No, indeed. I am sorry to report that not every woman in the world wishes to fall at your feet, swooning from the mere sight of you."

His hand was in her hair, and he was cradling her head, which felt unaccountably heavy and laden with far too many thoughts. The touch was achingly gentle. She never wanted it to end.

His smile returned. "Liar. Just as you dissembled about the books, you are lying now. I can't trust a word that comes from that pretty little mouth of yours."

No one had ever called her mouth pretty before. No one would have presumed to do so. She'd chased away her every suitor thus far with talk of sheep farming, beekeeping, science, and any other subject she thought might send them scampering away to find a more obliging dupe.

To her dismay, Virtue found that she liked the notion that Ridgely found her lips attractive, wrong though it was.

"You can trust these words," she lied some more. "I've told you, I'm not like most ladies." And with that resolute decree, coupled with the stern reminder that she must put thoughts of her home and her people before her own base longings, Virtue stepped away, extricating herself. "Might I have at least one of my books, Ridgely?"

There was an expression on his face she'd never seen before, and it was a dangerous one, she knew.

"No," he said, reaching for the first button on the placket of his trousers. "Now, if you don't mind, I'm desperately in need of a change of clothes. I suggest you remove yourself from my room before you see the rest of me."

Her eyes widened. The first button was already undone.

"You wouldn't."

He raised a brow, his long fingers hooking on the next fastening.

He would, she realized. And it was terrible of her, but she wanted to remain and watch. What a weak-willed disappointment she was to herself.

"Very well," she relented, hastily backing toward the door. "I'll go."

His laughter followed her into the hall, which was blessedly empty, no one present to witness her utter mortification.

The beginning, she very much feared, of her fall from grace.

CHAPTER 5

The hour was horrifically early—just after dawn. Standing hidden in the drapery of the portrait gallery's alcove, Trevor shuddered. The only occasion upon which he was ordinarily awake at this time was when he had yet to go to bed. Unfortunately, however, he hadn't spent the evening occupied by the pleasant distractions of feminine company and fine brandy.

Instead, he'd been through a fitful sleep in his chamber, tormented by the memory of how Lady Virtue Walcot had felt in his arms. Of how her luscious curves had come to life beneath his wandering hands. Of how her eyes possessed, when one looked closely enough, tiny flecks of gold that shimmered. Of how her palms had pressed against his chest along with her voluptuous breasts, and of how he had come ever so near to claiming her perfectly plump lying lips with his own.

A kiss.

When was the last time the promise of a mere kiss had wrought such agony? He couldn't recall. Nor could he recall ever wanting a woman as badly as he wanted her.

But that wild, uncontrollable yearning wasn't the reason he was presently looming in the shadows at this ungodly hour, watching the hall through which his delectable ward would have to pass.

No, indeed. It was because he didn't believe her when she promised she wouldn't slip to the mews and steal his horse for another dangerous jaunt. Just as he hadn't believed her when she'd said she was entirely unaffected by being in his arms. Utter rot, and they both knew it. Just as he knew she would soon come slipping through the hall like a lovely wraith, intent upon breaking her word.

Likely to spite him for the books. But what had the minx expected? He was charged with her welfare, which meant he could not allow her to go traipsing about in the early-morning hours, unchaperoned, putting herself at grave risk of footpads or worse.

Christ, he still had the lump on his head to prove London was a damned dangerous place.

No, he intended to catch her before she could do any more damage to her reputation or her person. His valet had not even shown a hint of surprise when he had requested the early call to wake. Old Soames was a consummate professional.

Something in the air changed then. He could feel it, a palpable difference that alerted Trevor not just of a presence, but of *her* presence. A subtle creak of the hall floor, followed by the hush of petticoats and skirts. And then the light floral scent of her. She was nothing more than a wisp passing by him, ethereal and haunting as she moved with the tentative care of someone unaccustomed to the darkness.

His eyes had ample opportunity to adjust. Trevor parted the heavy brocade curtains and stepped from the alcove. He moved with the silent stealth wrought by his days with the

Guild. This time, it was not a violent traitor to the Crown he stole behind, however.

And thank God for that, he thought grimly as he caught her waist in one arm and hauled her back against him in the same moment that he clapped a hand over her mouth, silencing her scream of alarm. There were some elements of his days as a spy he decidedly did not miss.

"*Mmmfff*," she cried out into his palm, the sound suitably muffled.

Trevor lowered his head, his lips unintentionally grazing the shell of her ear. "Quiet."

She stilled for a moment, and then she commenced a fight, struggling with him as she attempted to wrest free of his hold. For what purpose, he didn't know. But he wasn't about to take the chance of her escaping and running off to the mews to gallop away with Hera.

"Stop fighting," he commanded her. "You'll hurt yourself."

She said something else, but he couldn't make it out. And then she licked his palm, the cunning wretch.

White-hot flame shot through him. It shouldn't have been erotic, the touch of her tongue to his palm, for it was the act of a petulant child. And yet, his stupid prick twitched to attention.

No, not now. Not with her. He truly needed to take himself in hand. Close his eyes and pretend it was Virtue.

"Don't lick me again," he gritted.

"*Mmmrrr*," she said, sounding like nothing so much as an angry cat.

And then she did precisely what he had told her not to do. Of course she did, the brazen baggage. Her tongue darted over his palm, wet and hot and sleek, followed by her teeth as she caught the fleshy heel of his palm and bit.

Yes, she was just like a feline. An untamed one.

"Bloody hell," he growled, withdrawing his hand and giving it a shake. "What the devil did you bite me for?"

She escaped his hold and whirled about, a whisper of muslin and feminine outrage that stirred up the scent of flowers he still had yet to identify. "I couldn't breathe. Why did you attack me like a cutpurse?"

"I assure you, madam, that no cutpurse would be so gentle." If there had been light, he would have gestured to the proof on his head. In the darkness, it hardly mattered, and anyway, his hand still smarted from her sharp nip. "You knew damned well it was me, and yet you bit me like a wild animal."

"If you treat me like a wild animal, I have no recourse other than to act as one," she returned, her tone unapologetic.

Enough. Trevor wasn't going to stand here in the darkness at dawn, arguing with his devil's-spawn ward without being able to see her.

"And if you insist upon being a wayward, spoiled child, then I have no choice but to punish you like one." He took her arm with his uninjured hand in a light but firm hold. "Come with me."

He didn't wait for her response, but began pulling her in the direction of his chamber. His own rooms would have to suffice for privacy and, he hoped, illumination. He wasn't about to stumble about in the darkness down the stairs.

"Where are you taking me?" she demanded far too loudly for his liking.

He had no wish to send the few servants who had already awakened running after them.

"Hush," he instructed. "A familiar-enough place."

By God, it was dark. How she successfully wandered about Hunt House at this early hour without breaking her neck was a mystery to him.

Still tugging her along, he fumbled his way through the shadows with rather less grace than he would have preferred. He found the door to his chamber at last and pulled her through, closing it behind them.

Thankfully, the low light from the fire in the grate partially illuminated the space within.

He led her to a chair at the hearth. "Sit."

"But—"

"You dare to defy me now?" he interrupted, his voice bearing a sting he hadn't intended, wrought of his frustration with her. "Sit."

To his surprise, Lady Virtue sat, obeying him for what was perhaps the first time in their acquaintance. He turned away from her, finding some spills on the mantel, and lit the tapers on a candelabra, bathing this portion of the sizeable apartments in a warm glow. Satisfied with his efforts, he moved the armchair flanking hers so that it was opposite. And then he sat, seeking her soft brown gaze.

"You were intending to sneak away and to thieve my mare, in express violation of my warnings," he said grimly.

Concern flitted over her lovely features before she fixed a smile upon her lips. "I wasn't intending to ride at all."

Did the minx think him an utter imbecile?

Now that the room was properly lit, he cast a glance over the gown she wore, a Florentia blue merino and Mechlin lace affair that hugged her curves in the very best of ways.

His gaze lingered for a moment on the bodice trim accentuating her breasts before he forced himself to look away. "No? Forgive me for finding it odd that you're wearing your riding habit, yet claim you have no intention of riding."

She bit her lip. "Ridgely, I can explain."

Her daring never failed to astound him. He would have laughed had he been feeling more charitable. As it was, rising early, coupled with his inconvenient lust for her and her continued flouting of his every edict, had quite spoiled his disposition.

"Indeed? I would dearly love to hear it, my lady. I would absolutely love to hear where you were going at dawn wearing a riding habit and sneaking from Hunt House like a lowly thief, if not to steal Hera and go riding in Hyde Park."

"Steal is rather a strong word."

"An appropriate one," he countered, realizing he was grinding his molars so hard that his jaw ached. "What would you call taking something that does not belong to you, without permission of the owner, if not stealing?"

Her lush pink lips parted.

No sound emerged.

For once, he had rendered her speechless.

And he could not quite quell the rising sense of elation at having bested the chit. "No other word shall suffice? I'll wait."

He drummed his fingers on his thigh as silence stretched on between them, no sound save the rhythmic drumming and the occasional crackle of the fire.

Until she heaved a sigh. "Borrowing."

He raised a brow. "The act of borrowing denotes consent. And just as I did not approve of your reckless invasion of my chamber yesterday, I did not give consent to your taking Hera this morning. Indeed, I forbade it."

Another sigh. The small, even white teeth which had sunk into his flesh not long ago emerged to catch her lower lip and draw it inward. The action was not intentionally erotic; he had no doubt that Lady Virtue Walcot wouldn't know how to conduct a seduction. Hers was a sensuality which had yet to be unleashed. It was merely there in the raw, inherent.

One day, a man would be deuced fortunate to explore it with her.

Not him.

Never him.

"Have you anything to say for yourself?" he asked sternly.

She pursed her lips, then folded her hands in her lap, the picture of aristocratic femininity, belying everything he knew about her. "I am sorry."

He blinked, thinking he misheard. "You're sorry?"

"Yes." She cast her gaze down to the gloved hands in her lap. "I shouldn't have defied you."

Had he gone mad, or had his spitfire suddenly sputtered from a roaring flame to a dull spark?

Trevor searched her countenance with a narrow-eyed gaze, feeling oddly bereft at her hasty acquiescence. "No, you bloody well should not have. However, that has never stopped you in the past, so why should it have done now? There is only one response I can have to this latest indignation." He paused for emphasis, allowing his words to hopefully penetrate her stubborn mind. "There will need to be a consequence stronger than the mere confiscation of your books for a fortnight and temporarily barring you from the library, as clearly that punitive action had no effect upon you whatsoever."

Her gaze jerked back up to meet his, her eyes wide, no longer obscured by the sweep of her long, silken lashes. "There need not be further consequence. You have my promise, Ridgely, that I will never again go for a morning ride without your permission."

"And a groom," he reminded her.

"And a groom," she repeated.

"Excellent." He drummed his fingers some more. "Your mere promise, however, shall not be sufficient, I'm afraid. I had it before, and look at how easily and hastily it was broken."

"No." Her sudden pallor indicated her concern.

Something inside his chest shifted at that look. Softened. There was a name for it, this odd feeling, he realized.

Compassion. It wasn't his intention to punish her, nor to douse her fire. But she had been reckless, and he didn't wish her to come to harm. His actions were for her own sake, damn it.

"Yes." He rose from the chair, forcing himself to remain stern. "You've left me with no choice but to see the books consigned to a safe place until your wedding day."

It was his only recourse. His sole means of forcing her to see reason.

She shot to her feet, a swirl of outraged blue woolen skirts pooling around her. "You cannot!"

He was grim, forcing himself to remain unmoved. "I must."

∼

VIRTUE LAUNCHED HERSELF AT RIDGELY.

She told herself it was in desperation.

But when she landed firmly against the forbidding wall of his hard, muscled chest, and when her hands found his broad shoulders and his arms wrapped around her in an instinctive gesture, she couldn't deny desperation hadn't been her sole motive. Because it also felt good being here, held close to him. Good being in his arms, his blazing warmth far more wanted than the dwindling fire's in the grate. He smelled of shaving soap and fresh linen, with the decadent musk that always accompanied him, telling her he had been awake for some time. Had prepared his toilette, knowing he would find her slipping from her room for her morning ride. He was a worthy opponent, the Duke of Ridgely. To that end, it had finally occurred to her what she must do. How she might finally best him and prove her point, that she belonged at Greycote Abbey.

Virtue rose on her toes, as high as she could manage in

her kid half-boots, the heels of which had already given her something of an advantage against his tall frame.

"My lady," he protested sternly, as if he were scolding a troublesome child in his charge, "what do you think you are do—"

Her mouth smothered the rest of his words, effectively ending his protest.

She froze for a moment as wonderment stole over her. How forthright, to kiss him, the act requiring a daring she hadn't thought she possessed. But she was doing it. Hadn't had any other choice, not truly. Not that it was a difficulty, kissing a handsome man, even if he was infuriating.

Her first kiss. She'd never known the heady rush of pressing her lips to another's. Hadn't expected it to feel so oddly delightful. She remained as she was, holding still, her mouth aligned perfectly with his, wondering if this was how it was done. If this was all there was to it. If so, it was hardly as wicked as she had supposed.

His mouth was warm, his lips surprisingly soft. And when he breathed, it was as if she was taking his breath from him, bringing it into her lungs. What a strange intimacy. Stranger still, she rather liked it. The contact made the same dangerous yearning she'd known the day before in his chamber steal over her again. Longing simmered in her belly, a need she didn't fully know what to do with making her aware of her own body in new ways.

She had read a great many books, most of which were not deemed suitable for the eyes of an innocent lady such as herself. Some of them had been bawdy, bearing descriptions of the carnal acts which could happen between a man and woman. Vague descriptions laden with flowery prose, it was true. None of them had successfully described the intensity of being so close to another, of having his hands on her waist, his lips on hers.

He jerked his head back suddenly, ending the contact, leaving her staring up at him, bereft.

"What was that?" he demanded, his dark eyes, almost obsidian in the glow of the candlelight, burning into hers.

She stared for a moment, looking at his mouth, thinking that she'd *kissed* him. That she had settled her own lips against his. That his lower lip was fuller than she'd expected.

I kissed the Duke of Ridgely, she thought stupidly.

And then she repeated the sentiment aloud, for his edification. "It was a kiss."

Those sinful lips curved upward, into a semblance of a grin. "No, it wasn't."

Her gaze flew to his. "Of course it was."

He couldn't diminish her accomplishment now. Virtue was proud of how bold she'd been, seizing the reins for herself. Here was how she would finally make far more trouble for him than he wished to call his own. Nothing else had done it. She would kiss him every day if she must, until he finally sent her away.

And hide under his bed, too.

"That was nothing more than a rather weak attempt at distracting me from my course," he said firmly, assuming that same tone again.

The one that made her feel like a nuisance, just as his insistence upon calling her *infant* did.

Both nettled. He was being deliberately cruel. Mocking her. Acting as if she didn't know what a kiss was. Of course she did. She'd just given him one. How dare he act as if her effort had somehow fallen short of the mark?

"I kissed you," she insisted.

The lips which had molded so well to her own quirked with ill-concealed humor at her expense. "To be fair, you merely pressed your mouth to mine. Calling that tepid demonstration a kiss is rather like referring to a drop of water as a deluge."

Embarrassment made her ears go hot. What had she expected, throwing herself into the arms of such a practiced seducer? Of course her inexperience could not compare to the other lovers he had known. But then, she hadn't kissed him to woo him. She had kissed him to remind him how much trouble she was, and how much happier they would all be should he simply return her to her home where she belonged, instead of his stubborn insistence upon carrying out the terms of her father's will.

"That is how I kiss," she told him coolly, feigning a vast collection of beaus she did not possess. "No one has ever complained before."

His lips turned down, his jaw hardening. "Just who the devil have you been kissing in Nottinghamshire?"

"A lady doesn't share her confidences. Dozens of gentlemen, however." She paused, realizing that for a man of Ridgely's reputation, that number would hardly be sufficiently impressive. "On second thought, I dare say it was more likely hundreds, actually."

His brows rose. "Hundreds, you say?"

She held his stare, unblinking. "Yes, of course."

"Hmm," he said, his fingers flexing on her waist.

Was it wrong of her to like the way it felt, his hands on her? Yes, it absolutely was. But it would seem she was willing to commit all manner of sins in the name of finding her way back to Greycote Abbey.

Virtue told herself it was the people she loved, the only home and family she'd ever known—Mrs. Williams, Mr. Smith, Miss Jones—that spurred her onward as she raised her chin, fiery determination taking root at the base of her spine and rendering it ramrod stiff.

"Hmm? What does that mean?" she demanded to know.

"It means that either your legions of suitors in Nottinghamshire are woefully inept at the art of kissing, or you're lying."

His drawl infuriated her. What was it about the Duke of Ridgely that made her long to simultaneously box his ears and wrap herself around him as if she were ivy? Did he have this same effect upon the entire female sex? Or was she alone in this vexing, peevish misery?

"I'm not lying," she insisted.

And yes, she was indeed lying, quite naturally. But blast him for suggesting she was being dishonest. No gentleman would accuse a lady of dissembling. Then again, Ridgely was no gentleman, and he had made that abundantly clear on many occasions. Including the day before when he had removed his shirt whilst knowing she hid beneath his bed, the utter villain.

"You are, and I'll prove it." His hands had crept from her waist to the small of her back, splayed and open.

So *large*. Large and bold, just as he was.

Burning her through the layers that separated them—petticoats, chemise, riding habit. In that moment, she cursed the wool and linen keeping those big hands from her skin. Oh, she liked how he moved her body subtly nearer, so that their forms were perfectly aligned, all her curves fitted to his stern masculine planes.

"How?" she asked, intending to be defiant and sounding instead—much to her dismay—breathless.

"By demonstrating what a kiss truly is," he told her, his voice smooth and deep, soft as velvet.

Laden with sin, that voice, and with promise, too.

Very well. What could be the harm?

She rose on her toes, intending to accommodate him. The sooner this was done, the more likely he would be to realize how wayward she was, and how much easier it would be to send her away.

"What are you doing?" he demanded, humor lacing his tone.

The sheer nerve of the man.

"Assisting you in your demonstration, of course," she answered primly.

"If that is what you call it." He frowned down at her. "Cease attempting to take control of the moment, Virtue. Relax. Allow me to show you what you've been missing with all your Nottinghamshire beaus."

It was the first time he had called her by her given name alone. Not the dreadfully condescending *infant*. Not *Lady Virtue*. Not even *my dear*. Merely *Virtue*. She tried very hard not to like the way it sounded in his delicious baritone, nor the intimacy it implied.

Virtue nodded. "Very well."

But apparently, Ridgely was in no hurry to proceed. One hand remained on her waist, the other traveling along her spine, up, up, up in a slow, languorous sweep to her nape. His fingertips brushed tenderly over the skin there before rounding to her face. He tucked an errant curl behind her ear and then cupped her cheek.

His head dipped, his nose nudging lightly along hers in a teasing fashion. His breath was hot and whisper-soft against her own lips, sending anticipation thrumming through her veins. And then, the most astonishing thing: his mouth on hers, hot and smooth and decadent. But not merely motionless as the kiss she had given him had been. Instead, his lips were moving. Chasing hers. Coaxing them to respond. Which she did, following his lead. Slowly at first. And then with increasing confidence as longing unfurled within her like a tight spring blossom newly hatched. She was awake and alive and aflame as she'd never been before.

Oh.

Oh.

How different this kiss was, gentle and yet masterful. Sinuous and seductive. How wonderful. Surely there were other, equally superlative means of describing it, but her mind fumbled with its thoughts, rendered rusty by a confluence of sensation. She made an inarticulate sound—it couldn't be helped. A soft, breathy sigh almost, that would have been embarrassing had not the entirety of her being been focused upon his kiss. Upon his lips. His wicked, knowing lips.

She had never imagined a kiss could be like this. That it would unlock all the mysteries inside her, that it would reveal secrets she hadn't known she possessed. Virtue swayed into him, their bodies pressing more firmly together in an intimate dance she instinctively understood. Her breasts connected with the wall of his chest, her nipples aching behind the abrasion of her stays with each ragged breath she took. As she shifted, a thick ridge pressed into her belly. How deliciously hard he was, everywhere. How muscled and masculine, his larger, taller frame enveloping her as his lips continued their sensual assault with such sweet diligence.

Her hands moved from his shoulders to twine around his neck, her fingers slipping into the silken hair at his nape. He slowed the kiss yet deepened it at the same time. Suddenly there was his tongue, seeking entrance. To her mouth, of all places! She parted her lips to inquire after his intention, and then his tongue was gliding over hers, sending a bolt of heat directly to the center of her.

He tasted of tea and sin.

Of course he did. He was a conscienceless rake. Little wonder all the ladies swooned at the mere mentioning of the Duke of Ridgely. If his kissing lesson was any indication, he could reduce a woman to a puddle of mad yearning with scarcely any effort at all.

That wild thought, flitting through her mind as he licked into her mouth as if she were some manner of dessert he wished to thoroughly consume, ought to have restored her wits. Ought to have reminded her of all the reasons why she must not continue kissing her roguish guardian. Lady Deering warned her often that a lady must never allow a gentleman to lead her astray, and surely that was what Ridgely was doing now.

Only, Lady Deering had failed to warn Virtue of how lovely it would feel.

She never wanted the kiss to end. Never wanted Ridgely to remove his lips from hers. He seemed to understand her need, for the hands on her lower back held her more firmly to him, their bodies molding together. She thought quite fancifully that she could feel every part of him. Even *that* part of him.

Abruptly, he ended the kiss, his lips leaving hers bereft as he raised his head.

Virtue blinked up into his diabolically handsome face. He looked like a ruffian with that bruise on his head, and yet it only added to his allure. He smoldered with a heady blend of passion and danger, and he was utterly and completely irresistible, the scoundrel.

Lady Deering certainly ought to have taught her how to steel herself against men like him, who could seduce with a look, a touch, a kiss.

Now she knew. Too late.

"There you are," he said smoothly, as if her entire world had not just been abruptly shifted on its axis.

As if he were entirely unaffected.

Whilst she...she remained quite desperately *affected*.

Afflicted was more like it. What had the handsome devil

done to her? Her mind tripped over itself. She was still holding him, arms around his neck, but his hands had fled the small of her back to wrap gently around her wrists, untangling her as if she were an inconvenient vine in his garden. One that needed to be weeded out and removed.

She licked her lips, still humming with the effects of his kiss, and tasted him. A shaky, inhaled breath brought more of his scent to invade her senses. How unfair, that he should appear so vexingly unruffled.

"One would suppose you go about kissing ladies every day," she observed curtly, finding her voice at last as she took a step in retreat. "You act as if such intimacy is commonplace."

The corners of his lips hitched into a small smile that failed to reach the depths of his dark eyes. "Indeed."

That lone word, his self-derisive acknowledgment, stung. Of course kissing was quite ordinary for a man such as him. Why had she possessed the idiocy to believe, just for a moment, that his kiss had meant anything more to him than a mere lesson, another way to exert his power over her and make her feel foolish and small?

"Of course it is," she said quietly, some ingrained training causing her to bob in a curtsy that was rather lopsided in her current state. "Thank you for the lesson. If you don't mind, I'll return to my chamber now to reflect upon the error of my ways."

Her cheeks were flaming, she was sure of it. Virtue didn't wait for Ridgely's response. She simply gathered her skirts and whirled away, running from him and from his chamber both.

But most especially running from the memory of his kiss.

CHAPTER 6

God, Trevor despised balls.

"God's fichu, but I despise balls."

Trevor turned from his present occupation—watching his beautiful ward dance a lively country reel with some insidious fop—and discovered his host, the Duke of Montrose, at his side.

He raised a brow, grateful for the distraction and the company both. He'd always liked Monty, as the duke was more familiarly known to friends. They'd found themselves in any number of disgraceful scrapes together. But that had been a few years ago now. The duke was a happily married man, desperately in love with his wife, God help the fellow. Rather akin to a lion being domesticated into a lap cat if you asked Trevor.

Not that anyone had.

"Odd sentiment for the man hosting this entire affair," he drawled pointedly.

Monty raised his glass of lemonade in mock toast. "Touché, Ridgely. However, in my defense, Her Grace tells me this is the sort of nonsense one is required to host at least once a Season. I'll do anything to make her happy. Even fill my town house with hundreds of people I scarcely know."

The poor, besotted prick.

Ridgely shook his head. "Better you than me, old chap. The mere notion of getting caught in the parson's mousetrap makes me shudder. Hosting balls? Ye gods."

Monty chuckled. "I'm quite contentedly caught, I assure you. I've never been happier than I have since becoming a husband and father. And as for you, I'd have sworn you were contemplating the parson's mousetrap yourself, given the way you've been watching a certain young lady."

He would have laughed had not the thought been so horrifying. "Marriage? To my ward? I think not."

But he *had* kissed her that morning, just after dawn.

He never should have done so, and no one knew it better than Trevor. He had allowed her to think the kiss had been nothing more than a lesson, but that was a lie. He'd *wanted* to kiss her. Had spent every second of each minute since remembering how soft and lush she'd been in his arms, those delicious breasts of hers straining against his chest, her equally delectable mouth so responsive once he'd shown her the proper way of it. And that husky sound she'd made—surrender and longing in one—*bloody hell*.

He shook his head slightly, as if to dislodge the thoughts.

"Oh, dear me," Monty said at his side. "I hadn't realized that was Lady Virtue Walcot you were ogling."

Ogling.

Trevor longed for some champagne. Some brandy. Anything. The only drinks at this ball to be had were lemonade and punch. On account of Monty being a reformed man, or so the whispers went. Their paths hadn't crossed with enough frequency in recent years for him to know the reason or to inquire after it.

He sighed. "I wasn't ogling her. I was *observing* her. I'm the girl's guardian. What else am I meant to do?"

Definitely not kiss her, said a taunting voice within.

That was true. He absolutely, under no circumstances, must ever set his lips to Lady Virtue's mouth again. Even if denying himself was akin to a physical ache.

"You seemed to have been scowling at young Mowbray over there," the duke drawled.

Well, perhaps he had been. And curse Monty for taking note of it.

"Is that the fop with the ridiculously high shirt points?" he asked, knowing it was.

He'd made it his business to ascertain who was sniffing about his ward's skirts. It was part of being a good guardian. Which he was decidedly not. But an effort to make amends for the morning's folly.

"The Viscount Mowbray," Monty elaborated. "He is the fellow currently dancing with your ward."

And hadn't Pamela claimed Lady Virtue required his presence here so she could gain suitors? It certainly didn't appear as if she required any aid in that regard. She had been dancing with a partner since the musicians had struck up their first quadrille. And there she was still dancing now, with that mutton-headed viscount, a thin, gaunt stick of a man who appeared to believe that he could make up for what he lacked in physical attributes with fabric.

He was bloody well wrong about that.

Why was Virtue smiling at Mowbray as they whirled about just now? Was she laughing at something the young vainglorious dandy had just said? Trevor's brow knitted together as he contemplated them, misgiving swirling in his gut. She was far too lovely and lively for a man like the viscount. He'd probably demand she stop reading books about science. Just *look* at him, the self-important weasel.

"It's a miracle he can even turn his head with those points," Trevor grumbled.

Would it be too much to hope that a wrong movement would result in one of those shirt points landing in the blackguard's eye?

"He seems to be turning it rather well at the moment," the duke pointed out as Mowbray crooked his head toward Lady Virtue in an intimate fashion, allowing him to tell her something that made her smile again.

Disgusted, Trevor cast an irritated glance around the ballroom. Just where in the hell was Pamela? Some chaperone she made, allowing her charge to be flirted with in such leering fashion before everyone who had assembled.

His sister was presently nowhere to be found in the considerable crush.

Tempted to stalk through the revelers and deliver his fist to Mowbray's eye—only fitting, if his shirt points didn't prove accommodating enough—Trevor turned back to his host. "When is this confounded reel at an end?"

"Her Grace would know better than I," the duke said cheerfully, grinning like a fool at a point beyond Trevor's shoulder. "And here she comes now. My love, the Duke of Ridgely is wondering when this cursed reel will be at an end."

The Duchess of Montrose approached, all glittering diamonds and a swirl of gossamer in celestial blue. She was dark-haired and lovely, with eyes only for her husband. The look passing between the two of them—a shared amusement, as if they alone were privy to some manner of secret joke—nettled. He couldn't deny it. Few displays rendered him as bilious as a couple so hideously in love.

It seemed to be a catching sort of disease. His own close friend and fellow former spy, Logan Sutton, was also terribly afflicted by it.

The duchess took her place at Monty's side, offering

Trevor a welcoming smile. "How good it is of you to honor us with your presence. I was so pleased when Lady Deering said you would be present this evening. Having my husband's friends in attendance is always a feather in my cap."

He offered a bow in deference. "The honor is mine, Your Grace."

In truth, he was only here because Pamela had demanded it of him. But no need to be graceless and mention that aloud. On occasion, he could be polite. A gentleman, even.

"To answer your question, I believe the reel is ending now," the duchess said, a knowing smile on her lips. "It looks as if your lovely ward is about to part ways with Viscount Mowbray. I took note of you watching them as I approached. They make a fine couple, do they not? Young Mowbray is such a pleasant gentleman."

Devil take it, had everyone been watching him? Did nothing go unnoticed? Clearly, his awareness and observational skills had suffered since he had left the Guild.

"If one considers insipid dandies with shirt points in their eyes pleasant," he said, quite forgetting his intention to be a gentleman.

Already.

But the dancers were indeed dispersing, and he needed to speak with Lady Virtue. He was not about to allow her to marry herself off to a fop whose only concern was for the cut of his coat.

"Ah," the duchess said, a wealth of meaning in her arch tone. "You do not approve of the match, then? I had understood you were hoping for Lady Virtue to wed this Season."

Did all the *ton* know his personal affairs so well, or was it merely the wives of his friends?

Yes, he would have affirmed mere days ago in answer to the Duchess of Montrose's questions. *I am indeed hoping to marry the chit off. It cannot happen soon enough!* But he was willing to admit—quite grudgingly, and never to another—that over the course of the time Lady Virtue had been in residence and in his care, something had altered. He no longer thought of her as quite the towering burden he once had. The chit was intelligent and fiery and, in his estimation quite rare. He'd never met another like her. And she damned well deserved better than Viscount Mowbray as her husband.

This opinion, he told himself firmly, had absolutely nothing to do with the kisses they'd shared that morning. Nothing at all. He'd kissed dozens of women in his day, and all of them had understood what a kiss was. Never had he needed to show a woman the proper way of it.

Even if that demonstration had been the single most erotic experience of his life.

Trevor cleared his throat, his gaze shifting to the dance floor, where his ward was fast disappearing into the crush of glittering lords and ladies. "Let us say that I merely wish for her to make the best decision for a lady of her nature. She has an inquisitive mind, you see. I cannot imagine her leg-shackled to a man whose chief concern appears to be the knot on his cravat."

"How thoughtful of you," the Duchess of Montrose commented with politic restraint.

"Thoughtful is one word for it," said her husband with considerably less tact, chuckling.

Where the devil had Virtue gone? A dowager's turban had obstructed his view for one moment, and now she was gone. If she was sneaking away to further her kissing lessons with Viscount Dandy, it very well could call for fisticuffs. Soames had carefully arranged Trevor's hair to cover the bruise on his forehead, and he was reasonably certain he wouldn't need to fear earning more should he clash with the viscount. The only bruised and bloodied man betwixt the two of them would be Lord Foppish Shirt Points.

"If you will excuse me, Montrose, Duchess?" he asked, his gaze fixed upon the throng of guests, his ward still nowhere to be seen.

"Of course," husband and wife said in unison.

This too, like the shared glance, was the sort of folderol that inspired biliousness. Love was for henwits and featherbrains. Another bow, and Trevor's feet were already in motion, taking him through the cumbersome swarm of guests.

Montrose's voice chased after him in what was presumably an aside to his duchess. "He rather reminds me of myself, my love."

What the devil did *that* mean?

Scowling, Trevor edged his way past the dowager wearing the atrocious turban, and nearly earned a feather in the eye for his effort. Then a couple exchanging flirtation in the midst of where he needed to be. Was there something contagious in the air tonight?

He jostled past a fellow from one of his clubs who attempted to strike up a conversation. Trevor pretended not to see him and carried on, wading deeper into the melee. Still, nary a hint of Lady Virtue. Where had the minx gone?

As he asked himself that question, grinding his molars, he caught a hint of her dark hair in the crowd. She was walking toward the periphery of the ballroom, aiming for a door. Trevor increased his speed, intent upon hunting her down.

∾

VIRTUE WAS TAKEN by surprise when someone suddenly approached her from behind and herded her into an empty chamber in the hall outside the Duke of Montrose's ballroom.

A most indelicate squeal tore from her as she whirled

about to face the offender who had dared to all but shove her into the room.

"What are you... *You!*"

"Me." The door closed behind Ridgely, and the two of them were alone again, just as they had been that morning.

Only, this time, they were in the midst of a ball, hundreds of fellow guests beyond these four walls. The circumstances were far less scandalous than that morning's. However, at dawn, there hadn't been half the *ton* present to witness their folly.

"You can't be in here with me like this," she hissed, gesturing between the two of them. "Alone."

Ridgely shrugged and then leaned his shoulder against the door in an indolent pose. "Of course I can. I'm your guardian, and you're my ward."

Well, yes. She supposed there was that. Virtue frowned, considering him. He was every bit as handsome by the glowing light of the sconces and lamp as he had been earlier in the carriage. And then again beneath the blazing chandeliers in the ballroom. There was something about Ridgely in evening clothes that made her heart trip over itself and unwanted longing flare to vivid life.

"But your reputation is terrible," she pointed out. "If anyone finds us in here together, they'll assume the worst."

"To the devil with everyone else. *You're* my concern." He slid the latch into place and pushed away from the door, sauntering slowly toward her, his expression grave. "What were you doing, sneaking away from the ball?"

She eyed him warily, aiming for a nonchalant air she little felt as she ventured deeper into the room and farther away from her sinfully tempting guardian. There could be no more kisses between them, regardless of how desperately she yearned for them.

Not here, anyway.

Not *ever*, she reminded herself.

Ridgely himself had proven the fault of her logic. She couldn't persuade him to send her to Greycote Abbey with wanton behavior when she enjoyed it. There was far too much danger in the way his kiss had made her feel. Too much vulnerability. No, she would have to find another means of convincing Ridgely to relieve himself of all duties related to herself and to let her return home.

To that end, Viscount Morbray had seemed an excellent means of making mischief. He was full of himself, he preened like a peacock, and he would be frightfully easy to outwit. Or was it Viscount *Mow*bray? Morbray, Mowbray. It hardly signified. He was a popinjay, and she'd pretended to laugh at his jests during the reel they had partnered in, most of which she hadn't even heard over the din of the orchestra.

"Answer me, infant," Ridgely demanded curtly, stalking her across the room like a cat in search of his prey.

She bumped into a rosewood table, the collision making her thigh smart. She rubbed it and glared at him. "Cease calling me *infant*, and perhaps I will."

"Unfortunately for you, I am the one who issues orders between the two of us," her guardian said smoothly, coming to a halt before her where she had paused on the sumptuous Aubusson. "Tell me what you intended. Were you meeting that fop I saw you partnered with last?"

"He is not a fop," she said, but only because she required Ridgely to believe her smitten with the fellow, and not because she disagreed.

Morbray/Mowbray was indeed a dandy if ever she had seen one.

"His shirt points were nearly blinding him," Ridgely said, his tone cutting. "Do not, I pray you, tell me you didn't take note. I'm reasonably certain they're visible from the moon."

She rolled her lips inward to contain her laugh. Here was

a pity in life. The Duke of Ridgely possessed a cutting, deliciously wicked wit. If he were anyone else—that is to say, if he were a Nottinghamshire suitor and not the evil guardian so intent upon selling her beloved Greycote Abbey and marrying her off—she would have been charmed by him. But he was Ridgely, and Ridgely was horrible with a capital *H*, which was the very worst sort of horrible there was.

Even if she did like kissing him.

Liked kissing him very, very much.

"The viscount takes care in his wardrobe," she defended her dancing partner lightly. "I find his attention to his dress admirable, if you must know."

"Admirable?" Ridgely's eyes narrowed to slits of sparkling obsidian in the lower lights of the sitting room. "I can think of rather a great deal of adjectives one might use to describe the peacock in question, and none of them are admirable."

"Don't be unkind." She forced a smile. "I think I am in love with him. Desperately, hopelessly in love with him."

The duke sputtered, and were she not so intent upon her performance, she would have enjoyed his discomfiture immensely.

"In *love*? By God, did he tell you to slip away from the ball and meet him in a private room so he could compromise you? It's like the scheming little worm has discovered you're to have a sizable dowry, and he intends to spend it on hideous cravats and vomitous waistcoats."

Virtue glared back at her guardian. "Do you suppose his lordship would only be interested in me for my dowry? Would not a gentleman wish to marry me based on my own merits?"

"A gentleman, yes. But not a scoundrel who attempts to lure you away from a ball. I forbid you from dancing with Viscount Mowbury again." Ridgely sighed, then brushed at the sleeve of his coat. "You'll come with me, and I shall return you to the watchful eye of Lady Deering, who will be reminded she needs to implement a shorter leash on you. Come."

Mowbury? Was that the viscount's name? Virtue was reasonably certain it was Morbray or Mowbray. But not Mowbury.

"His name is Morbray," she guessed, hoping she was right, for the correct title seemed more important now. She needed Ridgely to believe she was serious.

It only caused the duke's gaze to sharpen. "*Mow*bray, my dear. You see? You cannot be in love with the fellow when you don't even know his name."

Blast. Perhaps she had been wrong about the viscount's title.

"You called him Mowbury," she pointed out.

"Yes," he said slowly, as if he were explaining to a child, "as a slight."

Interesting.

"You dislike him, then?" she probed, not sure why it mattered to her; Ridgely's opinion of the viscount meant nothing.

She had no intention of marrying the man.

The stinging ache in her thigh had finally dissipated, and she reasoned this was as good a time as any to put some more, much-needed distance between herself and the duke. She slipped nearer to the hearth, where a fire was merrily dancing in the grate. Surely a servant would soon arrive to attend it and find the door latched.

Ridgely's stern voice followed her as she made her escape. "I dislike that he was attempting to lead my innocent ward astray. Where are you going? I'm attempting to have a conversation with you."

Away from you, she thought, rubbing at her bare upper arms where her kid gloves ended. Not from cold but to chase the awareness that would not stop seeping into her body at Ridgely's proximity.

She forced herself to turn back to him. "I thought you wanted me to marry with haste."

Looking upon him was unfair, she thought. He was a Gorgon, a veritable masculine Medusa. Only, instead of turning her into stone, one look at him reduced her to a puddle of wanton longing.

"Yes," he said, drawing nearer with those graceful, long-limbed strides, "but not to some witless fool who cares more about the cut of his coat than his wife."

"I shouldn't think it any of your concern how my future husband treats me," she pointed out, and not without bitterness. "The sooner you are freed of the burden of being my guardian, the better."

"I'll still be your guardian after you marry. Until you turn one-and-twenty, your welfare is in my hands, regardless of whether or not you wed. It is my preference, naturally, for you to marry a man of my choosing, that he may essentially take my place until you reach your majority. Mowbray is decidedly *not* that man."

Her ire rose as he stopped before her, his maddening scent mingling with the burning wood of the fire. "A man of *your* choosing?"

He inclined his head, his expression still somber, his jaw hard. "A man of whom I approve."

"And you do not approve of Morbray?" she asked.

The corner of his mouth curved upward in the semblance of a mocking grin. "His name is Mowbray, my dear."

Curse Ridgely. He had left her mind a confused jumble yet again.

She tipped up her chin. "And I am in love with him."

He scowled. "No, you are not. You've only just danced with him once."

"Once was enough. I am sure his lordship would never dream of confiscating my books and making all my decisions for me," she snapped, beyond vexed with him.

He was an overbearing rogue.

What *had* her father been thinking, leaving her at this man's mercy?

"Is that what this is about?" Ridgely's brows drew together, and suddenly, he moved.

Moved with such haste she hadn't realized what he was about until it was too late, and he had successfully caged her at the hearth, one hand planted on either side of the mantel, his arms barring her from movement unless she slipped beneath them. But to do so would be a retreat. A sign of weakness when she could ill afford to allow any to show. This was a battle between herself and her guardian, after all. A battle of wills and wits.

And she *would* emerge the victor.

"I don't know what you are speaking of," she denied, attempting to maintain her calm.

And to avoid kissing him again at all costs.

His head dipped nearer to hers, that dark gaze threatening to swallow her whole with its intensity. "Were you baiting me by dancing with Mowbray and then agreeing to an assignation with him?"

Partially, and curse him for being so astute.

She made a sound of indignation. "Not everything is about *you*, Ridgely."

His lips quirked into a full smile, the effect of which settled in her belly and descended lower, to a far more wicked place. "It ought to be about me. I'm a bloody interesting chap, in case you've failed to notice."

Oh, she had noticed. She had noticed a great many things about the duke. Including that the chest currently hidden beneath his crisp white-and-black eveningwear was nothing short of wondrous.

"Are you making an attempt at humor whilst you've locked me away in a room in the midst of a ball?" she demanded. "Lady Deering will soon take note of my absence, I have no doubt. We must return at once."

"Don't feign concern over propriety now, my dear. I'm afraid your little game is at an end. You can thank me later for coming to your rescue and saving you from the gaping maw of complete and utter folly." He leaned into her, so near they were almost touching. "*No. More. Causing. Trouble.* Am I understood?"

She smiled up at him and blinked her lashes slowly, as she had seen one of the coquettish debutantes do to a suitor. "*More* causing trouble?"

He growled. "You heard me."

Her smile deepened. "You could always send me back to Greycote Abbey. There is no trouble for me to find there."

"Even if I wanted to, I could not send you there. I am obligated to follow your father's wishes to the letter, and his wishes were clear. Greycote Abbey must be sold."

Stalemate yet again.

She heaved a frustrated sigh. "And yet, no one is concerned with *my* wishes, whilst I stand here before you."

"I *am* concerned with your wishes. As your guardian and a friend of your father's, I must attend to both."

The levity had fled his countenance now, but he remained motionless, keeping her neatly pinned by the fire, which was warming her back quite pleasantly. She felt languid and heavy all at once, his nearness and the flames enveloping her, desire pulsing to life between her thighs. The ache was most persistent. She pressed her legs together in an attempt to subdue it, but the action only served to make the longing worse.

"I'm in love with Mowbray," she lied.

His expression hardened as he abruptly pushed away from the mantel. "No, you're not. I can see there is only one way I'll put this nonsense out of your mind."

"Oh?" She moved away from the hearth, overheated and dizzied and knowing it had far more to do with Ridgely than the actual fire. "Pray, enlighten me, o ye wise and aged guardian."

"Not so very aged," he was quick to deny.

Ah, her small insult had found its aim.

Her lips twitched. "Nor so wise, one might argue, and quite reasonably, too."

"Has anyone ever told you that you possess the impertinence of a hundred men?"

A compliment, she was sure.

"Oddly, no."

"Come with me, o troublesome ward." He extended his arm to her, every bit the gentleman he looked.

She eyed him dubiously. "Where are you taking me?"

"To the ballroom. We will dance, and if my sister is correct, you will be swarmed with a host of suitors." His tone was grim. "Suitors who are far more worthy of you than young Mowbray."

Dancing with Ridgely sounded dangerous. She feared she would like it far too much. But she rather supposed she had begun her attack this evening. In matters of battle, it was often prudent to allow the enemy to believe he had gained the upper hand before mounting an offensive strike.

She took his arm. "If we must."

He grumbled something unintelligible beneath his breath. "Indeed, we must."

CHAPTER 7

Trevor woke in the darkness of the early-morning hours to the soft *snick* of a door closing and the rustle of linen. He rose into a sitting position, searching through the darkness. His first thought was that it must be Virtue. He'd been dredged from the depths of a dream about her. He'd been chasing her in a meadow, of all places. She'd been flitting away, forever beyond his reach, the tinkling music of her laughter taunting him, her hair a dark, wispy cloud behind her as she ran, barefoot through a field of forget-me-nots.

There was an odd heaviness in his chest as he jolted from that dream, the feelings it had inspired still very much real. Longing for her, desperate longing. Love. In the dream, he'd been in love with her. The feeling had been there, sure. And he'd thought to himself that he understood why Monty had looked so mawkish when gazing upon his duchess. That it all made sense.

Christ.

"Virtue, is that you?" he demanded into the shadows, his eyes examining the muck of the night for her familiar form.

And that was when his old instincts as a spy instantly woke him up, taking the helm of the ship.

For the shadow was far too tall, moving across the chamber, into the faint glow produced by the remaining fire in the grate. Wide shoulders, the gait of a man.

The trespasser was not his ward. And there wasn't anyone in the household sufficiently near to offer him assistance. Soames kept his own room, and the only people close enough were Pamela and Virtue. He didn't dare alert the most vulnerable members of his household to the presence of a thief—or worse. No, he would have to defend himself and his women as well.

Fucking hell.

"Must have been a dream," he murmured aloud, as if to himself, hoping to lull the intruder into the false hope that he wasn't lucid.

The shadow had halted, standing as a silent sentinel halfway across the room, so still and quiet that Trevor might have believed he had imagined the bastard. But he knew better. He laid his head back upon the pillow with a sleepy yawn that was also feigned, pretending to stretch and alter his position on the bed as he made a show of pulling at the counterpane.

As he did so, he kept his eyes carefully slanted in the direction of the shadow. The nearest object to a weapon that he possessed was a candlestick on the table by his bed. He'd have to allow the villain to get close enough so that he could defend himself.

And pray the bastard didn't have a pistol on him.

Trevor's fingers found the cool ormolu and he grasped the thankfully substantial weight of the candlestick. Another swift movement, and he had his weapon hidden beneath the counterpane, ready.

He feigned sleep breathing, remaining still in an effort to

lull the intruder into the belief that he had fallen back into slumber and would thus be vulnerable once more. But though his eyes were lightly closed, he could yet see beneath slightly raised lashes. He stared so hard into the darkness that his eyes began to twitch, his heart hammering hard, palms going damp.

How easy it was to return to the man he had once been, the man for whom danger was a common threat.

And then, at last, the shadow moved. More slowly this time, approaching with grave caution. Trevor was a serpent, coiled and prepared to strike. The fire crackled and a sudden pop of a piece of wood catching newly alight echoed, illuminating the figure for a fleeting moment.

A man for certain, the arm raised, the indistinct outline of a blade gripped in the hand. Trevor reacted, throwing back the coverlet and hitting the raised arm with his hidden candlestick. There was the thump of the dagger dropping to the carpet. The man who'd been about to stab him issued a grunt.

Trevor leapt to his feet on the opposite side of the bed. "Get the hell out of my chamber and out of my house," he said sharply, taking care to keep his voice from carrying in the night.

If his sister and Virtue awoke and emerged from their chambers, there was no telling what would happen.

There was a flurry of movement from the other side of the bed as the would-be murderer began running from the room.

Trevor started forward, rounding the bed, determined to give chase. If he could catch the fellow, tackle him perhaps, he could see him subdued until Bow Street was called. But the villain was hasty on his feet, running down the hall as Trevor stormed after him. There was a terrible crash as the man ran into a familial bust and sent it to the floor in the gallery.

On he chased, determined. His own bare feet made a distinctly different sound landing on the stone stairs than the man he pursued, whose leather soles made a clacking sound that cut through the darkness and stillness of the night. The bastard had paraded through his home to kill him, wearing a fine pair of boots. For some reason, this outrage occurred to Trevor, seemingly of utmost importance, in his shock at his brush with death. Beneath his feet, the stone was cold and unforgiving as ever, slippery too. He took care to keep from tripping over his own blasted feet and breaking his neck, his thoughts moving faster than the rest of him. The urge to apprehend the man who had attempted to stab him pumped to the fore, *catch him, catch him, catch him*, almost in time to the beat of his heart.

When they made it halfway down the Grecian staircase that twisted through the heart of Hunt House, the assailant lost his footing on the slick stone. With a cry of terror, the man pitched down the stairs. Trevor raced down the staircase to the din of the sickening crunch of bones and thumps of the other man falling down the stairs, flesh connecting with the cantilevered stone stairway in merciless fashion.

The man he had been chasing reached the bottom first and slumped, motionless on the floor. Trevor carried on to the base of the staircase and the cold marble in the hall below.

The startled voices of servants were emerging from their quarters below stairs, apparently awakened by the shouts and thuds. His butler Ames, dressed in banyan and nightcap, strode forth, raising a candle to illuminate the bottom of the staircase.

"Your Grace, what is the matter?" Ames asked, alarm tingeing his ordinarily august and unflappable tones.

"There was an intruder," Trevor managed, breathless from the frenzy of his reaction to the danger, not taking his eyes from the seemingly lifeless body of the villain he had just barely thwarted. "This man. I believe he intended to kill me. A weapon—someone find me a weapon."

"A weapon, Your Grace?"

"A fire iron," he said, his gaze never wavering. He had pistols locked away, but there wasn't sufficient time for them to be retrieved now. The prone figure didn't appear to be breathing, his head at a strange angle, blood beginning to pool on the marble. "Someone fetch me a fire iron."

On the odd chance the bastard hadn't managed to break his own neck in his tumble, Trevor intended to defend himself and his household against the man however he must. And in this moment, nothing would feel more satisfying than taking a fire iron to the villain's skull.

Curious as to the man's identity, Trevor used his foot to nudge the lifeless body, rolling him over. Blood and bruising from the impact of his fall down the stairs made it difficult to discern the features, but he could see well enough to know there was nothing familiar about the man. He was a stranger to Trevor. Why would a stranger be intent upon killing him? If his interest had been in thieving some Hunt family heirlooms, surely he would have made away with the silver or some paintings or a vase.

It made no sense. The man's sole aim appeared to have been stabbing Trevor.

"Good heavens, Ridgely, what is all this commotion about?" Pamela demanded suddenly from above, intruding on his mind's attempt to make sense of this muddle. "What has happened?"

He glanced up for a moment to see his sister's worried face illuminated by the glow of yet another taper from above, the open, circular staircase giving her an unimpeded view of the base of the stairs.

Blast.

She screamed, the shrill sound echoing off the stone and marble.

"Bloody hell," he muttered, his attention returning to the felled stranger as he winced at the sharpness of his sister's alarm.

Quite the lungs Pamela possessed.

Her lady's maid pushed to the vanguard of the collection of worried servants. "May I attend her ladyship, Your Grace?"

The would-be murderer had neither, as yet, moved nor taken breath that Trevor had seen. An eerie calm had settled over him that he recognized well from his days as a spy. There was always first the action, then the shock, followed by an odd surge of the need to take command of the situation. To see the traitor captured, the revolutionary caught in his trap, the murderer felled. And then afterward, to clean up the mess of it, literally and figuratively.

He nodded to the lady's maid. "Please do attend to Lady Deering, and my ward as well."

Certainly, Virtue would have been awakened by this dreadful affair. If nothing else by Pamela's scream. Unless…

New fear rose within him, sudden and jarring, swelling like an uncontrollable tide. His heart clenched, his mouth going dry. If the bastard had dared to harm a hair on her head, he would… Christ, what *would* he do? He didn't want to contemplate it. Couldn't bear it.

He had to make certain she was safe.

"What is happening?"

Virtue's confused voice cut through his wild thoughts, filling him with relief. Another glance up confirmed she was safe. And by God, wearing some sort of diaphanous night rail which ought to be outlawed. Where the devil was her dressing gown?

"Return to your chambers, ladies," he called sharply, his voice echoing in the eerie stillness which had fallen in the hall. "I have this matter firmly under control."

"Who is that man?" Pamela was demanding, hand over her heart.

"I haven't an inkling," he answered honestly. "Now kindly take Lady Virtue to your room, if you please, while I see this matter sorted."

At least his sister had the common sense to cover herself with a dressing gown. He had no doubt that it was new and had cost him dearly, but at least half the footmen weren't gaping up at her. He cut his gaze to the shocked domestics gathered, the size of which was growing by the moment.

One of the footmen finally reached Trevor, rushing forward with the fire poker he had requested. He accepted it and returned his gaze to the man at his feet who, it was more than apparent by this juncture, was dead.

He'd likely broken his neck in the fall.

For once, the stone steps which had been the pride of his father and which Trevor had always loathed—they were so damned cold and hard, just like his sire's heart—had actually proven beneficial. Difficult to credit, but there it was. The former Duke of Ridgely was likely turning in his grave at the prospect.

"What shall I do, Your Grace?" Ames asked.

Trevor looked down at the dead man at his feet and made a sudden, unwanted realization. First the blow he'd taken to his head the other night, now a knife-wielding assassin in his chamber in the midst of the night. These were not poorly timed coincidences.

Someone was trying to kill him.

Someone wanted him *dead*.

Dead enough to attempt to murder him in his own bed.

Was it just the man on the floor before him, or were there others? Trevor knew not. All he did know was that there were few men on this earth he trusted like the men who had been a part of the Guild. They were like brothers to him, in bond if not blood. He needed them at Hunt House, and he needed them now.

"Send word to Logan Sutton and Archer Tierney," he told his butler. "I want them here first."

"Right away, Your Grace," Ames said.

∽

"Dead, is he not?" Trevor asked of the sleepy-eyed friends who had dashed to Hunt House at his request.

And in the very bowels of the night, no less. Thank God not everyone in London thought him a base scoundrel. Then again, perhaps these two did, but he would entrust his very life to their hands, and he was damned glad they had answered his call.

They were gathered at the base of the stairs, where a coverlet had been summoned to cover the body of the man in question. The better to assuage the tender sensibilities of the servants and ladies of the household, all of whom had been told to remain in their quarters until any traces of lingering danger could be assessed by Trevor, Sutton, and Tierney.

Tierney sank to his haunches by the still, blanket-clad form and flipped back the corner to take a look within. "Quite."

"Gone to Rothisbones," Logan Sutton concurred grimly, gazing down at the body. "Didn't know you were in the business of hushing calls, Ridgely. I thought you were only in the flesh trade."

He ignored the jibe, for he employed no prostitutes at The Velvet Slipper. *Saint's teeth*, it was a club. A very exclusive one which catered to very particular tastes, but a club nonetheless.

"I didn't kill the bastard," Trevor said. "He did, however, try to kill me."

Tierney rose, his expression grim, his green gaze sharp and intelligent. "Tell us what happened, from beginning to end."

Trevor relayed the tale, from waking in the night to the sound of someone entering his room, to the subsequent battle for his life, the lost knife, and the assailant's frantic attempts to flee.

"Which ended," Trevor gestured to the body on the marble hall, "in this fashion, as you can see. He slipped on the stone stairs and couldn't right himself in the darkness. Broke his neck in the fall, unless I'm mistaken."

"Do you recognize 'im?" Sutton asked.

A man born and raised in the rookeries, Logan Sutton's roots sometimes showed in his speech patterns and odd turns of phrase. One look at the auburn-haired man before him, however, and no one would see Sutton as anything but the elegant gentleman he appeared to be. Trevor, however, knew what Sutton was capable of. He was clever, loyal, and fearless.

Well, he'd been relentlessly loyal to the Guild until he'd met his wife. Now, Mrs. Sutton retained much of the loyalty Sutton had once devoted to the Guild, and the Guild had been disbanded.

Love, or some such rot.

"I've never seen him before," Trevor said of the bastard who would have slain him. "Do either of you recognize him?"

He was thinking of their former work for Whitehall, of course, and the many criminals they had dealt with during the time they had operated the Guild.

"No," Tierney said. "I've never seen him."

"Nor have I," Sutton added.

"Damn it," he muttered, running a hand through his hair.

That would have been too easy, he reckoned.

Sutton whistled through his teeth, his gaze going to the healing knot on Trevor's head. "That's quite the knock you took to the old knowledge box, Ridgely. It doesn't look new, either."

"It isn't new," he admitted on a heavy sigh. "Nor is this the first attempt on my life."

"What the devil, Ridgely?" Tierney shook his head. "Why didn't you call for us after the first attempt?"

An excellent question. He'd been foolish to believe, he realized now, that a footpad would hit him over the head with such exuberance. Most pickpockets were skilled enough to merely jostle a victim and relieve them of their coin, without the target ever being aware of what had happened.

Another sigh. "Because I thought I'd merely been robbed. Considering what happened tonight, I've realized how wrong I was to make assumptions."

"Given your state of dress, I take it you were in bed when you were attacked," Tierney said.

He'd had the presence of mind to fetch a banyan as he waited for his friends to arrive and throw it over his nightshirt, but he was still in his bare feet.

"Yes," he said, his mind returning to the moments in the darkness when he had first realized someone was in his room, his heart beginning to pound again. "I was asleep in my chamber when he came into my room. I've made some inquiries with the household, and from all accounts, nothing has been stolen, and nor was anyone else's chamber entered."

"The bastard knew where to find you then," Sutton surmised.

"I cannot think otherwise," he agreed. "Hunt House is not a small residence. He knew directly where to go."

"Hunt House is a bloody castle," Tierney said wryly.

It was obscenely large. Trevor couldn't argue the point. His father had created a monument to his own vanity and wealth.

"Aye, the bastard would have been more concerned with the silver and anything he could easily transport that was of value if he were a cracksman," Sutton agreed. "That nothing was missing, and he went straight to your chamber, is telling."

"What became of his weapon?" Tierney asked, his manner businesslike and brusque.

As if it were every day that he dealt with matters such as attempted murders and dead bodies. But then, since Tierney had been the leader of the Guild, Christ only knew what he'd seen and done. Trevor had never asked.

Now didn't seem the moment to begin, either.

"He had a knife," he said, remembering the glint of the firelight on the blade as the man had raised it high. "Not a small affair, either. I was prepared for him and hit him with a candlestick, knocking it from his hand."

Tierney nodded. "The knife fell, presumably to the floor. What happened then?"

It was a blur of sound and shadows, protective rage and shock and fear. Nothing seemed as clear and distinct as it had in the moment, when he'd been forced to defend himself. But then, that was rather the way of it with the mind. Violence and upheaval did strange things to the memory, rendering it hazy and confusing at times and at other times obscenely clear.

"He ran," Trevor said, forcing himself to remember. "I chased after him, intent upon catching the scoundrel before he could do any further mischief. We rushed into the hall and through the picture gallery, and then reached the staircase."

"Take us to your chamber," Sutton said. "We'll be needing to find that knife. It may give us some manner of clue."

It was an excellent point. His mind had been so scattered earlier when he'd retrieved his banyan that he hadn't even thought about the blade or finding it.

He inclined his head, grateful anew for the friendship of these two trusted men. "Follow me."

They climbed the stone stairs that had proven the dead man's downfall, Trevor leading them on the same path he and his assailant had traveled not long before. Now, the sconces in the halls were blazing, every corner of Hunt House filled with light from the efforts of diligent footmen, who had ventured past the body when housemaids were kept below stairs.

They were through the picture gallery and proceeding down the hall when a door popped open. And there stood Virtue, still clad in nothing more than a night rail, her dark hair a tangled mess around her lovely face. It shouldn't have been at all endearing and yet, it somehow was.

"Ridgely, what is happening?" she asked, her gaze darting to the two men flanking him.

By God, he could see the silhouette of her lush form, clearly delineated beneath that excuse for a garment she wore. Even in his present state of alarm, he could not look away from the glory of her curves lovingly illumined by the light at her back. A careful glance at both Sutton and Tierney revealed they had averted their gazes in deference to the lady's state of dishabille. Thank Christ. He'd hate to have to challenge the only men he could currently trust to a duel over Virtue's honor.

"My lady, please return to your chamber until you are otherwise instructed," he snapped at her, not surprised at her latest inability to do as she was told.

When had she ever?

The chit was a walking, breathing, magnificent study in rebellion.

"Not until you tell me what has occurred," she said stubbornly, her eyes darting to his companions. "Ah, Mr. Sutton, how good it is to see you again. Whatever are you doing here at this time of night? And you, sir…"

Truly? She expected him to perform introductions at half past four in the morning, after an assassin had just broken his neck on the staircase, and whilst she was *nearly nude*?

"This isn't a ballroom, Lady Virtue," he corrected her sharply. "Nor are you dressed for company. I suggest you return to your chamber and await further direction from me."

As if belatedly realizing how scantily clad she was, Virtue glanced down at her night rail, a becoming flush rising to her cheeks. "Oh dear, I do suppose I ought to have put on a dressing gown, at least. Forgive me."

"You are forgiven," he said curtly, recalling the godawful ache in his gut when he had momentarily feared something ill had befallen her and relenting. "Given the shock of the evening, it's only to be expected."

She was safe, thank God. And so was Pamela. As was he, for now.

The ominous reminder spurred him on, forcing him to add, "Mr. Sutton, Mr. Tierney, and myself are examining my chamber for clues. If you will excuse us, my lady?"

"Clues for what?" she asked, stubborn and maddening as ever. "Lady Deering was screaming, but I couldn't decipher much of what she was saying. There appeared to be a dead man at the base of the staircase."

Her composure was impeccable. How did she manage it? His own sister had dissolved into hysterics, and Pamela was as hardened as an anvil.

Trevor cleared his throat. "There is indeed a body at the base of the staircase."

"Who is he?" she asked, lingering at the threshold and making no effort to fetch the dressing gown she'd mentioned.

This damned ward of his was going to prove the death of him.

If whomever it was who wanted him dead didn't first.

"We don't know," he ground out. "Lady Virtue, please return to your room."

"Oh, but I would dearly love to be of assistance."

Why was he not surprised?

Trevor stifled a groan. "No."

"Why not?" Tierney asked, slanting him a diabolical grin.

The cunning wretch likely scented his desperation to be rid of his ward's unwanted and unnecessary temptation. Archer Tierney was like a damned shark.

"Because it isn't done," he countered, *sotto voce*. "She's my innocent ward."

Sutton snorted. "Couldn't be innocent for long with you as her guardian."

Had he considered these two his friends as recently as approximately one minute prior? For some incomprehensible reason, yes, he had.

More fool he.

Trevor glared at Tierney and Sutton and then at his ward for good measure. "Back in your room, infant. At once."

Her face fell, and he rather felt as if he'd kicked a puppy.

He, who had nearly been slashed to death in his own bed, not long ago.

He was a candidate for Bedlam, clearly.

Trevor waited for the door to close, and then he carried on, leading the still-snickering Tierney and Sutton to his chamber where the knife—and hopefully some answers—awaited.

CHAPTER 8

Someone had tried to kill Ridgely.

The thought had haunted Virtue for hours. Ever since she had spied him in the hall at half past four that morning, looking somber and yet handsome as ever in his bare feet and silk banyan as he led his friends toward the scene of the crime which had almost occurred.

She shuddered again to think of it now as she moved stealthily toward the library, how close he had come to death. It was…well, the thought still robbed her of breath, making her lungs go tight in her chest. Ridgely was so vibrant, so magnificent, so big and strong and powerful and…

No, she had best not continue to enumerate all the pleasant attributes of her guardian. It would do her no good to dwell upon them. Instead, she would take advantage of his distraction—understandable, given the mayhem which had ensued after the night's upheaval, which had bled into the morning hours and then the afternoon as well. Yes, she would use his diversion to find something with which she might entertain herself.

She didn't dare attempt to steal back one of the books Ridgely had taken from her chamber. However, what would be the harm in finding a tome to distract her within the walled shelves of his library with no one about to deny her access? There were so many books that she had no doubt he would never miss just one. Would never be the wiser that she had defied his edicts yet again.

At last, there was the room she sought, its door conveniently ajar as if in welcome. Calling to her, she might even say, were anyone to ask. Not that anyone would. Lady Deering had been notably absent at breakfast and later as well. Virtue had been informed that her ladyship was suffering a megrim and would be keeping to her rooms for the remainder of the day. Naturally, all social obligations had been regretfully declined.

With Ridgely busied by the events of the night before and Lady Deering conveniently indisposed, Virtue was free to roam. She paused as she reached her destination, checking the hall outside the library in both directions to ascertain that she had not been seen. Nary a soul.

And that was to be expected as well.

It wasn't every day that someone attempted to murder the master of the house. Her guardian may have attempted to keep the truth from her, but he ought to have known the servants possessed tongues. The below stairs gossip was ever so much more interesting than that above. Whenever Virtue wanted to know anything, she spoke with the domestics. In that sense, life at Hunt House was not so very different from life at Greycote Abbey.

With a sigh of relief that she remained unseen, she closed the door at her back, giving herself complete and utter privacy. Nothing but herself and walls of books and a crackling fire in the hearth and…

What *was* that sound?

It sounded rather like a bear.

Virtue ventured deeper into the chamber and that was when she made the discovery. It was not simply herself, a wall of books, and a crackling fire in the hearth.

It was also a snoring duke on a divan.

The Duke of Ridgely, to be precise.

Whatever was he doing, sleeping in the library? She had supposed that after the mayhem of the night and morning, he had gone to wherever it was he disappeared during the day. Instead, he was still here. Looking unfairly handsome in repose, as if all the troubles of the day had been abandoned to the ethers of slumber.

She should go. Allow him his privacy and small sense of peace in the wake of such brutal upheaval.

Virtue's feet, however, had other ideas. Because they were taking her closer. Across the Axminster. It was the angle of his head, she suspected—a deuced uncomfortable-looking degree—which was prompting the bearish snores. He would likely have a sore neck when he awoke.

She hovered over him, feeling oddly proprietary. Someone had tried to murder this beautiful man in his bed. And whilst he was a vexing guardian, she was startled to discover a strong burst of emotion in her heart as she gazed down at him. A hot rush. Quite unique and unusual. Some elemental force of yearning, as if he were gravity and she a celestial body being pulled.

She *cared* for the Duke of Ridgely.

When had it happened, and how? Was it a natural reaction born of his skillful kisses? Had it begun when she had watched him disrobing and spied the masculine perfection of his muscled back and chest? Or perhaps the reason was far less reliant upon the corporeal and instead produced by something else—the shock of learning someone had attempted to take his life.

She supposed the origin of the unwanted affection mattered not.

It was there, beating inside her heart, and she had no notion of how to excise it as she stood there, her greedy eyes drinking in every detail of his form. His strong jaw was shaded with whiskers. He hadn't shaved. But of course, he hadn't. He would have dressed out of necessity. Unbidden, the memory of him earlier that day, barefoot and disreputable in his silk banyan, made forbidden warmth burn in her belly. She had seen him as his lovers had, in that rare and private lack of polish, sans cravat and waistcoat and gleaming boots or shoes. More than once.

And she was seeing him now as the women he'd gone to bed with must have. In repose, his even breaths making his chest rise and fall, the natural smolder and almost raffish charm he possessed absent in his relaxed features. He looked, she thought, almost innocent. Young and free of the weighty responsibilities that ordinarily kept his jaw clenched and his eyes flinty.

Less ducal.

Less like the arrogant guardian who had punished her by taking her books.

The air was chilly in the library despite the fire in the hearth, for the room was cavernous, with a second level of books ringing its periphery. And Ridgely had no counterpane. She looked about for something which might be used to cover him, unwelcome tenderness creeping over her. Truly, she ought to simply reach for the nearest book and flee, making do with whatever tome she secured for distraction, before Ridgely was ever the wiser to her forbidden foray into the library.

But instead, she found a fur blanket draped over one of

the armchairs flanking the fire and returned to his side, spreading it over him with care. She was about to make good on her escape when he shifted, his hand shooting out to grasp her wrist in an almost punishing grip.

"Virtue?" He sat up, scowling, and released her hand. "What the devil are you doing in here? I thought for a moment... Christ, I could have hurt you. I *didn't* hurt you, did I?"

He looked tired, dark half circles beneath his eyes from a lack of sleep, marring the otherwise flawless perfection of his countenance.

"You didn't hurt me," she said quietly. "There's a chill in the air. I was merely trying to keep you warm."

His gaze narrowed. "Are you certain you weren't trying to smother me in my sleep?"

"Of course not," she said, frowning down at him, startled that he would make a joke about such a serious matter so soon after he had been attacked. "I may not like you, Ridgely, but I do not wish any harm upon you. Perhaps a well-timed splatter of bird offal upon your favorite hat, or a misstep in horse dung with your favorite boots, or too much salt in your soup, or a sudden fit of sneezing..." Her words trailed off as she realized she was chattering inanely and also revealing rather too much about the fantasies his smug treatment had inspired. She cleared her throat nervously. "Well. As you can see, nothing so fiendish as plotting your murder."

But someone else was. She bit her lip and wished she could recall her words, their gazes colliding.

"I'm vastly relieved by your munificence," he said wryly, sweeping back the fur she had spread over him and rising to his full height. "Such a caring, tenderhearted ward I have."

She winced. "I am sorry, Ridgely."

He raised a brow. "What are you sorry for, infant? Trespassing in my library?"

Well, er, yes. There was that. He had told her she was barred from entering, had he not?

"For what happened to you," she elaborated. "The man who attempted to murder you in the midst of the night. You must have been terrified."

He scrubbed a hand over his jaw, his scowl deepening. "You weren't meant to be told about that. Who informed you?"

"All the household knows," she answered indirectly, not wishing to cause harm to any of the domestics who had shared their confidence with her that morning. "It's hardly a secret."

He sighed heavily. "Very well. Someone wants me dead. Since I've never seen the fellow who met his end on the stairs last night, I can only surmise he was a hired assassin."

Which meant that whomever it was who had made the attempt on Ridgely's life was still out there somewhere in London, with a deadly vendetta against him. A cold spike of fear burrowed itself deep in her heart.

"An assassin?"

"Yes, and not a terribly successful one, thankfully." He flashed her a grim smile. "And one who is now happily out of commission."

"You shouldn't jest about such a serious matter, Ridgely." She frowned at him. "You could be in grave danger."

He gave a bitter little laugh. "You needn't fear for me, infant. This isn't the first time I've been in danger, and nor, I haven't a doubt, shall it be the last."

He was speaking of his past, she suspected. Ridgely had been a member of a secretive group known as the Guild before she had come to stay with him. She knew his work had been perilous. But then, her gaze caught on the lingering bruise on his forehead, partially covered by a wave of dark hair.

She gasped. "The footpad, you mean. Are you suggesting he was more than a thief?"

Ridgely inclined his head. "It would seem so, given my nocturnal visitor."

"Do you think it was the same man who attacked you before?"

The duke shrugged. "I'm ashamed to admit I wasn't paying attention. I was ambushed from the shadows and my only recollection is a staggering blow to the head. Now, if you don't mind, I've had rather enough of your questions. I've one for you instead. What are you doing in my library?"

Ah, he hadn't forgotten his edict, it would seem.

She folded her hands together at her waist, attempting to look demure and innocent. "I heard a snore as I walked past in the hall, and I came to investigate. When I found you sleeping, I thought only of your comfort. I intended to leave forthwith, but you stayed me."

With that firm grip. She'd startled him, but given what he'd endured the night before, it was understandable.

"Let me see your wrists," he said, extending his hands, palm up.

"I'm perfectly fine," she returned, not wanting him to touch her or lure her nearer for fear of the effect both would have upon her. "I'm not delicate."

"Nonsense. I want to see."

He moved forward, ending the meager distance between them, and took her forearms in a gentle grip, turning them over. Her clasped fingers unthreaded themselves, and then he was simply holding her hands in his, his thumbs tracing lightly over the pale skin and blue veins of her inner wrists.

"You see?" she asked, striving for a brisk tone. Instead, her voice was thick with an embarrassing combination of emotion and desire. "I told you no harm was done."

"I shouldn't have been so rough with you." His head was

bent, perilously close to hers, thumbs still swirling over her skin, doing astonishing things to her pulse. "Forgive me. I hadn't intended to fall asleep in the library, but after Tierney sent his bodyguards over this morning, my weariness finally hit me. I couldn't sleep in my bed, however. Not yet…"

Bodyguards? Whatever Ridgely found himself ensnared in, it was clearly dangerous.

His words trailed away, and he glanced up at her, the searing connection of his gaze on hers rendering her breathless. Was it his bare hands on hers, the maddening swirl of his thumbs against flesh she had never realized was so starving with need? Was it his mentioning of a bed, his nearness, the shock of nearly losing him?

Strange to think how dependent she was upon him. Her entire life had been at Greycote Abbey. Now that she had been plucked away from her home and everyone she had known, the Duke of Ridgely and his sister were truly all she had.

But no, it wasn't that pointed fact which made her sway toward him now.

"You're so soft," he murmured, almost an accusation, though there wasn't any sting in his voice.

She should extricate herself. Recall that Ridgely was a practiced seducer. The man who was currently withholding her books and demanding Greycote Abbey be sold and that she enter into a bloodless union with a man of his choosing.

But he was also the man who had kissed her with such sweet and tender passion. The man who touched her with gentle caresses that brought all the fire she'd never known was burning inside her to vibrant life. Who had danced with her at the ball last night with such flawless elegance.

And he was the beautiful sinner who watched her now with a dark, hooded stare. So intent upon her that she felt his gaze as if it were a touch. Felt it everywhere, from her lips to the tight buds of her nipples straining against her stays, to the heaviness in her belly and between her legs.

Longing. Forbidden and reckless, yet far too potent to resist. Of all the lures that had ever pulled her, the Duke of Ridgely was the strongest, his magnetic attraction drawing her almost against her will.

"Ridgely," she said, half whisper, half plea.

"I was dreaming of you," he told her, his baritone a low, pleasant rasp to her senses. "First in the night, when that bastard came into my chamber and just now, here, in the library as well."

Dreaming of her? The intimacy of it—she'd been inhabiting his very thoughts—secretly thrilled her every bit as much as his wandering thumbs did.

Breathlessly, she asked, "What was your dream?"

"I was chasing you in a meadow. You had forget-me-nots in your hair the second time. A crown of tiny blue flowers adorning your head."

He was serious, his expression inscrutable. The air between them seemed to vibrate with awareness.

She swallowed hard against a rising tide of yearning. "Did you catch me?"

His brow furrowed. "Never."

But he'd caught her now. And she liked it. Didn't wish to move and sever the contact. Not now. Perhaps not ever. Her own foolishness shocked and disappointed her. *This is Ridgely*, she reminded herself sternly. *Be cautious where he is concerned.* And yet, it mattered not. Because Ridgely had become so much more than the rakish guardian who taunted her and called her infant. He was also the first man—the only man—to ever kiss her. And he had nearly been killed. She'd almost lost him. The stark horror of what had occurred was written in the shadows in his eyes. She hated that someone had dared to enter his home with the intent of doing him harm.

"I'm so relieved you are safe," she said on a rush. "That man—"

"Hush." He cut off the rest of what she would have said. "I don't want to think about him just now."

And then slowly, his gaze never leaving hers, he lifted her wrists to his lips, delivering gentle kisses to each before moving to her palms, pressing his mouth to first one, then the other, before lowering both.

Heart beating hard, she crushed her hands into fists, as though she could keep those sweet kisses there forever. She might have asked him what he *did* want to think about. But in the next moment, his mouth was on hers. His hot, delicious lips claimed hers, bold and possessive, knowing and wicked, all at once. He took her in his arms, drawing her into the heat radiating from his tall, lean form.

He was kissing her, and it was wrong, but it was also so wickedly, deliciously *right*.

And nothing and no one else mattered just then.

∽

HER LIPS WERE every bit as silken and alluring as her inner wrists. Sweet. Soft. Not for him. Forbidden. She was his ward. He should stop kissing her. He *would* stop kissing her...

In a moment.

Perhaps in a few minutes.

A year, a decade.

He didn't know when he could bear to drag his mouth from hers. Mayhap never. A lifetime. *God.* She felt so good, pressing her womanly curves into his body as she curled close—so wonderfully, perfectly close. And lush, her breasts crushing into his chest, her arms wrapping around his neck, fingers threading through his hair, then catching handfuls and tugging. A little bit wild suddenly, his innocent minx. As if she could not be near enough, could not have enough of his lips and tongue and teeth, his body that wanted inside hers so badly that he ached with it. They moved together, frantic and restless, hands traveling over each other, kisses breathless and greedy. Not just eager, but desperate. She made a low sound of need that went directly to his cock.

Somehow, it seemed as if he must have nothing but her mouth forever, as if no kiss would ever be this rousing, nor this necessary, all sweet innocence laced with carnal seduction. He must kiss her or perish from the need. No other kiss, no other woman, would do.

Only Virtue.

He kissed her voraciously, forgetting to be gentle, forgetting to be a gentleman, forgetting everything but her and the way she opened for him, her tongue boldly seeking his. She tasted like sugar and that, too, seemed right. Because he wanted to eat her up. He wanted to lick her and devour her and revel in her. To savor her like the most decadent confection he'd ever known.

Trevor had been so perilously close to death mere hours before, but this, the woman in his arms, the heady sigh of delight she made when his hands coasted up the small of her back and he settled her firmly against his raging cockstand, these were all reminders of how very alive he was. Of how precious each breath, each second, was, none of them guaranteed.

Some dim, gentlemanly part of his brain told him to slow down. This was not like the game they'd played in his chamber, when he'd known she was watching from beneath his bed and he had taunted and teased her, nor was it like their kissing lesson. This was different.

But then his innocent little lamb caught his lower lip in

her teeth and nipped him, and his prick promptly told his conscience to go to the devil.

Restraint, control, honor, ability to think straight... All were lost. *Gone.*

Without even knowing how he'd managed the action, Trevor had taken her into his arms. He'd lifted her from the floor, and he was carrying her over the Axminster, his whirling thoughts a flood of possessive need. Thinking *mine, mine, mine* with each step that he took. He wanted to consume her, to carry her away, to keep her only for himself.

She'd driven him to the edge of madness. Living in his house, leaving her scent and her books where she'd been, like a wraith haunting him. Tempting him at every turn. Smiling at him with those full, pink lips, the lips that any courtesan would have given her eye teeth to possess, so plump and full and inviting. Invading his territory. Watching him disrobe.

Kissing him.

She hadn't known how to kiss the first time. He'd pretended to laugh at her, had acted as if her lack of instruction amused him. In truth, it had inflamed him. Had driven him here to this precipice of ruinous want, where the desire to make her his was stronger than ration or reason.

He wanted her with a furor that seized him in its relentless grip. And why could he not have her without ruining her? Why could he not revel in being alive, in the sensual abandon of her kiss? It all made complete and utter sense to his fractured mind as he kissed her with painstaking care and laid her on the Grecian divan, his body following hers.

The sofa was oversized, the cushions leaving room aplenty for him to join her so that they were both situated on their sides, facing each other. The fur she'd spread over him was still atop the cushions, and it was sleek and plush beneath them. All he could think about was Virtue naked on a fur by the fire, wearing nothing but diamonds at her throat as he sank into her.

The thought drove him as his lips sought hers with wicked, singular intent. He wanted her mindless. Wanted to seduce. Not fully, he reminded himself. He would put an end to this. Soon. But first, there was Virtue and the fur and her succulent lips, and he was settling them together on the sofa, their bodies fitting together everywhere they should. So smooth were his motions, guiding them as one, that their mouths never parted. They kissed as if the world itself were about to upend, and these final, fleeting moments might be all they had remaining.

He did something he didn't ordinarily do when he kissed a woman and opened his eyes. Virtue's eyes were closed, her thick, luxurious lashes fanned against her cheeks. She was beautiful. Every part of her. He didn't want to miss a detail. Not a second.

And then, because he had to see more of her, he broke the kiss, dragging his lips reverently along her jaw, to her creamy throat. How finely and delicately she was formed. If he were an artist, he would paint her like this, lying flushed and gorgeous on a library sofa, the innocent in the act of being deliciously debauched. He would capture the sweep of her jaw, the precious curve of her ear. A few curls had sprung free of her elegant chignon, the hint of dishevelment utterly entrancing.

He lowered his head and buried his face in the miraculous place where her neck and her shoulder met, unimpeded by the open, blue satin spencer she wore atop her white muslin gown. She had a tiny beauty mark there that captivated him. He kissed it, then inhaled deeply of her glorious scent.

The desire roaring through him hadn't abated one whit.

Instead, the fire was raging, the flames licking ever higher as his hand traveled from her fine-boned shoulder to cup one of her breasts. The heavy roundness spilled over his palm, even constricted as it was by her stays. And through the layers of her gown and undergarments, there was no mistaking the pebbled nipple. She was so responsive and soft and lovely, a sigh leaving her as he caught her earlobe in his teeth and nipped as she had done to his lip.

Then he couldn't resist kissing the hollow behind her ear, his tongue dipping to taste her there. She shivered and pressed closer to him, saying his name.

"Ridgely."

But that was his title.

He didn't want that. It seemed wrong whilst they were entwined thus and he was intent upon giving her pleasure. Because he'd decided somewhere between holding her wrists and guiding her to the divan that he was going to do everything in his power to show her what passion was truly like. Just this once. Nothing irreparable. He wouldn't take her innocence. No, that wasn't his to take. But kissing her, bringing her to the heights of bliss…this, he could do.

And he could do it so very well.

"Use my given name, darling," he murmured into her ear. "I give you leave."

Just this once, he wanted to say. Should have said. Just as he should have gathered up a shred of honor and left her alone on the divan. But he didn't do that, either.

His thumb circled over her nipple instead, and his lips made constellations over her throat, finding his way back to the beauty mark, then higher, along her jaw once more, to her chin, the corners of her lips. Lips that were swollen and dark from his kisses. *God.* How luscious she was. He'd never wanted to be inside a woman, buried deep, claiming her as his, so badly.

The depth of his reaction to her astonished him, for it was even more potent now than before. He was lost in her.

And it was utterly ridiculous. He, who had seduced his way through London, brought to his knees by a mere miss who had only just learned to kiss. The very last woman he should want, to say nothing of hold, in his arms. The last woman he should touch, kiss, or corrupt.

"I don't know what it is," she whispered, her hands cupping his face in a hesitant gesture that belied the fierceness of her kisses.

He should have shaved. He wondered if his whiskers pricked her tender palms. And then he had the urge to rub his whiskers all over her naked breasts and belly and thighs. On her sweet cunny, too. To mark her as his. But even as the mad desire rose within him, he knew it could never be.

What had she been speaking of? He felt almost as if he were in his cups. Drunk on her.

"What don't you know?" He searched her gaze, falling into the honeyed warmth, the golden flecks hidden in her irises.

Her thumbs traced his cheekbones in a slow, gratifying caress. "Your given name."

"Trevor," he told her, and then he couldn't resist kissing her deeply again.

"Mmm," she said into his mouth, the sound one of carnal delight, as if she had just bitten into something delicious.

He knew the feeling. This wasn't supposed to feel so bloody good. Nor was he meant to be kissing his ward in his library. Or anywhere else, for that matter. Not that the reminder of propriety and duty stopped him. He'd come very near to dying today, and he was going to celebrate his victory against death in the very best fashion he could fathom, by covering Lady Virtue Walcot's lips with his and parting them until he fed her his tongue and she sucked on it as if she wanted to swallow him whole.

And then he thought about what other parts of himself

she might swallow, and his cock went harder, rising against the placket of his trousers. She hadn't said his name. Perhaps he should leave her mouth for a moment, allow her to catch her breath and will his raging cockstand to abate before he did something even more foolish than the liberties he'd already taken.

This was wrong and he was in agony.

Apparently, Trevor William Hunt, sixth Duke of Ridgely, Marquess of Northrop, Baron Grantworth liked very bad things. Forbidden things. Wicked things. But then, he had never claimed to be a good man, and nor had anyone else accused him of being one. He reckoned no one would be surprised to have their bleakest suspicions of him confirmed.

Trevor took a moment to study her as he lay on his side, still wearing whatever he'd donned that morning in between the departure of his friends and the arrival of the Bow Street Runners they'd called for, who had made their inquiries concerning the dead man. He didn't recall his heart ever pounding this quickly. Not even in the darkest depths of the night when he'd been racing after that murderous villain down the stairs.

He wanted to tell her how beautiful she was. To tell her the power she could possess over every man in London, should she wish it. If he'd had a modicum of poetry in his soul, he would have composed a sonnet then and there to the wonders of her sensual allure. But all he could think about was how she had tugged at his hair and thrust her curves against him in all the right places, and the sharpness of her teeth on him.

She was a tigress, and good God, he *loved* it.

"You bit me," he said, his lip still throbbing where she'd nipped him, rather like a naughty kitten.

Her eyes were wide, her breathing ragged, her breast rising and falling against his eager palm. "I didn't."

"You did." He released her breast with the greatest of reluctance and tapped his mouth where she'd done it. "Here."

Her cheeks flushed pink. "Forgive me. I didn't intend to hurt you."

There was only one pain when it came to her, and it was the pain of not being able to take her as he wanted.

"And you pulled my hair," he added for good measure, not certain why.

Perhaps to distract himself from his desperate lust. Perhaps to celebrate her ferocity. Her boldness had both vexed and drawn him to her in equal measure, from the moment they'd first met.

"I am sorry," she apologized again, her flush deepening.

"I'm not," he told her, holding her gaze, cupping her cheek and forcing her to meet his stare when she would have looked away. "I'm not sorry because I liked it."

Her lips parted as she struggled to make sense of his revelation. "You did?"

"You're a bit wild, aren't you, Virtue?"

Of course she was. She defied him at every opportunity, crossed verbal swords with him whenever she could. She stole his damned mare and rode Rotten Row at six o'clock in the bloody morning. She slipped into his bedroom to find the books he'd taken from her. She was wild and wayward, and he suddenly, very badly, wanted all that energy focused upon him. He wanted to lose himself in her, with her. To worship her as she deserved.

What an arse he'd been, supposing he might hastily marry her off. She deserved so much better than a marriage of convenience with some tepid lord who was no match for her keen wit and unbridled passion. But what an inconvenient time for this realization, when he had someone trying to murder him and he was all but ruining her.

"I'm not wild," she denied softly, brushing a lock of hair from his forehead. "Surely you are more so than I."

He smiled at her, brushing his thumb over her lips, stroking the seam. She'd licked him yesterday morning, the minx. And he'd liked it far too much. Testing the boundaries between them, he pressed inward with the lightest of pressure, awaiting her reaction.

She took his thumb into her mouth and sucked. Ah, Christ. He felt that suction in his throbbing cock. Felt it as an ache in his ballocks. A driving, almost blinding need. She was perfect.

"Do you want another lesson?" he asked softly, already knowing the answer.

They may ordinarily be enemies on the battlefield, but here in the library, they'd struck a temporary pax, driven by their mutual shock over the events which had unfolded the night before. Her body responded to his in ways he'd never experienced. And his to hers.

She released his thumb. "Yes."

Ah, the effect her acquiescence—simple and unabashed—had on him. His tip was leaking, leaving a wet smear of mettle on the fall of his smallclothes, as if he were an eager virgin about to bed his first woman. But that couldn't be helped now. He'd come this far, and he couldn't stop until he pleasured her. He wanted to be the first man to bring her to release, just as he'd been the first to kiss her. Even if he couldn't have her completely, he could have this. He could show her, teach her. A lesson in restraint for him, a lesson in desire for her.

He caught her waist in his hands and rolled neatly to his back—no easy feat on the Grecian divan—pulling her atop him as he went, so that she was astride him as if they were coupling. Trevor held her there, cradled between his thighs, his rigid cock burrowing into her softness. The weight of her atop him, her curves molded deliciously to his body, nearly undid him. There was nothing more erotic than being at this bold Siren's mercy as she discovered her innate sensuality.

Her hands were splayed on his chest, hair mussed and beginning to come undone, and she was the most beautiful sight he'd ever beheld. She gazed down at him as if in wonder, her kiss-bruised lips parted. "What are we doing?"

What, indeed?

They were being reckless. Foolish. Courting scandal and ruin. What could be better?

He caressed her waist. "Whatever you want to do. You're in control."

She frowned down at him, and he swore he could almost hear her clever mind churning. "But I thought this was a lesson."

"It is." He smiled up at her, thinking there was a possibility she would unman him with record haste. "It's a lesson in taking what you want. In claiming your power over a man."

"I have power over you?"

If only she knew. More than he ever cared to acknowledge. In this moment, he'd crawl to her over broken glass just for the chance to please her.

"God, yes," he admitted, his hands sweeping up her back.

Now that he had her where he'd wanted her—well, one of the places he'd wanted her, for his fantasies were rather copious—he wasn't about to waste the chance to touch her freely. He smoothed his touch over her shoulder blades and higher, to her nape. His fingers found their way into her chignon and began removing pins. Heavy tendrils of silken, mahogany hair began to fall.

The expression on her face was a potent aphrodisiac. The knowledge that she had power over him excited her.

"Power enough to make you return my books?" she asked.

The minx.

He laughed, and then she kissed him, and his mirth instantly died, because it was apparent that he wasn't the one teaching this bloody lesson. It was her. And the lesson was how quickly Lady Virtue Walcot could bring him to his knees.

CHAPTER 9

Virtue was certain Ridgely had cast some manner of spell over her. It was a spell that rendered her aching and throbbing in wicked places and made her want to hold him tight and never let go. It was also a spell that made her forget all the reasons she did not like him and instead told her to claim his smiling, sinner's lips with her own.

And so she had.

Because his body was big and strong and hot beneath hers, and his manhood was insistent and thick prodding her, and he'd told her she had power over him, and she believed him. Because she felt it now, in their kiss. She had always taken to any task quickly; it was her great pride to excel at every skill she tried. And it was no different with kissing. She'd followed his lead, her lips moving with his, until she found the rhythm of it, until she knew what made him groan low in his throat.

He held her more tightly to him, pulling her hair from its careful chignon until his fingers were sifting through the strands, and then he grabbed a handful, mooring her to him as she feasted on his lips. Ridgely matched her kiss for kiss, his mouth ravenous, and soon, she was breathless again.

Some small part of her mind that maintained a foothold in ration told her she would never have this opportunity again. That she would never be so free and bold with the Duke of Ridgely's delightfully muscled person. She ought to take advantage whilst she could. And so she did.

Her lips left his mouth and traveled over his angular jaw, the prickle of his shadowy whiskers a thrill to her senses. His scent wrapped around her like an embrace, musky and so very Ridgely. She explored him as he had her, kissing to his ear, then down his throat until his neatly tied cravat proved an impediment. Her fingers tangled in the knot, undoing it, and pulling it out of her way so that she could continue on, her mouth grazing over his skin in new, previously unexplored places.

He had told her he'd liked it when she had bitten him, so she nibbled lightly on his neck, delighted when he made a deep sound of approval. But all too soon, the flesh she'd revealed was not enough. She wanted him as he had been in his chamber the day she'd watched him from under his bed. Wanted him bare and magnificent, his chest and back and arms hers to touch and kiss.

She was aching for him, the need building between her legs an exquisite agony which could not be soothed. Virtue rubbed herself over him, seeking more contact, searching for relief it seemed could only be had from him. A moan tore from her, part frustration, part desire. His hands were everywhere, caressing Virtue with a tenderness that surprised her.

"Do you want me to touch you?" he asked, his voice a seductive rasp.

She writhed against him, her body seeking answers her mind didn't comprehend, and kissed the protrusion of his

Adam's apple, then the underside of his jaw. "You *are* touching me."

And she liked it. Far too much.

"Not like this," he said, a hint of amusement lacing his tone.

She kissed his sharp cheekbone. "How?"

"Beneath your gown. I'll find the place where you ache, between your legs. Stroke you there, pleasure you. Do you want that?"

Her curiosity was profound, but no more so than her desire. He could ask her anything and she would agree to it, willingly and desperately.

"Yes," she murmured into his ear, relishing this shocking proximity they were sharing.

How would she ever be able to *not* touch him after this? To look upon him without remembering in vivid detail what his lips felt like beneath hers?

He rolled them together, somehow keeping them on the cushion of the divan, before her frenzied brain could form further coherent thought. And then she was the one on her back, with the heady weight of Ridgely anchoring her to the cushions. He braced himself over her on his forearms, a rakish sweep of hair falling over his eyes as he looked down at her with a gaze burning hot with the same restless longing inside her.

"You're still in control," he told her, his voice low. "Whenever you want me to stop, say the word, and I will."

She nodded, mesmerized by him hovering over her, the underside of his jaw beckoning to her lips until she set them upon it, kissing him.

He stiffened, then rubbed his cheek against hers. "I'll go slowly."

She inhaled again, filling her lungs with the clean, lovely

scent of him. "If you go any slower, I'll burn up before you finish."

Ridgely chuckled. "Patience, darling."

Darling.

How wicked the endearment sounded in his dark, deep voice. How much preferable to *infant*, his customary jibe at her age. If only she could insist he forever referred to her thus, from this moment forward. But this was just a temporary madness between them, and she knew that even if she made the demand, Ridgely would never comply.

He moved his knee to the outer edge of her thigh, balancing his weight as he reached between them, pulling her gown and petticoats past her ankles, over her calves. Good heavens, her stockings were on display. And he was watching his progress with an expression of great concentration, as if nothing would tear his gaze from her slowly revealed flesh.

Where did he intend to touch her? The wait only served to heighten her awareness of him, the vital heat emanating from his big, powerful form. His fingertips brushed her shins as her muslin and linen traveled north until her garters and the tops of her thighs became visible. He was still watching her with undivided intensity, drinking in the sight of her splayed limbs as if he wished to emblazon it upon his memory.

But surely he would stop there, leaving her some modesty.

No, he didn't. Her hems drifted past her hips and pooled at her waist, cool air kissing her bare skin.

"Ridgely, I…" She was breathless again, but not from kissing. From anticipation. From need.

It shocked her to realize how much she wanted him to touch her there, at the juncture of her thighs. At the center of her very being, or so it seemed.

"Trevor," he reminded her, slanting a glance toward her from beneath his long, lowered lashes. "Shall I stop?"

She would die if he did.

"No," she murmured, licking her suddenly dry lips before swallowing hard. "Don't stop."

"Beautiful," he said thickly, stroking her inner thigh as he continued bracing himself on one forearm, their bodies aligned.

She had never thought of that part of herself as anything more than serviceable. Limbs and feet to take her where she wished. A body with needs she quietly met in the dark haven of her bed at night. But never had she dreamed how decadent it would be for a man to see her thus, to eat her up with his hungry stare as if she were the most bewitching sight he had ever beheld.

His praise made her blood sing. She hadn't realized she'd been clamping her thighs together—a nervous reaction, she supposed, uncertain of what to expect—but now she relaxed, allowing them to fall apart, showing more of herself to him.

"My God," he said, awe in his voice as his fingers stroked higher. "So pretty and pink. And glistening. Is this where you ache, darling?"

That knowing touch skated nearer to where she wanted it most, and she inhaled sharply, her hips lifting from the fur robe still spread over the divan.

"Yes."

"And you want me to touch you?"

Wicked fingers traveled over her mound, tracing a circle around the pulsing nub that throbbed with desperate desire for his caress. He was taunting her, teasing her. The blood was coursing through her body, rushing in her ears. She was lightheaded and desperate with want.

"Please," she managed to say when he failed to give her what she wanted.

"I do like the way you beg."

And then there it was, the briefest hint of his forefinger gliding over her swollen flesh. She wanted more. Needed more. And he knew it, the wretch.

She said something and clutched at his arms, hips wriggling, about to come out of her skin.

His given name. *Trevor.*

Yes, that was what it was that she'd said, and how good it felt on her tongue.

His finger strummed over her aching bud as if she were an instrument.

Not enough. He was torturing her. She remembered belatedly that she had hands of her own which were up to the task and reached between them, her fingers flying furiously over herself.

"Jesus," he hissed. "You *are* wild, aren't you?"

Perhaps she was after all.

She was touching her most intimate place, and the Duke of Ridgely was watching her. Virtue ought to have been ashamed, and she knew it. But there was something about the scandalous and forbidden nature of the act that excited her. She rubbed over her swollen clitoris, luxuriating in how slick she was and how good it felt, little sparks shooting from her core and up the base of her spine, a quickening she recognized beginning in her belly.

He rubbed her inner thigh and pressed a kiss to her still-covered breast. "That's it, darling. Make yourself come while I watch."

It was all too much. The rumble of his wicked words, his touch, the exquisite pulse of need within her, his mouth on her breast, his body pressed to her side, burning into hers, and his dark eyes devouring her. She was flying higher, heart pounding, the coil of desire tightening like a spring.

She couldn't hold it back.

The rush of pure, liquid bliss hit her with so much force that she couldn't contain her cry, and then his lips were there, on hers, smothering her moan. And he was kissing her hard, his tongue taking her mouth as if it belonged to him, as if it always had and always would. And her mind didn't doubt the veracity of that claim. She felt and understood it to the very depths of her soul. Her thighs had clamped together, holding her hand and his imprisoned there as wave after wave of ecstasy pounded through her.

And as the roaring in her ears began to slowly fade, that was when she heard the stunned feminine gasp from across the library and the accusatory voice of Lady Deering.

"Ridgely, what have you *done*?"

∞

As far as Trevor was concerned, the question wasn't so much what he *had* done as what he *hadn't* done. He could have done a great deal more. Had wanted to more than he'd wanted to take another breath.

Still wanted to, in fact, and there was no denying it.

However, there was no better cure for a raging cockstand than facing the shrill disapproval of one's proper sister after thoroughly debauching one's innocent ward on a sofa.

In the whirlwind which had followed Pamela's disastrous discovery of Trevor and Virtue on the Grecian divan in the library, his ward had been sent to her room and Trevor had secured himself a glass of brandy before facing his sister for the inevitable reckoning in his study. He had nearly poured it down his throat in one fluid motion, and he was still waiting for the expected dulling of his senses to descend. Much to his everlasting shame, he had licked his finger clean of every trace of Virtue just before Pamela had stormed over the threshold like a general about to rout an enemy. He could yet taste her sweet musk on his tongue, and it was driving him to distraction.

Clearly, a second brandy was in order.

"Will you tell me what happened, or am I to guess?" Pamela demanded, pale and tight lipped when he was filling his glass anew.

He took his time before lifting his glass to his sister in a mocking toast. "Need I elaborate?"

He would rather not. For he could scarcely make sense of it himself, it was true. One moment, he'd been sleeping on the library divan, and the next, his ward had been there. Tempting and hauntingly lovely. And there had been a strange confluence of relief that he was still alive mingling with his unbridled attraction to her. He never should have touched her. That had been the start of it. Those silken, warm wrists of hers.

"Ridgely."

Pamela was not impressed by his question. Had she forgotten he was her elder brother and that his largesse provided her with her teeming wardrobe, the jewels at her throat, and the roof over her head? Deering had been a wastrel. Pamela had loved him desperately. He'd died destitute, having drained his family coffers, and leaving her with nothing.

But he would not remind his sister of past pains. To do so would be wrong. And for some reason, Trevor had decided he had committed enough wrongs for one day.

He took a fortifying sip of his brandy and then sighed, relenting. "After the guards were in place, I wandered to the library and fell asleep."

"That doesn't explain how you came to be atop Lady Virtue on the divan," his sister pointed out, *sotto voce*.

Thankfully, none of the servants had overheard her outrage earlier, and Pamela was exercising extreme caution now to preserve the illusion that nothing untoward had occurred. No one was the wiser for his transgressions against the innocent lamb in his care. An innocent lamb who was, just as she had previously taunted him, not quite as innocent as he had supposed.

She knew how to make herself come.

Bloody hell.

Lady Virtue Walcot, flushed and rumpled on his divan with her hems around her waist, creamy thighs parted to reveal her glorious cunny as her fingers flew over her swollen clitoris, was a memory that would live on within him forever.

Beyond eternity.

A sculpture ought to be commissioned to preserve the moment and commemorate it a hundred years from now, so that men could see that once a goddess had roamed the streets of London, bringing mere mortals to heel like mongrels. And none of them a bigger mongrel than he.

"Have you nothing to say?" Pamela asked, her outrage making her quiet voice vibrate beneath the intensity of her emotions.

"I've quite forgotten your question," he admitted wryly.

He'd been thinking of Virtue. *Again.* When he ought to be thinking about the ramifications of his actions and the very real possibility that someone was trying to have him murdered.

Pamela's nostrils flared. Trevor and his sister had always been opposites. She favored their mother with her golden-blonde hair and her bright-blue gaze. He physically looked like his father, with dark hair and eyes. It was one of the reasons, he suspected, that their mother loathed him. And where Trevor eschewed propriety and had spent years avoiding his familial duty like the plague it was, Pamela had been the dutiful daughter, marrying a duke's son. It hadn't been her fault that Deering had died before inheriting, leaving her with nothing save her widow's portion. Nor had it been her fault that her husband had been an abysmal gambler.

"My question," his sister repeated, an edge to her voice which had been initially absent in her flustered state, "was what happened between you and Lady Virtue in the library?"

What had happened was that everything he'd thought he'd known about himself had been torn asunder and rearranged. He felt rather like a map that had seemed complete, but had in truth been drawn hopelessly incorrectly.

But he wasn't about to confide any of that to his furious sister.

"She's still a virgin, if that's what you're asking," he said instead, intent upon avoiding offering further details.

Pamela's face turned an alarming shade of red. "That is *not* what I was asking, though I am gratified to hear it. Good sweet heavens, Ridgely. This is beyond the pale, even for you."

She was damned easily embarrassed for a widow. He didn't think he'd ever witnessed his ordinarily composed sister so agitated.

"Well." He waved a hand dismissively into the air, flashing her a self-deprecating smile. "Allow me to alleviate you of any concern in that regard, nonetheless."

"How long has this been happening?" Pamela gritted from between clenched teeth. "Have you been debauching her for the entirety of her stay at Hunt House, beneath my very nose?"

"Such matters tend to be delicate and require privacy," he drawled. "I'd never dream of debauching my ward whilst you watched, Pamela. What manner of scoundrel do you take me for?"

"Cease jesting!" she hollered, her voice echoing in the cavernous room like the lash of a whip. "How can you dare laugh about this, Ridgely? Are you completely callous and cold, utterly without conscience? Do you not feel badly about what you've done to Lady Virtue?"

What he'd done? Why, the minx had bit him. And pulled his hair. And then she had grown impatient with his teasing and tended to herself. The chit was a menace.

"I'm not laughing, sister dearest," he said, changing his tone. "I'm being perfectly calm. You, on the other hand, are rather making a spectacle."

His jibe was apparently too much for Pamela.

She stormed forward, eyes flashing with uncustomary anger. "How long, curse you? How many times have you trifled with her? I warned her against the dangers suitors might bring to her reputation, but I never dreamed the greatest danger would be here in her very home."

He was hardly a danger to Virtue. If anything, he was attempting to protect her. To show her the way of the world so that she might make a better match for herself. She deserved a husband who appreciated her, damn it. Not some pompous fop with shirt points in his bloody eyeballs.

The reminder of Viscount Mowbray was timely. What had happened to her protestations of love for the silly prig? She'd been quite silent on the matter with Trevor's tongue in her mouth.

"It was a mistake," he told Pamela coolly. "One that won't happen again. That is all you need concern yourself with."

Only, he wasn't certain about that. He didn't trust himself with Virtue. Not after what had happened between them in the library.

"I am her chaperone. Only think of the damage it will do, not just to Lady Virtue, but to me, were it to become common fodder for the gossips that her own guardian had ruined her beneath my nose?" Pamela threw her hands up in despair, and then looked about, as if she were seeking an object she might throw.

But that made no sense. This was Pamela. Pamela was calm. She was never angered. She was always calm and implacably proper.

Just as the warring thoughts settled in his mind, his sister picked up the inkwell from his writing desk and hurled it into the fireplace. It shattered within, sending ink splattering all over the interior brick.

He stared at the aftermath in disbelief for a moment. Perhaps he'd finally driven her to the edge of madness. He couldn't blame her. He was reasonably certain he'd driven himself there. Trevor had never meant to debauch his ward. He'd been doing everything in his power not to ever since she had arrived at Hunt House. It had simply…happened.

"I am exceedingly fortunate you have excellent aim," he said, keeping his sangfroid intact as much for his sister's benefit as his own. "I should hate to think of how all that ink would look on the wall coverings."

But Pamela was not finished. She raised a scolding finger, all the better to berate him. "If you touch her again, next time, I shall aim for your head. Sow your rakish oats anywhere else in London. Go to your sordid little house of ill repute. Take a mistress if you haven't one. But leave Lady Virtue *alone.*"

Why did everyone insist upon calling The Velvet Slipper a brothel? It wasn't one. But the mulish expression on his sister's face told him now was not the time to argue the matter.

He nodded. "I intend to do precisely that. As I said, what happened was an unfortunate lapse in judgment. It won't occur again."

It couldn't, regardless of how desperately he longed for it

to. But what his sister didn't know, and what he couldn't possibly tell her, was that there was only one woman he desired. And she couldn't be found at The Velvet Slipper. There was no cure for what ailed him save Virtue, and he couldn't have her.

"If it does, you'll have no choice but to marry her yourself," Pamela warned. "There won't be any other way to protect her from the damage."

Leg shackle himself to Virtue? Why did the notion not make him shudder with abject revulsion? He'd never wanted to marry. The institution held no appeal for him. And yet, the thought of Virtue in his bed every night…

No. It wouldn't happen. He was not the man for her. Someone hated him enough to want him dead, for Christ's sake. He couldn't forget about the price upon his head. Tierney had been reasonably certain the bastard who had broken his neck on the stairs had been a hired assassin.

"Rest assured that I have no intention of marrying Lady Virtue or anyone else," he told his sister smoothly. "I promise I shall keep my distance. You, meanwhile, will encourage her to marry. Quickly." He paused, thinking better of that particular directive. "But *not* to Lord Mowbray."

"What is your objection to the viscount?" Pamela asked, indignant.

"I don't like him. He isn't good enough for her."

"Hmm." His sister's eyes narrowed as she studied him. "They seemed taken with each other last night at the Montrose ball when they shared a dance."

"I said no," he bit out curtly. "Now, is there anything else you wish to take me to task for, or are we done?"

"Will you tell me why there are suddenly ruffians sauntering about Hunt House?" she demanded next, apparently not finished. "There is a man called *Beast* roaming about as if he were an honored guest. It is all quite scandalous, even for you."

He didn't think he liked this new Pamela very much.

"They're trusted men here to ensure the safety of the household," he told her firmly. "You needn't concern yourself with them."

Tierney had assembled the best and most fearsome men in his acquaintance for the task, within hours. He didn't give a damn if the men's names were Beelzebub or Mephistopheles. If Tierney said they were reliable guards, he believed it. He wasn't taking any chances with his life or the lives of those in his care.

"This is because of the dead man, then?" his sister asked, her countenance turning grave once more. "I thought he was a common housebreaker."

Apparently, Pamela was not nearly as well-informed as Virtue. Somehow, Trevor wasn't surprised that his enterprising ward had ferreted out the truth before anyone else.

He sighed wearily, for after being harangued by his sister for the better part of the last half hour, he didn't wish to also explain the complexities of someone trying to have him murdered.

"There is a possibility he was not," he said simply. "The guards will remain until I deem them no longer necessary, for the safety of everyone within Hunt House."

Pamela was once again pale. "I don't like the sound of this, Ridgely. What are you not telling me?"

He summoned a false, reassuring smile. "Nothing, my dear. I am merely being excessively cautious. Now, will that be all?"

"I do hope they will be sleeping in the stables," Pamela said.

Another sigh. "Thank you for your concern, sister. I'll take it into consideration."

She dipped into a reluctant curtsy. "Thank you. But be warned, brother. I meant what I said about Lady Virtue. If you compromise her any further, you'll have to marry her."

Marry her, indeed. As if he would ever be foolish enough to find himself alone and tempted with Virtue again.

CHAPTER 10

Virtue eyed the stack of books that had been brought to her room earlier that day by one of the chamber maids, knowing all too well what the unexpected delivery meant. There was no lingering doubt. Not even the slightest hint.

Ridgely was avoiding her.

She'd suspected it for the past few days, when he had been notably missing from the breakfast table and every other engagement afterward. At first, she had supposed that he was limiting his presence at Hunt House because of the potential danger surrounding him. However, days had passed, and with the guards present and no further attempts having been made on his life, it had become apparent that there was another reason for his absence.

Virtue herself.

She could not forgive him for such callousness. To touch her so tenderly and hold her so close to him—they had almost been one—and then to simply disappear and act as if none of it had ever happened…

She shouldn't have been surprised. Nor should his defection have felt like a dagger sliding directly between her ribs. She shouldn't have spent her days hoping he would appear, thinking of his deliciously wicked kisses, wondering what else might have happened had not her chaperone interrupted them.

Lady Deering, meanwhile, had been disapproving and somber in the wake of the library incident. She had reminded Virtue of the perils of allowing herself to become embroiled in compromising situations.

"*Ridgely is a rake, my dear,*" she had admonished sternly. "*You must never find yourself alone with him. If you do, the consequences may be far greater than you can possibly imagine.*"

Consequences.

Virtue would be ruined, she had implied. Ruination, if it meant she returned to Greycote Abbey, would have its merits. However, for now, she was still mired firmly in London where she least wished to be. With a sigh, Virtue decided to seek out the library. The books Ridgely had returned to her held little appeal at the moment, and she could only suppose that his relenting suggested she was no longer forbidden from entering that particular room.

She had sufficient time to dress for the next ball she would be attending with Lady Deering, an affair being held by the Marquess and Marchioness of Searle. She left her chamber and began down the hallway. Passing one of the guest rooms, Virtue heard raised voices from within and paused. The female voice was easily recognizable as Lady Deering's. The male voice, however, did not belong to Ridgely. Curious, Virtue wandered closer, discovering the door to the guest room was ajar.

And within, there stood her stoic, composed chaperone, in the arms of one of the guards Ridgely had brought into Hunt House. The fellow who was known only as Beast, unless she was mistaken.

"Do you know what I think, Marchioness?" the dark-haired man was saying, his voice so low that Virtue almost couldn't hear it, tinged with the slightest hint of an unfamiliar accent.

"No, and nor do I care to know what you think," Lady Deering responded. "You, sir, are a brute."

"A brute whose mouth you fully enjoy," the guard taunted her.

Virtue's eyes went wide as she realized she was witnessing an intimate moment between the two. That Lady Deering was not pushing away from the man, but instead her arms were curled around his neck.

"You are vile," she said, and then she tugged his head down to hers for a kiss so passionate, Virtue's ears went hot and her belly did a strange little flip just watching.

Lady Deering always seemed so concerned with propriety. She was a stickler for societal dictates. Virtue hadn't supposed there was another side to her chaperone...

But she was eavesdropping.

Virtue wrenched herself away from the door and turned to flee, colliding instead with an all-too-familiar wall of male chest.

Ridgely's hands caught her waist, steadying her when she would have lost her balance and gone tumbling to the floor.

"Virtue? What are you doing tearing about in the hall?" he demanded, frowning down at her.

Good heavens, what if he discovered Lady Deering kissing the guard? She had to distract him. But at the moment, she was rather distracted herself. Her breasts were crushed into his chest, and without the added barrier of her stays which she'd foregone this afternoon, her nipples went instantly hard at the contact.

He was dressed as if he had been fencing, his shirt sleeves rolled back to reveal his forearms, a simple knot in his cravat above a well-tailored waistcoat, and breeches instead of his customary trousers. Something about his lack of formality rendered him even more wickedly handsome.

"I was…" she struggled to form a suitable reply for his question. She couldn't tell him she had been intending to find the library when she'd instead discovered his sister in a heated embrace with one of the guards.

A man named Beast, no less!

"You were…" he prompted, sounding annoyed.

"I was looking for something," she suggested, seizing on the first excuse that entered her mind.

"Looking for what?" His voice was icy, but he'd yet to release her.

Instead, he was holding her far too close, as if he feared she might flit away if he released her.

"A book," she said, the first object that rose to her mind, for she had been going to the library to find one.

His gaze narrowed. "And in one of the spare bedchambers?"

Curse it, he had seen her at the door to the room where Lady Deering and the guard were.

"It is not within." She flashed him a bright smile, aware she was speaking far too loudly. "I had thought perhaps I had left it there earlier whilst I was exploring."

"Exploring?"

"Yes," she lied blithely. "Hunt House is so vast that I am still finding new rooms."

"Hmm," he said noncommittally, his countenance making it plain he did not believe her.

Fair enough. She *was* lying. But she had to lure him from the chamber where Lady Deering and the guard were hidden away. She owed her chaperone that much, at least.

"Perhaps you might aid me in finding it," she suggested to the duke.

Ridgely released her. "I am only just returning from Angelo's. I was on my way to my chamber when you ran into me."

"I believe I may have left it in the music room," she fibbed. "Or was it the library?"

"You and libraries do not go well together," he muttered.

And she knew what he was referring to. Those kisses. Those unbearably erotic moments they'd shared together on the divan. Her stomach flipped again, an answering warmth settling low.

"Will you help me find it, Ridgely?" she asked as sweetly as she could muster. "Please?"

"If I must," he relented. "But only so that I needn't worry about you invading every room in search of it. How did you lose it so quickly? Were the books not only just returned to you?"

She moved in the direction of the spiral staircase. "It wasn't one of those books that I lost. It was a different one."

Ridgely followed her, his long-legged strides keeping easy pace with hers. He was wearing gleaming Hessians today, and with the breeches he had donned for fencing, they accentuated his muscular calves quite nicely.

"I thought I told you no more books," he drawled wryly.

Virtue sent him a smile. "Lady Deering took me to a book shop."

That much was true, but she wasn't so frivolous that she'd abandoned one of her precious finds in the music room. Ridgely needn't know that, however.

He muttered something that sounded distinctly like *Pamela and her blasted shopping*.

"Besides, you've returned my books to me," she reminded him. "Was there a reason for your change of heart concerning my punishment?"

"Lady Deering suggested that if you had something with

which to occupy your mind, you may find yourself in fewer scrapes." His tone was grim as they descended the stairs together, almost arm in arm if not touching. "It would seem she was wrong yet again."

"I have been a most dutiful ward these past few days," she defended herself.

They were approaching the main hall, and she steeled herself against the grim memory of what had happened on these very stairs not long ago, and the attack which had preceded it.

"I was told you went for a ride in the park with Lord Mowbray," he said.

And so she had. Her campaign of causing Ridgely trouble hadn't ended, and nor had her desire to return to Greycote Abbey.

"I did," she said agreeably.

"Despite my concern that the viscount is not a worthy suitor," Ridgely intoned, as stiff and proper as she had ever seen him.

Perhaps that was because they were in plain sight of the servants. Not that any were currently about. The well-trained domestics of Hunt House were as quiet as mice and every bit as difficult to find, unless one rang for them.

"Lady Deering disagrees," she told him, leading the way to the music room.

"Lady Deering is wrong," he snapped. "Mowbray is a witless dandy."

"His phaeton is lovely," Virtue told him airily as she ventured across the threshold and began the premise of wandering about in search of her nonexistent book.

She made the mistake of casting a glance over her shoulder at the duke as he prowled behind her. There was something about his forearms so blatantly revealed to her avid eye that made her almost weak in the knees.

"His phaeton," Ridgely said, lip curled in a sneer, "cannot possibly compare to mine."

"I wouldn't know." She shrugged. "Never having been taken for a ride in yours."

And having been quite soundly ignored by you for the last few days, she thought, still feeling hurt. Four. Not that she had been counting.

"Perhaps we shall have to remedy that," he said, "and I can show you the difference between the silly pretensions of a fop and the refined taste of an intelligent man."

Indeed. What did he think rendered him so superior, she wondered, suddenly vexed. But then in the next rush, it occurred to her that Ridgely was a duke and Mowbray a mere viscount in comparison. And he was a great deal more handsome and charming.

There was no comparison, curse the man.

"Such harsh words you have for Lord Mowbray." She spun away from Ridgely, making a show of inspecting the pillows on a window seat, as if she had perhaps left the mysterious tome there.

"And not without merit." Instead of searching the chamber for her book as she had supposed he would, Ridgely had followed her. He was perilously near now, his presence burning into her with a heat that would not be contained.

The man was like a flame.

And she was very much ready to combust.

"Hmm," she said, echoing his noncommittal hum of earlier. "Lady Deering says I must wed soon, and the viscount is most amenable to a match. He has already told me so."

"When, damn his eyes?" Ridgely snarled. "In his phaeton?"

The anger in his tone took Virtue by surprise. He was so often relaxed, his every reaction and tone languid and laden with easy charm.

She whirled about to find him looming over her, the picture of aristocratic refinement with an edge of roughness and danger she couldn't help but to find alluring.

"And if it was then?" she asked, testing him.

Testing the both of them, it was true, and she didn't quite know why. She had successfully baited Ridgely into irritation. He fairly vibrated with disapproval.

"Did he kiss you?" he demanded instead of answering her.

Was the Duke of Ridgely *jealous* of Viscount Mowbray? How impossible it seemed. And yet, if true, the anger he was exuding made sense. As did the rigid set of his shoulders and the angle of his jaw, the fury glittering in the dark, chocolate depths of his eyes.

In truth, the viscount had been a perfect gentleman. He'd also proven himself the sort of company who delighted in droning on about himself whilst never asking her a single question about herself. For the number of times she had spoken, Mowbray may as well have been alone in his sleek phaeton.

She hesitated, deciding upon the answer she would give to Ridgely. He had all but disappeared from her life following the incident in the library. The passion she had known with him had produced a sea change in her. Every part of her had come to life in a new, previously undiscovered way. And he had merely carried on with his every day without her in it. Nary a word. Not a look, not a touch. Not even a note upon the books he had sent to her room.

Virtue tipped up her chin and sent the duke what she hoped was a wicked smile, one that said Mowbray had kissed her witless and she had adored every moment of his imaginary attentions. "Of course, he did."

Ridgely's nostrils flared and his hands balled into fists at his sides. "That scoundrel. I'll challenge him to a duel for this.

How dare he importune my ward with his unwanted attentions? This will not stand."

A duel? Good heavens. She hadn't supposed he would be so inflamed by her falsehood that he would challenge Mowbray to pistols at dawn.

"You mustn't," she said lamely. "It would cause a dreadful scandal."

"No more a scandal than daring to take liberties with you in his phaeton," Ridgely countered. "I'll tear off his shirt points and stuff them down his gullet."

Oh dear.

How had her trip to the library so dramatically drifted away from its intended port of call?

"He didn't do it," she admitted on a shamed rush.

"Are you denying the kiss so that I will change my course?" he asked grimly.

"No." She tore her gaze from his, staring at the designs on the Axminster. "Lord Mowbray didn't kiss me in his phaeton. Nor did he kiss me anywhere else. The only man who has kissed me is you, and you have been ignoring me, you insufferable, arrogant, book-thieving lout!"

The moment the words left her lips, she clapped a hand over her mouth, shocked at the furor of her own response. She hadn't intended to reveal so much. Hadn't wished for Ridgely to know just how deeply what had happened between them had affected her. Most definitely hadn't wanted him to realize his absence had been the source of such consternation and hurt on her part.

Everything was fast unraveling. And she had only herself to blame.

TREVOR OUGHT to have been ashamed, he knew, for the surge of possessive pride that swelled in his chest at Virtue's cross revelation that Mowbray had not kissed her in his phaeton as she had initially claimed. The chit had been lying, and quite boldly. There was no reason his discovery of her duplicity ought to leave him with a hard cock save one.

He was depraved.

Depraved enough to be absurdly pleased at the knowledge that he was the only man who had ever kissed Lady Virtue Walcot, the ward who had driven him to the very brink of madness with desire. The woman he had spent nearly every waking hour thinking about since she had pleasured herself on the Grecian divan in his library. He had stroked his cock into submission more times than he'd believed possible to the memory of those dainty fingers working over her swollen clitoris, her creamy thighs open to reveal the pink petals of her sex.

She had a hand pressed over the lips that had also featured quite prominently in his sordid fancies. Her honey-brown eyes were wide, and well they should be. She'd lied to him and then insulted him. Any other man in his position would have been outraged.

But he was not any other man. And all Trevor wanted was to press her down on the window seat behind her and slide into her dripping cunny until they were both mindless and she forgot the existence of every other man.

Especially the Viscount Mowbray.

"You lied," he said softly, instead of giving in to the foolish urge.

Her hand fell away, and a look of guilt crept over her expressive features. "Yes. Forgive me. I shouldn't have. Mowbray was quite the gentleman. He doesn't deserve to face you at dawn for a sin he didn't commit."

"To the devil with Mowbray," he said. "Tell me why."

"To make you angry, I suppose," she admitted then paused, nibbling pensively on her succulent lower lip before continuing. "I was vexed with you, and you have made your disapproval of the viscount plain. I seized the moment, not thinking of the consequences."

Now was the time for him to accept her apology and take his leave of the chamber. He never should have ventured to the music room alone with Virtue to begin with, let alone engaged in a conversation about kissing. She could bloody well find her own book. Lingering with a cockstand and the diabolically tempting ward he couldn't seem to stop touching was nothing short of madness.

But Trevor was a Bedlamite. Because he had to know. He had to stay. He had to keep testing his own resolve just a bit more.

"Why were you vexed with me?" he asked, newly fascinated by the trim on her bodice, an *X* which crossed over her bountiful breasts and somehow served to make them appear larger.

Good God, were her nipples hard? Could he *see* them through her gown and stays?

The answer hit him as he forced his gaze upward, back to her lovely face and moving lips. Virtue wasn't wearing any stays.

"You disappeared," she said. "After the library. It was…you kissed me so…and then nothing. Lady Deering warned me you're a rakehell and that you seduce a different woman every day. I dare say I should have listened."

Frowning and hugging herself about the waist as if she were holding in her emotions, Virtue made to slip away from him.

"Don't go," he ordered, catching her elbow and keeping her from fleeing as she'd intended. "Wait."

Had his sister truly told Virtue that he was a rake? That

he seduced a different woman every day? If so, she had a rather exaggerated opinion of his prowess.

Virtue's countenance was a mask of indecision and hurt. The hurt was what hit him in the gut like a punch. *He'd* caused it. He hadn't intended to, but he had, nonetheless. And he hated himself for producing even a second of her pain.

"I've been keeping my distance for your sake," he explained gently.

"How like a rake to make his inconstancy sound heroic," she said, her tone smart.

He deserved her scorn. He was older, infinitely more experienced, her guardian, for Christ's sake. He should have known better than to touch her, to kiss her.

To lie with her on a library sofa.

And yet, he could not resist. Not any more than he could keep himself from reaching out with his free hand to tuck a stray wisp of mahogany hair behind her ear just now. Nor keep his fingers from lingering there at the silken patch of skin, the warmth of her burning him like fire.

"It is not inconstancy that keeps me away," he admitted, his voice rough with emotion he couldn't begin to understand. "It is the need to protect you from myself."

She was still, her gaze searing his, her expression inscrutable. "I don't need your protection, Ridgely. I am capable of looking after myself."

He wanted her to understand who he was. To chase her away, for her own good.

"Yes, you do," he countered firmly. "My sister was correct in one matter. I *am* a conscienceless rakehell. I could devour you right now. I could take you on the window seat of this music room, and I wouldn't regret it for a moment."

He'd hoped she would recognize the danger of lingering here, within his reach, alone in the music room with the door firmly closed and no one else about. He'd hoped she would gather up her skirts like most virginal chits would and flee the clutches of the dastardly rogue. He was what mamas warned their debutantes about. His own sister thought him capable of seducing an innocent for sport.

And the sad truth of it was that he most definitely *was* capable of seducing Virtue. Not for sport. Because he wanted her more than he wanted anyone or anything he could ever recall desiring in his thirty years of life.

But she was Virtue, and Virtue was fearless and reckless and, as he'd pointed out to her that day in the library, a bit wild.

So she tipped her chin up in defiance. "I wouldn't regret it either if you did."

Her words were like a bolt of lust being shot directly into the heart of him. His reaction was instant and uncontrollable. His hand, the one near her throat, trembled beneath the force of it, and then he cupped her nape and pulled her nearer, into him, whilst his other hand released her elbow and settled on the small of her back. He could not shake the feeling that here was where Lady Virtue Walcot belonged.

In his arms.

"You shouldn't feel that way," he murmured, still trying not to kiss her, even if her mouth beneath his was all he desired—more than for the sun to rise on another day.

"Don't tell me how to feel, Trevor," she said boldly.

And that was it. She'd called him by his given name. Had *scolded* him. God, he loved it. Loved every wicked, wrong, forbidden second of being alone with her, of her lush curves pressing into his hardness in the most delicious of ways, her sweetly floral scent invading his senses.

"I'm your guardian," he reminded her.

Reminded them both.

But the warning faded as he caressed the soft skin of her

nape. His thumb found its home in the inviting dip where her hairline began, and without conscious effort, he was cradling her head, lost in the glittering depths of her gold-flecked eyes. She was, he thought in the wildness of that moment, a goddess meant for him. *Made* for him.

"I don't want you to kiss Mowbray."

The admission was torn from him. He hadn't meant to say it. Who was this man he'd become? What had she done to him, the minx?

"Ever," he added for good measure.

"Why not?" she asked, pushing him as she always did.

He liked her boldness. Liked her daring. Liked the beauty mark he knew hid at the crux of her neck and shoulder. Liked the color of her lips, stained with his kisses. Liked the avid working of her mind, her cleverness, her indomitable spirit. Here was a woman unlike any he'd ever known, her determination to be herself and live life by her own rules something to be not just admired, but savored, too. Savored in the same way he savored her loveliness, her curves, her sensual response.

"Because I want to be the only man who kisses you," Trevor said.

They stared at each other in the wake of those words, words which had fled him of their own volition. Words which were reckless and bloody stupid. What was he saying, that he wanted to be the only man who kissed her? Did he even mean it?

Yes, he did, Trevor realized, to his united astonishment and dismay. He wanted Virtue for himself alone. He was selfish and greedy and he wanted to claim her and keep her and kiss her and pleasure her and…

And…

No, he would not allow himself to think the last aberrant, wholly unwanted thought.

Not *marry* her. Surely?

She kissed him, and the madly whirling contemplations scattered instantly, swept away by a rush of pure, animal lust. It seemed that the more he kissed and touched Virtue, the greater the effect she had upon him. One touch of her mouth to his, and he was lost.

With a growl—yes, like a wolf intent upon devouring his prey—he deepened the kiss, his tongue slipping into the welcoming wet warmth of her mouth. She tasted of sweetness as she always did, and he couldn't seem to get enough of her. Virtue responded in kind, clawing at his shoulders, thrusting those delicious breasts of hers against him so that he swore he could feel her nipples poking into his chest. No stays, he thought again. Scarcely any barriers to keep his hands and lips and tongue from what they wanted most.

This was going to end badly.

Or wonderfully.

Either way, he couldn't stop. Didn't want to.

He closed his eyes and surrendered to the potent lure of Virtue's mouth answering his.

CHAPTER 11

Virtue clung to Ridgely and returned his fierce kisses with all the mounting hunger within her. Anger and frustration were dashed by desire. His admission had left her feeling strangely giddy and wanton all at once. She could hear it again, echoing in her mind as his mouth ravished hers. *I want to be the only man who kisses you.*

Yes, please.

Ruin me, she thought as his tongue tangled with hers, and to her shame, she wasn't thinking of Greycote Abbey or the events her shredded reputation would likely set in motion. No, she was thinking only of herself just now. Of what she wanted.

Ruin me as he kissed a path to her jaw, tongued the whorl of her ear.

Ruin me as he dragged his lips down her throat and then found a particularly sensitive place in the crook of her shoulder where he sank his teeth into her for a nip that she felt between her legs.

"Oh," she gasped, clinging to him, head falling back. "My." Trevor sucked on her neck. "Heavens."

"God, I could eat you up."

His low, guttural words made the pulsing and heaviness of her sex increasingly pronounced. She ached more than she had that day on the divan, and he had scarcely even touched her yet.

He found the tapes on her gown and undid them. Her bodice sagged, and he pulled down the little cap sleeves, taking her chemise with them. The sound of threads popping and tearing mingled with the harshness of their breaths. Her chemise would need to be mended. Perhaps her gown as well.

She didn't care.

He dragged handfuls of fabric down to her waist, and the cool air of the music room, which had no fire lit, kissed her bare skin and made her already stiff nipples pucker. Her breasts were large, she knew. Embarrassingly so, she'd thought since she had grown into them a few years before. And yet, there was no shame when Ridgely took them in his palms, his thumbs unerringly finding the sensitive peaks and rubbing.

"Sweet Christ above, you're perfect," he said, voice hushed. "May I?"

She didn't know what he was asking permission for—he was already touching her, and the only problem they would have was if he stopped, as far as she was concerned. He gave her breasts a gentle squeeze, and oh how she loved the sight of his big, capable hands kneading her flesh. Of his thumbs teasing her nipples, then catching them in his forefingers and rolling them until sparks of pleasure shot through her.

"Yes," she managed to say. "Yes to everything. Do anything."

He cast her the devil's own grin, and the wicked intent there made her knees nearly give in. "You mustn't give me *carte blanche*, darling. There's no telling what I'll do."

"It matters not," she said with brutal honesty. "Whatever you do, I will like it. Love it, in fact. Of this, I have no doubt. Just as surely as I know the sun rises in the east and sets in the west."

"But soft, what light through yonder window breaks?" He kissed the curve of her breast.

Oh, yes. His kisses on her there seemed a fine plan indeed. His query possessed a familiarity. She'd heard those words, strung together in such lovely fashion, before.

She searched her lust-addled mind and found the answer she'd been seeking. "Shakespeare."

"Romeo and Juliet," he confirmed, his mouth traveling steadily over her other breast now, as if to mark every part of her skin with his kiss. "It is the east, and Virtue is the sun."

She might have laughed at his play on words, but in the next breath, he took her nipple into his mouth and sucked hard. Virtue cried out, and this time, her knees did give way, but he caught her and guided her gently backward, down onto the window seat with its cushioned bench. He went with her, dropping to the furniture but taking care to keep his full weight from pinning her there, the sunlight streaming in through cracks in the curtains to cast them in a golden glow.

It might have been a dream, so surreal was the sight of the Duke of Ridgely looking down at her with raw desire in his expression. But then his beautiful head bent, and his tongue painted a lazy circle around her nipple, and the pulsing ache between her thighs told her no dream could ever be this delicious.

"This." He paused and flicked the peak of her breast with his tongue. "Is." Another pause as he sucked hard until releasing her nipple with a lusty pop. "Your." Yet another pause, and his lips coasted over the pink tip. "Warning." He kissed between her breasts. "Leave." *Kiss.* "While." *Kiss.* "You can."

"I'm not going anywhere," she breathed, her hands roaming freely over any part of him she could touch. Shoulders, arms, the broad plane of his back, his hair. She caught handfuls, relishing the silken strands passing through her questing fingers.

Another kiss from Ridgely, and then he sucked hard on her nipple. His hand had grasped the skirt of her gown, petticoats and chemise, and now slid beneath, skimming over her stockings. Past her garters.

His warning didn't alarm her. Not in the slightest. She wanted this. Wanted the Duke of Ridgely for herself. Wanted his touch, his kiss, his lips. Wanted him with a furor, clamoring and trembling inside her, that was stronger than the desire to return to her home.

How had he done it? How had he unmoored her with nothing but his clever hands and lips?

He kissed his way back to her mouth and his hand found her inner thighs. She parted for him as he stroked higher, unerringly discovering the center of her need. His fingers slicked through her folds, until he rubbed tantalizing circles over the place where she was most sensitive, the nub that she instinctively knew was swollen and wet.

"Anything?" he whispered against her mouth, the word dark and mysterious and sinful.

Laden with promise.

"Yes," she whispered, for his fingers were already making her hips jerk into his touch, seeking more. Completion. "Anything you want."

Their faces were impossibly close, their breaths mingling, lips brushing as he spoke. "I want you to come for me. Come for me the way you did in the library, only lose yourself from my touch this time."

She wanted that. Told him so without words, kissing him hungrily instead and thrusting her tongue into his mouth. He made a low sound of approval and sucked on her tongue, increasing the pace and pressure of his fingers all the while.

They stayed that way, a tangle of limbs on the window seat, hidden away from the world in the privacy of the music room. Their kisses were ravenous and deep. Ridgely—or Trevor, as she must think of him in this moment of startling intimacy—surrounded her. The breaths she took were his. Each beat of her heart a frantic rhythm he stoked by working her into a stunning crescendo. Faster now, fingers working her, tongue licking into her mouth until everything within her tightened just before exploding.

The bliss, when it hit, was so sudden and forceful that she couldn't contain the loud moan that escaped her. He swallowed it down, continuing to stroke her until her thighs were quivering and she was so unbearably sensitive she thought she'd burst. And only then did he break the kiss, his head lowering to lavish attention on her breasts once again.

But his fingers weren't finished.

Instead, they dipped lower, unerringly finding another part of her that was aching. He played with her, teasing her entrance with slight pressure. It was new, this sensation. Maddening and delicious at the same time. Her body moved, instincts taking over, undulating against him.

One finger dipped inside her in a shallow thrust.

She gasped at the unfamiliar intrusion, and the feeling of it, of him.

He kissed her nipple, slanting her a heated glance. "Tell me when to stop."

But she wouldn't. She didn't wish for him to.

She shook her head, which was lolling about on the cushion, half her chignon undone, hairpins pricking her scalp and she did not care. "Don't stop."

"I want to use my tongue," he said. "Will you allow it?"

Use his tongue for what? She didn't know. Couldn't fathom. He'd already used it so very much, and she found herself much the better for it.

"Yes," she said, for there was no other answer.

Whatever he wanted, she wanted more.

She grew confused as he appeared to withdraw, the heavy weight of his body leaving hers. Virtue reached for him in protest, but he kissed her fingers and sank to his knees on the floor, rearranging her body to his liking, so that she faced him instead of lying horizontally across the cushions as she had before. And then, he did the oddest thing yet.

He flipped her hems up with one deft motion, and with the other, he hooked each of her knees over his shoulders. Reaching beneath her to cup her bottom, he pulled her toward him.

"Tr-Trevor," she stuttered, shocked. "What do you intend?"

She had read about such matters, of course, in the sinful books she had managed to find, but she had thought the scenes she'd read were the hyperbolic imaginings of wicked authors.

"Relax, darling," he said soothingly, dropping a kiss on her inner thigh. "Let me show you."

Surely, she had thought, a man would not place his lips on a woman's... Trevor's head settled firmly between her legs.

Oh.

This man would. And that was his tongue upon her, lapping gently at first, as if he were consuming something delicious that he didn't wish to devour all at once. How wonderful it felt, the warm glide of his lips and tongue. He made another sound, a low *mmm* that rumbled against her flesh.

"So sweet," he murmured against her aching sex. "Sweet as honey, just like your lips."

All she could offer as a response was a weak moan as he had his way with her, feasting on her sex until she was squirming beneath him, breathless, gasping. Shameless, arching into his wicked mouth, her fingers seeking purchase once again in his hair. She tugged and he answered by lavishing more attention upon her nub, licking faster before suckling.

"Oh," she breathed, the quickening already beginning in her belly.

He released her and then placed a kiss atop the throbbing bud.

"Not yet," he said, as if he sensed her body's terrible need. "I want to savor you a bit first."

Savor her. She shivered, and not because of the lack of fire in the grate. He licked into her, following the same path his fingers had taken, his tongue sinking inside, then out again. Another noise left her, a strangled moan and plea in unison.

If she didn't take care, she'd bring all the servants down upon them.

"Bite the back of your hand," he ordered her gently, and then traced the seam of her back to her clitoris.

She obeyed, catching her knuckles in her teeth and biting down as he sucked on her whilst one of his fingers returned to her entrance. There was the same delicious pressure, heightened by his demanding mouth, the hard suction and light nips of his teeth alternating until she was writhing beneath him, the pleasure so exquisite she could scarcely bear more.

His finger slid slowly, out and then in, with each pass moving deeper. Filling her in a way his tongue had not. And then more. Another finger. She was impossibly stretched. His mouth gave no quarter, demanding a release as his hand pumped in time to her labored breaths.

Harder. Faster. Her heart was galloping in her chest. Until she came apart. This release was quicker than the last, shooting through her like fireworks into a night sky. Glorious bursts, so beautiful, so very good. She was certain she was going to die from the pleasure of it.

In the aftermath, she lay there, utterly spent and limp, a languid lusciousness settling over her, and thought she may have, quite unintentionally and ridiculously, fallen in love with the Duke of Ridgely.

~

What had Trevor done?

Restraint? He clearly possessed none. Honor? Had he ever owned a shred of it? If he had, the last bit had been obliterated the moment he'd lifted Virtue's skirts and licked her until she'd come on his tongue and fingers.

The taste of her lingered in his mouth, on his lips.

Honey and musk. Sweet and sensual. Just like her.

Regrets? God, not a single one.

With hands that trembled from the force of his reaction to her, he reluctantly flipped down her hems, restoring her modesty and ruining the most bewitching sight he had ever beheld: Virtue on the window seat, nearly naked and looking thoroughly ravished.

By him.

He rose from his knees and leaned over her with the intention of restoring her bodice to rights. Instead, he paused, mesmerized by the dreamy expression on her lovely countenance. He had been wrong before. *This* was how he would paint her—dark tendrils of mahogany escaped from her chignon and framing her face, lips swollen and dark, full breasts spilling from her gown, all creamy and perfect and tipped with hard, pink nipples. Sunlight streaming down on her like gilded gossamer.

No Venus captured in oils had ever been so alluring.

There was only one solution for the current dilemma in which he found himself.

He'd spent the last few weeks convinced he must marry Lady Virtue Walcot off with all expediency so that he could carry on with his life. But it was apparent that the only man he could marry her off to was himself.

His achingly hard cock told him it was the sole way. Eventually, he must marry someone. Produce an heir. Otherwise, his odious cousin Ferdinand Clutterbuck would inherit the title and run the estates and all their people firmly into the ground.

Why not marry Virtue? Two birds, one stone, etcetera.

It wasn't ideal. He wasn't prepared for a wife. But then, there had been attempts on his life. Someone wanted him dead. Perhaps even Cousin Clutterbuck. That reminder did something to mollify the raging need to claim Virtue here and now. To finish what he'd begun. To give them both what they wanted most.

Death and Cousin Ferdinand did wonders to wilt a fellow's cockstand.

"Let me help you," he told Virtue as he awkwardly attempted to pull her bodice back into place.

No easy feat when her bountiful breasts were everywhere. They were like prisoners escaped from gaol, and now that they had their freedom, they had no wish to be contained by linen and muslin.

"I suppose I'm indecent," she said, still breathless, her

cheeks flushed prettily. She rose to her elbows, which didn't serve to help his attempts at righting her chemise.

"Blast," he muttered. "Your breasts are as willful as you are."

"Allow me," she said, chasing his hands with hers. "I think you may have popped some of my stitches."

God. He was a brute.

He swallowed hard at this knowledge, the way she so easily reduced him to nothing but raw, animal lust. The way she brought him to his knees. It had been mere weeks since she'd swept into his life with the force of a summer thunderstorm. And he was helpless to resist her.

With quick, efficient motions, she righted her chemise and bodice. He ought to have done it for her. Lord knew he'd helped his fair share of lovers back into their gowns after frantic trysts. But he was still too shaken by his realization to be of much use.

"We'll marry, of course," he blurted.

Not quite the manner in which he had intended to deliver the news of their impending nuptials, it was true. And the moment Virtue froze, the stubborn expression he knew all too well crossing her features, he recognized the misstep.

He ought to have asked instead of making the announcement. What was the ordinary method of such nonsense? He'd never before requested a lady's hand in marriage.

"I fear I misheard you," Virtue said, rising to her feet and shaking the wrinkles from her skirts.

Her tapes were yet undone. His hands clamped on her waist and spun her gently about. Trevor was suddenly grateful for a task to occupy himself with.

"You didn't mishear me." He knotted one of the ties. "After the liberties I've taken with you, there is no other recourse for us. We will marry."

And then he could happily have her in his bed, where she belonged.

She whirled about, pulling the remaining ties from his fingers. "No."

He blinked, feeling unaccountably awkward and bereft. This wasn't like him. He was known for his charm. He'd used it to persuade many ladies to part with their gowns and undergarments.

Now, surely he was the one who had misheard *her*.

He frowned down at her. "No? What do you mean, no? Precisely what are you refusing, my offer of assistance with your gown, or my offer of marriage?"

She raised a brow. "Did you offer to marry me? I confess, I heard no offer. All I heard was a pronouncement."

"In this instance, the offer and pronouncement must be the same," he told her, hating himself for how stiff and proper he sounded, even to his own ears. "I've gone too far."

"Nonsense."

Nonsense? Did the stubborn chit think to chastise him?

"You're an innocent," he added. "What I've done is unconscionable."

"Not so innocent," she reminded him pointedly.

And although she had alluded to her lack of innocence before, on this occasion, he knew who was responsible for her education. Trevor cursed himself for the surge of possessive pride at that fact. He was despicable.

"I am your guardian, Virtue."

"So I have been told with relentless frequency." Her cheeks were still flushed, but she was frowning at him now. "I don't care if you are my guardian, and your honor and sense of duty can go hang. I'm not marrying you."

She could have knocked him down with a feather.

Her words at the ball returned to him, mocking. *I'm in love with Mowbray*, she had claimed. This absurdity he plainly refused to entertain, that she could fancy herself in love with a spineless dandy like the viscount and yet refuse to marry Trevor himself.

"Neither are you marrying Mowbray," he warned her sternly. "So you may as well get that particular maggot out of your head. You will marry me, and that is final."

"And what shall you do if I don't?" she demanded, crossing her arms. "Steal into my chamber and take the books you've only just returned? Banish me from the library again?"

She was angry with him, he realized dimly. The force of her passion had quickly given way to indignation, and he was the source of both. She was far less prickly when he was kissing her. Likely, he ought to have asked her to marry him when his tongue had been on her and his fingers had been deep inside the drenched heat of her cunny. Her answer would have decidedly been *yes*.

"The repercussions of our actions extend far beyond mere books," he told her. "Boundaries have been crossed which cannot be uncrossed. We must wed."

Three words he'd never thought to say. And yet, here he was, saying them to Virtue, of all the women in the world. To this beautiful, magnificent woman who was intelligent and bold and stubborn and maddening. To his own dead friend's daughter.

Ah, Pemberton. The marquess would have likely told him to name his second after what he had done. And Trevor wouldn't have blamed him one whit. He never should have surrendered to temptation. He never should have touched her. Kissed her. Tasted her.

But he had. And now, even without Pamela there to verbally box his ears and issue dire warnings of consequences, he knew what had to be done. There was only one way to make amends for his lack of control, and it was marriage.

His ward, however, remained unconvinced.

"Why must we wed? No one has seen us. No one knows what has happened here except the two of us." As she spoke, her fingers were investigating the damage which had been done to her chignon.

It was almost completely undone. Her sleek locks rained around her shoulders, and his fingers itched to touch them.

"*I* know what has happened," he said grimly, "and that is sin enough. Your father entrusted you into my care. I have a duty to do right by you, and in this instance, there is no other way to ameliorate my inexcusable actions save a union between the two of us."

"My father scarcely remembered my existence when he was alive," Virtue countered. "I hardly think he'll care about what has become of me now that he is gone."

Her assessment of Pemberton was harsh. It occurred to Trevor that he'd never asked his friend about his relationship with his daughter. Christ, now that he thought of it, he'd imagined the marquess's child had been little more than a babe. Certainly not a woman fully grown. Virtue was not entirely wrong. Pemberton had scarcely mentioned her. The realization angered him on her behalf. What manner of man would simply ignore his own flesh and blood?

"Regardless of the relationship you had with Pemberton, you are my responsibility," Trevor bit out, furious with himself as much as with his old friend, now that the fogs of lust had been banished from his mind. "I trespassed. I took advantage of you whilst you are in my care. A gentleman would never—"

"Would you cease this nonsense?" she interrupted crossly. "Pray do not pretend that you are a gentleman, Ridgely. You are a rake. What happened just now was likely as commonplace to you as breakfast."

That rather stung.

He clenched his jaw, wanting to reach for her and yet restraining himself. "Nothing about what we just shared was commonplace."

Damn her for suggesting otherwise.

He wasn't a stranger to bed sport, and he'd readily admit that. Trevor wasn't certain he was quite the rakehell Pamela suggested. But he was no neophyte to the art of lovemaking, that much was certain. However, he could honestly say that he had never, in all his thirty years, been as profoundly affected as he was whenever he so much as stood in Virtue's presence.

She transfixed him.

"You must think me a fool, Ridgely." She shook her head. "I know you don't want to marry me."

She wasn't wrong.

He didn't *want* to marry anyone. Not truly. Good God, the mere thought of that vaunted institution was enough to induce body-wracking shudders. To hang, draw, and quarter his soul.

But if Trevor *must* wed at all, then there was only one woman he would consent to shackling himself to in holy matrimony. And it was Virtue. Virtue, with her flashing honey-brown eyes and reckless defiance and love of books and questions and flippant air after he'd just made her spend all over his tongue and fingers. With her rebelliousness and her plain speaking and disregard for society and above all his title.

God, she was maddening. Infuriating. He wanted to kiss her and fuck her and bask in her presence and never let her go.

This time, he did reach for her, catching her waist and

pulling her against him, all her delicious curves melting into his hardness. "I don't think you a fool, and I must marry you."

"You *must?*" She pursed her lips. "Look around the music room, Ridgely. No one else is here save us."

"It doesn't signify." And it didn't, did it? *He* was here. He knew what he'd done. And to his own friend's daughter. To an innocent.

He knew what else he wanted to do. Far more. He'd only just begun. Depraved was what he was.

"If I'm truly ruined, then you must send me back to Greycote Abbey. There is your answer, Ridgely. Not marriage. Never *that*."

It took Trevor a moment to understand the implication of her words. Was it possible that she believed her ruination would mean a return to Nottinghamshire? If so, she was horribly misguided.

"What do you mean, I must send you back to Greycote Abbey?" he asked. "You must know I cannot send you there. Even if I wanted to, I could not. It has been sold."

Her lips parted, and he felt her reaction to his news—news which he hadn't intended to impart in such fashion—as she recoiled as if she'd been struck.

"Sold?"

He'd been so caught up in trying to figure out who the devil was trying to see him dead that he hadn't given proper attention to the correspondence he'd received concerning her father's estate. He damned well should have told her before now. He knew how strongly she felt about Greycote Abbey. Although they'd both known it was inevitable—the terms of her father's will had demanded the sale—he took no pleasure in carrying out Pembroke's final requests.

Particularly not when doing so hurt Virtue.

Her eyes glistened with unshed tears, and he hated it, the sight of his firebrand struck with the knowledge that her beloved home was gone. He took no pleasure in her pain. Hadn't wanted the cursed duty. The obligation.

Since inheriting, his life had become a myriad of tasks. He'd never bloody well wanted to be duke. Hadn't been born to it. He'd been the third son, not even the spare, until Matthew and Bartholomew had become unexpectedly ill. Mother still didn't forgive him for her golden children's passings, and Trevor knew it better than anyone. But that was neither here nor there.

"It's been sold, the legalities completed two days ago," he repeated quietly, giving her waist a gentle squeeze. "You cannot return."

"You...oh, I cannot believe it. How *dare* you sell Greycote Abbey?" She pushed at his chest, the action so forceful and unexpected that he took a step back, releasing her. "And without me even knowing? How could you, you utter scoundrel, you...you *tyrant*?"

She was a head shorter than he, but damn it, let it never be said that Lady Virtue Walcot was not strong. She *was* strong. Physically, emotionally, mentally. In every way. He accepted her fury. Her sadness.

"I hadn't a choice," he said firmly, needing her to understand. "The terms of your father's will were clear. The estate had to be sold, Virtue. To that end, it *has* been sold." He paused, searching her countenance, realization dawning on him anew. "Do not tell me you believed I would send you back there, all this time, to Nottinghamshire?"

She said nothing, fat tears rolling down her cheeks.

"Christ," he muttered. "I thought you understood."

"And I th-thought I was to be informed before the sale happened," she said, sniffling through her tears in a valiant attempt at composure. "Should I not have had a say in the matter? Should I not have been told? Asked?"

He felt quite suddenly as if he'd swallowed a stone.

"I'm your guardian," he explained needlessly. "I made the decisions on your behalf."

"How could you do this to me, to my home and the people I love? I'll never forgive you." Her voice broke on the last word, and she whirled away, fleeing the music room.

Trevor watched her go, feeling every bit as shattered.

CHAPTER 12

"Marriage," Pamela repeated, her tone incredulous as it echoed through the private confines of his study. "You?"

Trevor winced. He couldn't fault his sister for her shocked reaction to his announcement that he intended to wed Virtue. No one had ever wanted to find himself leg-shackled less than he. But he couldn't be trusted with his ward.

That was the plain truth of it. Where Virtue was concerned, he possessed neither restraint, nor compunction. Nothing save the all-encompassing need to greedily have her any and every way he could, for the rest of time.

He was doomed.

And not just because someone wanted him dead. But because of his own recklessness. His own foolishness. This ridiculous, utterly unprecedented need for her that was a poison in his blood. The venom could not be removed. Nothing would cure or quell it.

"Me," he agreed, inclining his head to acknowledge the irony. He was standing by the window, where moments before his sister had joined him, he'd been watching a deluge of rain falling from the gray-cast sky. The gloom beyond seemed a perfect reflection of the day. "Marriage. To Lady Virtue."

"But…you…she…"

Christ, Pamela was sputtering. The rain lashed against the windowpane, mocking him.

"Yes. I intend to marry her." Trevor paused, then sighed. "I *must* marry her."

"You must, you say." Understanding dawned on his sister's countenance. She'd been still, hovering at the threshold, but she was a flurry of movement now, the blue muslin of her gown frothing as she began to pace the length of the chamber. "What have you done this time?"

Everything but ravish his ward in the music room.

Pamela gave him no quarter. She marched toward him, holding his stare, daring him to speak the awful truth aloud. His ears went hot. He wouldn't do it.

"I have compromised her," he said instead, retreating from her outrage. He moved away from the window and stalked toward the hearth, where the evidence of her last vexation with him remained in the form of a black ink stain on the bricks. The fire crackled, the flames licking low. There was no reprieve to be had within its red-orange depths. He turned back to Pamela. "Quite beyond repair."

His sister's shoulders sagged, defeat overtaking her. "It has only been three days since the last incident."

"Four," he muttered, wondering if she would throw a different object into the fireplace this time.

It had been four days since he'd last touched Virtue. Which had obviously been far too many days. He'd fallen upon her like a starving man given his first meal in a decade.

"You *promised*." The last word was issued as an irate hiss. "You swore you would keep your distance from her."

"Apparently, I'm no better at keeping my word than our father was."

It was an unpleasant discovery to make about himself, that he was not so very different from his sire. He had liked to believe he possessed nothing in common with the cold-hearted, conscienceless villain who had fathered him. How lowering it was to realize he had been wrong. But whereas their father had compromised their mother to seize her dowry, Trevor had compromised Virtue for no reason other than his own desperate need to pleasure her.

"Your lack of control is appalling," Pamela said coolly. "Truly, Ridgely. Could you not have found one of your light-skirts and dallied with her instead?"

He could have. Should have. *Would* have. However, no one else was Virtue, and that was fast becoming the crux of the matter. He didn't want anyone but her. No one else would do. But how to explain that to his sister when Trevor himself didn't quite understand the ramifications of such a revelation? The profound realization was astonishing, really.

He'd never been so moved by a woman before; he wasn't certain he liked it.

"I am a scoundrel," he admitted easily to his sister. "It is one of the reasons, I dare say, why my own family reviles me."

"We do not revile you."

"Mother does," he pointed out.

"Mother reviles everyone," Pamela countered.

And not incorrectly.

He raised a brow. "I challenge you to find someone she reviles more than I."

"Why are we speaking of our mother when the subject at hand is your egregious conduct?" His sister sighed and shook her head. "Tongues will wag quite furiously. Everyone will assume you have ruined Lady Virtue."

"Let them wag." He waved a dismissive hand. "I don't give a damn about gossip. I never have."

"But *I* do. Of course, you have not thought of the effect this news will have upon Lady Virtue or myself. I have been acting as her chaperone, and I have failed quite abysmally at the task of keeping her safe from you. She will be scorned in polite society if there is the slightest whiff of scandal."

His sister's assessment stung. And partially because she was right. He hadn't given thought to what would happen for Virtue and Pamela.

"She will be a duchess," he said. "Surely that will ameliorate the pain of having to marry a rogue. As for you, no one will find fault with you for the match. You have performed your duty as chaperone well, and you're a paragon of virtue. Everyone will have no doubt I am to blame."

Which he was.

Color flared in his sister's cheeks. "I do try, but I am far from perfect. I fear I have been remiss in my duties."

He disliked the guilt in Pamela's voice. "You have hardly been remiss. I am at fault. Not you."

"Nonetheless, it shall reflect on me."

"I will do everything in my power to make certain no hint of scandal taints either of you," he vowed. "You have my word."

"You will make a good husband for her, will you not?" Pamela was frowning, as if she had already arrived at the answer to her question and found it disappointing in the extreme.

A good husband. He hadn't even contemplated the notion of being a husband, let alone one of merit. What to say? Their own parents were a classic example of the epic tragedy a marriage could become. Mother and Father's mutual enmity had only been eclipsed by their own selfishness.

Trevor swallowed hard. "I shall try."

"Try?" Pamela's eyes narrowed as she continued pacing about his study, her gown swirling as she went. "That is hardly reassuring."

"If you intend to throw something, please reconsider," he drawled, attempting to lighten the grim mood. "I've only just replaced the inkwell."

"I was overset when I threw the inkwell," she defended herself. "And it was your fault then. Just as this is your fault now."

Yes, he was to blame. But he couldn't summon much regret. At the moment, he wanted nothing else the way he wanted Virtue in his bed. Curious, that.

The heat from the fire became too much. Trevor returned to his vigil at the window. "As we have already established, I am a rogue," he told her with a languid air.

"And one who is utterly without compunction." Pamela's voice was tart. "Where is Virtue now? I will need to speak to her."

He thought of Virtue's flight from the music room and winced again. "I'm afraid she isn't entirely pleased with me at the moment, having just learned that Greycote Abbey has been sold. She has refused my suit, and quite soundly, too."

Guilt lanced him at the thought of her in tears. He hadn't imagined she would be so devastated by the news, and the sight of her anguish had torn him apart. Her words echoed in his mind. *I'll never forgive you.* How he had yearned to hold her and comfort her then, but he had known she wouldn't have welcomed it.

"If she is displeased with you, how did you also happen to compromise her?" Pamela frowned. "Surely you did not *force* her?"

"Saint's teeth, Pamela." He scowled, infuriated and insulted all at once. "What do you think of me? I would never harm a woman. You bloody well ought to know that."

"I should hope not." She sighed heavily. "Forgive me. This is all quite a shock. Not entirely a surprise, given what I witnessed in the library. But a shock, nonetheless." Pamela paused in her furious strides suddenly. "What do you mean she has refused your suit?"

Trevor turned away, staring out the window, watching the rains lash the world beyond Hunt House. "She says she has no wish to marry me. Apparently, she intended for me to send her back to Nottinghamshire."

"She cannot refuse you," Pamela said grimly. "She hasn't a choice now."

"Then perhaps you might have a talk with Lady Virtue," he suggested, "and persuade her to see reason."

He had yet to change after his return from Angelo's, and a cursory glance at his pocket watch revealed that it was just one quarter hour until he was expected to pay Tierney and Sutton a call. Trevor hadn't intended to propose marriage today; he had been rather more concerned with finding out who wanted him dead before it was too late.

"You have created quite a disaster, brother," Pamela observed wryly.

He didn't bother to argue, for he had indeed. There was only one way to make it right. He had to make Virtue his duchess.

With all haste.

~

FROM THE WINDOW in her chamber, Virtue stared down at the street and square, a tapestry of carriages and people blurring together, muddled by rains. Everyone was carrying on with their day despite the murk. But her world had come to a shuddering, crashing halt.

Gone.

Her home had been sold without her permission. Without warning. She hadn't even been afforded the opportunity to bid farewell to Greycote Abbey and the people she loved.

She wasn't certain which was worse, the knowledge that they were all forever lost to her, or the knowledge that *he* was responsible.

Trevor. No, not Trevor. Ridgely, as she must think of him now. Her enemy once again.

A knock sounded at the door to her chamber. She stiffened, hoping it wasn't him. She needed to form a new plan now that she knew Greycote Abbey was lost to her. And that plan would not involve marriage to the Duke of Ridgely.

"Who is it?" she called.

"Lady Deering," said the familiar voice of her chaperone. "May I come in?"

Ah. It would seem he had sent a proxy. The coward.

She sighed and turned to the door. "You may."

Lady Deering swept into the room, her countenance a study in worry and dismay. "What has happened to your gown?"

Oh dear. Virtue glanced down at her bodice, finding the seams still gaping at her sleeves. She'd quite forgotten in her upset when she'd stormed back to her rooms that Ridgely had ripped the threads.

Her face went hot at the memory, and her traitorous body warmed in sinful places before she tamped down the unwanted longings.

"My gown was caught," she lied lamely. "I will have to repair it."

"Caught?" Lady Deering's expression was shrewd. "By whom?"

The knowing tone of her voice told Virtue that her chaperone knew precisely whom.

"I suppose he has sent you here to me," she said instead of answering, hugging herself around the waist.

"He has." Lady Deering approached her, looking grim. "There is no alternative for the both of you now save marriage."

Virtue's answer was instant and vehement. "I'll not marry him."

Not after what he had done, selling Greycote Abbey without warning. Nor before then, either. She had no intention of wedding anyone, and particularly not Ridgely. Her attraction to him was maddening, but she had no doubt that time and distance would cure her of the affliction.

"You haven't a choice," Lady Deering said gently, giving her shoulder a consoling pat. "You've been compromised."

Compromised was a thoroughly genteel manner of describing what had happened in the music room. Bloodless and cold. Thinking about it now, the way Ridgely had made her feel with his clever mouth on her body, made Virtue distinctly warm. Too warm.

Still, her reaction to Ridgely was purely carnal. She didn't like him. She wouldn't marry him. His insistence that they marry was the height of foolishness, considering they were the only two witnesses to their folly.

"No one knows," Virtue countered, just as she had earlier with Ridgely.

"Yes, but *I* know," her chaperone said, frowning. "There also remains a possibility that the servants are aware as well. All it requires is one person to whisper a hint of scandal. Believe me, my dear, bad news travels with far greater alacrity than good."

She didn't doubt it was so. Still, she would not relent. Ridgely had betrayed her. Her heart was crushed into a thousand jagged shards, and he was responsible.

"I won't marry him, my lady," she said.

"If we are to be sisters, you should call me Pamela," Lady Deering told her, giving Virtue another shoulder pat. "And you *will* marry Ridgely, dearest. You must now, after today's indiscretions."

Frustration rose to a maddening crescendo within Virtue. "From the moment my father died, I have been told what I must do. I must have a guardian, I must go to London and leave Greycote Abbey and the only home and family I've ever known, I must find a husband, and now I must marry Ridgely. I am sick to death of hearing what I *must* do. What about what I *want* to do?"

Lady Deering's expression turned wistful. Almost sad. "I am afraid ours is a life of duty rather than wants."

The other woman's calm acceptance only served to heighten Virtue's frustration. "Did you never want something more than the life you were told you should lead?"

But of course Lady Deering must have. Virtue thought of what she had seen and overheard earlier between her chaperone and the guard known as Beast.

"It wouldn't signify if I did," Lady Deering said quickly. Far too quickly, Virtue thought. "We are, all of us, governed by society. We must follow its dictates or suffer the consequences. I do not think you are prepared to pay the price, Virtue."

"What price is dearer than marriage?" she asked, shaking her head, more stubbornly determined than ever. "No, I'll not marry him. Not after the way he sold Greycote Abbey without a word of warning to me. I didn't have a chance to say goodbye, nor to see it one last time."

Tears pricked at her eyes as she thought of Mrs. Williams with her kindly blue eyes and ruddy cheeks and ready smile. Of Miss Jones who had taught Virtue all her finest recipes in the kitchens. Of the doting and kindhearted butler Mr.

Smith, who had been a fatherly figure to her when she hadn't one because her own had been perennially absent.

All lost to her now.

She hoped they would remain with whomever it was who owned the estate. Greycote Abbey was as much the home of its many loyal domestics as it had been hers.

"I understand you are frustrated with my brother," Lady Deering was saying. "However, he was only acting in your best interest as he was charged, carrying out your father's wishes. As Greycote Abbey has been sold, and you have been compromised, there is nothing that can be done to change what has been set in motion."

She moved away from the window at last, her agitation sending her feet flying across the Axminster. "He cannot force me to marry him. I'll leave Hunt House and absolve him of all duty related to me."

She opened her wardrobe and began hauling her belongings from it and laying them systematically across the bed. Where were her cases? She'd have to see her books properly packed. Naturally, they would come with her wherever she went.

Lady Deering followed her, placing a staying hand on her arm. "Don't be foolish, my dear. Where would you go, a young lady alone in the world, with no one to protect you? You haven't even access to your own funds."

Blast him! Her chaperone was correct. How neatly and thoroughly Virtue was trapped. Ridgely was her gaoler. She hadn't enough pin money for rooms of her own; she'd used almost everything he had given her to buy books. And to obtain more money, she would need the duke's aid. The very man she was intent upon escaping.

She wilted onto the bed, atop her morning gowns and petticoats, and stared at the ceiling with its Roman-inspired plaster medallions. It was stunningly lovely. A regal prison. She hated it.

"You will accustom yourself to the notion of marriage," Lady Deering suggested with a reassuring tone.

"I won't," she said to the ceiling.

The mattress dipped as Lady Deering settled herself primly on the edge. "I do believe he possesses the ability to be a good husband to you. He has been wild, heaven knows, but I've never seen him so attentive with another lady before you. When you are in a room, you are all he watches. His reputation is well known, but it isn't like Ridgely to dally with innocents. He usually prefers widows and unhappy wives."

Virtue hated the thought of anyone else he had kissed. Anyone else who had received his smiles, his knowing caresses, anyone who had been held in his arms. It made no sense, because she certainly didn't wish to have any claim upon him herself.

Did she?

No. Of course she didn't.

Still, however…

"I shouldn't like to think of anyone else the duke has preferred just now," she said grimly.

Because he *was* a rake. He was the sort of beautiful, charming, devil-may-care scoundrel to whom women flocked. And she had been no different. Wooed by those wicked lips and dark eyes filled with sinful mystery.

"No other will be his duchess," Lady Deering told her softly. "That right will belong to you alone."

And she understood then, the magnitude and gravity of what Ridgely's sister was telling her without directly speaking the words. A chill swept over her as she turned her head to face Lady Deering, whose elegant profile showed no hint of her true emotion. She was so still she might have been a statue, and had Virtue not previously witnessed her shocking display of passion with the guard, she wouldn't have believed it possible.

"He will take mistresses, you mean," Virtue said.

"He may," Lady Deering agreed. "It would be his right."

Virtue sat up, her stomach feeling as if it had been cinched into a knot. "Did Lord Deering have mistresses?"

Lady Deering flushed. "No, he did not."

"How would you have felt," she asked, "if he had taken one?"

"It would have broken my heart," Lady Deering answered solemnly. "Ours was a love match. But you are not in love with Ridgely, are you, dear?"

Yes.

No.

Oh, she did not know.

"Of course not!" she denied, with perhaps far too much emphasis. "And what would my match to Ridgely be? A pity match?" She hated the thought. "I'll not do it."

"Not a pity match, but a match of good sense," Lady Deering said. "You require a husband. Ridgely must marry eventually anyway. The two of you clearly share some manner of connection, or else you would not have found yourselves in this predicament."

They had indeed shared a connection. One he had severed the moment he had sold Greycote Abbey without her knowledge or consent. And to think he had dared to reprimand her for trespassing in his chamber. His sins against her were far greater.

"I cannot forgive him for what he has done," she told Lady Deering. "Nor can I bind myself to him forever. We would never suit."

We would suit in some ways, said a wicked inner voice.

One she promptly stifled, along with all unwanted

reminders of just how lovely it had felt to have his mouth between her thighs. The pleasure had been beyond the realm of her fanciful imaginings. But that was the way of it with rakes, she reckoned. They were masters of seduction.

She must not forget that the Duke of Ridgely was also arrogant and overbearing. He was the man who had stolen her books and barred her from the library. Who had sold Greycote Abbey. Who had called her *infant* in such mocking tones, his perfect mouth always twisting in a half smile as if she were a joke only he found amusing.

To the devil with him. He could take his proposal of marriage and stuff it in his ear as far as she was concerned.

"Give yourself some time to contemplate the matter," Lady Deering advised. "I'd wager you will change your mind."

"Never," she vowed firmly.

No, she would not marry the Duke of Ridgely. Nor would her opinion alter. Her decision had been made.

CHAPTER 13

"Come." With a rude sneer and nod of his head that no well-trained servant would ever make, Archer Tierney's butler turned on his heel and stalked away.

Apparently, Trevor was meant to follow the fellow.

He stepped into his old friend's new town house for the first time, seeing the door closed at his back. No one offered to take his hat and gloves, but then, this was hardly a social call. Trevor had made the journey from Hunt House in an unmarked carriage with an armed guard accompanying his coachman. After two failed attempts on his life, he wasn't interested in taking further chances.

If the bastard wanting him dead tried again, he'd have the fight of his bloody life next time. Bad enough Trevor had to be kept from sleep by the dreams which continued to claw at him, until he woke sweating in the night, half-convinced a new assassin had come to deliver him to his bloody end.

He traveled over the marble entry and up a set of carpeted stairs, trailing the large, scarred guard. The house was elegantly appointed, with a noted dearth of wall hangings. Not an ancestral bust or portrait to be found. Also not surprising, a reminder that Archer Tierney hadn't inherited his wealth. He'd earned it.

"In 'ere," the butler growled, opening the door to what Trevor presumed was Tierney's study.

Trevor crossed the threshold, finding Tierney and Logan Sutton already within, seated at a pair of armchairs by the hearth. Tierney held a smoking cheroot in his long fingers, looking menacing as ever. They stood in deference at his arrival.

"Thank you, Lucky," Tierney told his scowling butler. "That will be all for now."

The servant—inaptly named, judging from his unfortunate countenance—tugged at his forelock and quit the chamber, leaving Trevor, Tierney, and Sutton alone. They were old friends from disparate heritages. Sutton had been born to the rookeries. Tierney was the bastard son of an aristocrat. Trevor had been the third son, a wayward devil-may-care no one had given a damn about. They had worked together as spies, ferreting out the secrets of traitors and revolutionaries, catching dangerous men on behalf of Whitehall.

Until Trevor had unexpectedly inherited after his father's and brothers' untimely deaths. First his brothers, one after the other, and then his father. And suddenly, Trevor had been an unlikely duke with the weight of the world upon his shoulders. Estates and people who depended upon him. A mother who resented him. Now a ward. Soon—*God*—a wife. He had stepped back from the Guild after becoming duke because he'd had far too many familial obligations suddenly calling him. They'd only mounted since then.

He found himself suddenly missing the days when they had worked together. How simpler life had been. Dangerous, and yet in the danger there had been a deep and abiding camaraderie. A greater sense of purpose that had been strangely absent from his life. Or, at least, it had been until Virtue had arrived in London.

"Still alive, I see," Tierney observed, unsmiling. "My men are taking their duties seriously, yes?"

Thank Christ Tierney still possessed so many connections with cutthroats. He was the eyes and ears of London's underbelly. And Trevor was damned glad to have the guards Tierney had sent him watching over Hunt House. If Tierney trusted them, he had no doubt they were loyal and fierce.

"Quite seriously," he said. "Thank you for that."

"It is the least I can do for an old friend," Tierney said magnanimously. "Besides, I trust you'll pay handsomely for the effort."

Tierney's days as a moneylender were showing. But no matter. The ducal coffers had coin aplenty.

Trevor inclined his head. "Naturally."

"Good man." Tierney grinned then. "I've made some inquiries on your behalf, and I believe I may have news for you concerning the chap who broke his neck on your stairs."

"Word from Bow Street?" he asked.

"We're a step ahead of them as usual," Tierney said.

"A young actor has recently gone missing," Sutton added. "His brother reports that he hasn't been seen for nearly a week, and that he has failed to appear at the theater for the drama in which he was a player."

The news was most unexpected.

"An actor?" he repeated, startled by the knowledge, for he may have dallied with his fair share of actresses and even an opera singer in recent memory, but he knew of no actors.

Why the devil would a man he'd never met attempt to murder him in his bed?

"Yes." Tierney nodded. "I've spoken with the brother. He gave me a description of the missing man, and I believe it is your dead body. The age, hair color, and build he described his brother having all match."

"His name is John Davenham," Sutton said. "Do you recognize it?"

Trevor shook his head. "I've never heard the name."

His temples throbbed as a headache threatened to descend. After the upheaval of the day, this latest development was as perplexing as it was unwanted.

Tierney took a puff from his cheroot. "You're certain?"

He surrendered to the temptation to press his fingers into the ache in his head. "I'm thinking. But honestly, the name doesn't sound familiar to me at all. I can't say I've crossed paths with any actors, at least not that I am aware of."

"What about at The Velvet Slipper?" Sutton asked. "Your first attack occurred there, correct? Is it possible that Davenham could be one of your patrons? Or perhaps a jilted lover from one of the ladies who frequent the establishment?"

Thump, thump, thump went his head.

Only he would manage to compromise his ward whilst some mysterious villain was attempting to murder him.

"Not that I am aware of, however there are many who come and go as they please at The Velvet Slipper," he said. "For privacy reasons, patrons to the club don't use their given names or titles. Members often wear masks to spare themselves any hint of scandal."

And that anonymity meant, he realized now, that virtually anyone could be present there at any time. Including this Davenham fellow. When he had first begun The Velvet Slipper, Trevor had wanted it to be a haven for those who wished to seek diversions outside pleasure houses. The club members were mutual participants in everything that happened within its walls. He had been younger, wilder, more reckless then, difficult as it was to believe. He'd never imagined the club would have the potential to lead to his own demise.

"Damn," Sutton muttered. "I was hoping you might have a record of members or visitors. It would have certainly made our work easier. What of Mrs. Woodward? Does she have information that might be of use, do you suppose?"

"I will ask Theodosia if she knows of Davenham," he said, referring to the more-than-capable woman who managed the daily operations of the club on his behalf.

Mrs. Theodosia Woodward was clever and shrewd, with a business acumen that could easily eclipse that of any man he'd met. Except Archer Tierney.

"Perhaps she might make some discreet inquiries amongst the patrons," Tierney suggested. "If the man who tried to kill you was indeed Davenham, we need to find out why he was motivated enough to commit such a crime. It's damned unlikely that a man who is unknown to you would seek to murder you for no good reason."

"Is there ever a *good* reason for murder?" he drawled, but then recalled who he'd issued the question to. This was no drawing room chatter, and Archer Tierney was the furthest one could get from a *ton* gentleman.

Tierney raised a brow. "It all depends upon who is being murdered."

"Christ," he muttered. "I shouldn't have asked."

"No," Sutton agreed with a wry grin. "You shouldn't have."

Trevor sighed. "I've been thinking the attempts on my life had to be related somehow to our work with the Guild. Quite ironic that we faced some vicious, dangerous men in our day, and yet the source of all my woes should be a pleasure club I started on a whim."

"We aren't ruling out the possibility of someone with a grudge against the Guild," Tierney reassured him. "However, if that were the case, it stands to reason that you wouldn't be the sole target. Myself, Sutton, and some of the others would likely have been attacked as well. Moreover, you've been out of the Guild for the longest of any of us."

"Instinct tells me this ain't related to the Guild," Sutton said grimly. "As Tierney said, others would have faced danger by now, not just you. No, it looks as if you've somehow made an enemy of someone angry enough to try to send you off to Rothisbones."

A way with words, Logan Sutton had.

"How fortunate for me," Trevor said, and not without a trace of bitterness.

He had problems enough facing him at the moment, without fretting over would-be murderers he'd never bloody well met. He had Virtue to contend with, and now that she was furious with him over the sale of that blasted estate, only the Lord knew how he could bloody well convince her to marry him. Imagine that—the Duke of Ridgely, desperate to persuade a woman to *wed* him.

What had the world become?

"We need to be certain Davenham is the dead man," Tierney interrupted Trevor's thoughts then, all business. "If he is, we'll make inquiries accordingly. We need to know who he is involved with and why he'd want you dead. If the bastard was acting on another's behalf, we need to find out who that person is before they try again."

"For now, you'll be safe with Tierney's men keeping watch," Sutton added. "We are investigating everyone we can, including the cousin who is currently your heir. From the information we've gathered, it seems unlikely he is behind the attacks, but he certainly has the motive, given he's next in line. If you can think of anyone with whom you've had conflict recently, that would certainly aid our cause."

Ah, Cousin Clutterbuck. Ferdinand was an avaricious weasel, it was true. But he rather doubted his cousin was capable of committing murder merely so he could inherit. He wasn't willing to rule out the possibility, however.

Trevor winced as he thought of others he had recently clashed with, thinking of only one person. "Just my ward, but our conflicts often lead to circumstances decidedly different than murder."

"Ah," Sutton said, his tone knowing, watching Trevor with a smug grin. "I was wondering about the two of you."

Trevor had kept Sutton's wife safe at Hunt House during Sutton's final mission for the Guild. He didn't think he liked the expression on his friend's face.

"There is nothing to wonder about," he blustered.

Because there was, of course. But he wasn't prepared to discuss it. Not with Sutton and Tierney. Bad enough he'd had to humble himself by revealing so much to Pamela.

Sutton's levity only increased. "There's one reason for a man to wear the expression currently on your face. I recognize the signs all too well, old friend."

Trevor scowled at him. "Go to bloody hell, Sutton."

"Never say Ridgely has been afflicted by the same ailment you're suffering, Sutton," Tierney said, his tone dripping with disdain.

"Love," Logan Sutton crowed. "Ridgely here is a cove who's falling in love if I've ever seen one."

Falling in love? Him?

With Virtue?

No. It wasn't possible. Was he in lust? Decidedly, resoundingly, yes. There was a great deal of that happening on his behalf. His poor cock had never been so thoroughly abused as it had been these last few weeks. But love? He didn't believe in that tender emotion. Never had. Never would.

"You're a Bedlamite, Sutton," he said. "The only thing I'm in love with is my ability to stay on this side of *terra firma*.

Now, if the pair of you chortling rogues will excuse me, I have other matters to attend to."

Such as persuading his stubborn, maddening, delicious ward to marry him. But Trevor very wisely kept that to himself. Sutton and Tierney would make a feast of his abject humiliation, he had no doubt.

Sutton and Tierney rose, the latter taking another puff on his cheroot. "Stay safe, Ridgely."

"I shall try," he said grimly. "Thank you for your work on my behalf. Do let me know if you hear anything from Bow Street about this Davenham fellow. I'll contact them myself as well, and if Theodosia has information, I'll pass it along."

"Don't fight it, Ridgely," Sutton counseled him sagely. "Love is the best bleeding thing that ever happened to me."

"Go to the devil," he muttered, and then took his leave.

He was not falling in love with Lady Virtue Walcot.

Not now.

Not ever.

No, indeed. His primary concern was convincing her to become his duchess. And as he took up his own gloves and hat in the entryway of Tierney's town house, the perfect plan began to form.

∼

VIRTUE NEEDED A PLAN.

She heaved a sigh as she paced the carpets in her room, trying not to look at the wrapped parcel which had been delivered to her chamber earlier along with a note from *him*.

For my future duchess, the missive said, written in his bold, masculine scrawl. Signed simply *Ridgely*.

"Future duchess indeed," she muttered to herself.

She'd refused to open the parcel on principle, an action which had cost her greatly since the gift—a shocking token she hadn't expected to receive—was heavy and sturdy and felt very much like a book. Undeniably like a book.

Ridgely had bought her a book.

She'd not lie, the realization was steadily undermining her determination to withhold her forgiveness from him for all eternity. Which book could it be? The anticipation was making her fingertips itchy with the need to peel back the simple brown paper and see.

Her feet ached. Her head ached. Her *heart* ached. And she had yet to seize upon a solution for the dreadful predicament in which she found herself unceremoniously mired.

Greycote Abbey was *gone*. Sold. Lost to her forever. She had known, of course, that her father's will had demanded the sale because she was unmarried and the funds of the sale were meant to be placed in trust for her and used for her dowry. But she had believed, quite erroneously it now seemed, that she had ample time to circumvent the requirements of the will. Greycote Abbey was unentailed. There was no reason for it to be sold. It ought to have been hers. It *was* hers. Or, at least, it had been, until Ridgely had directed the sale of it.

Now, her future was desperately uncertain.

And everyone remaining in her life was adamant that she must marry the man responsible for its loss. She had pleaded a headache that evening to avoid dinner with Ridgely and Lady Deering, requesting a tray to be sent to her chamber instead. She was still furious with him for his lack of communication with her concerning the sale. He had been far more concerned with thieving her books from her than he had been with warning her of what lay ahead. He could take his gift and go to the devil, as far as she was concerned.

A knock sounded at her door.

She paused mid-stride. "Who is it?" she demanded crossly, thinking that if it was her guardian, daring to encroach upon the privacy of her chamber, that she would gladly box his ears.

"It is Abigail, my lady," said a cheerful voice.

One of the maids, then.

"Come," Virtue called.

The door opened to reveal the apple-cheeked domestic who often aided her with her *toilette*. Instead of a tray of dinner in her hands, however, the girl held nothing. On her countenance was a look of expectation beneath her mob cap.

"I'm to help you dress for dinner," Abigail explained.

Virtue summoned a sweet smile for the servant's benefit; after all, her quarrel was not with the maid. "There will be no need for that. I'm not attending dinner this evening. I've already informed Lady Deering she should expect my absence."

Abigail hovered at the threshold, looking uncertain. "Of course, my lady. But His Grace himself has requested me to attend you, saying you'd changed your mind."

Oh His Grace had decided Virtue had changed her mind, had he?

She ground her jaw in frustration. "And I have requested dinner in my chamber this evening. I'm afraid there has been a miscommunication. You are dismissed, my dear."

"I...please, my lady." The maid plucked at her skirts, her uncertainty giving way to dismay. "The duke was quite clear on his wishes. I was told that I wasn't to accept *no* for an answer."

"Indeed." Boxing his ears gathered appeal by the moment. "What are the consequences for you if I do not accede to His Grace's wishes?"

"I don't know, my lady. But I do wish to make His Grace happy," Abigail said earnestly. "I depend upon this position to send money to my mother, to help with the wee ones at home."

Of course she did, like many domestics thus employed. Virtue relented, not wanting to cause problems for Abigail any more than she was prepared to face Ridgely.

"Very well," she allowed. "You may help me dress for dinner."

The maid's smile was blinding and gap-toothed. "Thank you, my lady."

It required all the patience and goodwill Virtue possessed to refrain from grumbling as she allowed Abigail to assist her in dressing for dinner. She chose her palest gown—a simple white muslin, with a fichu for modesty, and kept her hair simple and severe. A tightly scraped chignon. No further adornment. She was a woman in mourning anew. If she had brought her black gowns with her to London, she would have donned one of those to emphasize her displeasure.

Her gowns. The reminder left a bitter taste in her mouth as she descended for dinner at the appointed hour. And all the books she had left behind. The library at Greycote Abbey which had kept her such company...

What had become of the fragments of her life she'd abandoned at Greycote Abbey, thinking to return for them soon?

Ridgely was waiting to escort her into dinner, dressed in customary elegance, his slashing jaw freshly shaven, his hair newly trimmed, the bruise having faded. If she didn't know better, she would have said he had taken extra care in his appearance this evening, whilst she had decidedly done the opposite.

He bowed formally.

She dipped into an abbreviated curtsy, unsmiling. "Your Grace. Where is Lady Deering?"

He smiled, his dark eyes glittering. "She accepted a prior engagement. She won't be joining us."

Oh dear.

No proper Lady Deering whose icy primness would keep them both in check?

Virtue frowned at him. "We cannot dine alone. It is unseemly."

His finely molded lips twitched, as if to suppress mirth. "I am your guardian. It is perfectly acceptable."

She never would have agreed to attend dinner if she had known it was to be with Ridgely. Alone. And she suspected he was more than aware of that fact. Indeed, Lady Deering's absence was undoubtedly why he had insisted she attend dinner.

"I find my hunger has abated," she said. "I will return to my chamber."

"No you won't, my dear." His hand shot out, snaring her elbow when she would have attempted her escape. "You will dine with me."

His hold was firm, but she knew she could break it if she truly wished. Still, she was cognizant of the servants traveling quietly about in preparation of the meal. She told herself that she had no wish to cause a scene, and that was the reason she lingered, far too near to him for comfort, his scent taunting her. Why did he have to smell so decadent, like a rare, expensive treat?

"I don't want to dine with you," she said quietly, taking care to keep her voice from carrying. "Have you sent your sister away intentionally this evening?"

His smile deepened, the corners of his eyes crinkling. "Of course not."

He was lying, she was reasonably certain of it.

"I don't believe you."

He chuckled then, the sound low and inviting. Good heavens, he was handsome when he smiled. Sinfully so. How was she to maintain her defenses when one charming laugh from him was akin to a wall of cannon fire? To say nothing of his hold on her arm.

It burned her through her kid gloves.

"Don't believe me then, if it pleases you to do so," he said softly, releasing her arm. "But come to dinner with me. We need to talk, you and I."

"There is nothing I want to say to you," she informed him.

"Do you intend to remain angry with me forever?" his voice was teasing. "If so, our marriage will be a deadly dull one."

Not his nonsensical insistence upon marrying her again. She had hoped that as a seasoned rakehell, he would have seen reason now that the fogs of lust had faded from his mind.

"We aren't marrying, Ridgely."

"Yes, we are." He took her gloved hand in his and tucked it into the crook of his elbow. "We'll discuss it at dinner."

Her stomach possessed the utter gall to rumble at that moment, completely ruining her ire.

He heard it of course, the cad. "You see? Even your stomach agrees with me."

Her stomach was a traitor just like the rest of her. Fortunately, she had her wits. She was far stronger than the weak, physical part of her body.

"Very well," she relented, but only because she was hungry. And what could be the true harm in dinner? It wasn't as if he intended to ravish her over the first course, was it?

His smile turned predatory. Positively wolfish. "Excellent decision, my dear. Come along."

CHAPTER 14

The second course had been laid out on the table. Trevor was separated from his true quarry by a decadent sea of food. Roast fowl, quail, asparagus in butter sauce, raspberry gelée, soufflé, peas *à la française*. Pity he wasn't hungry for anything but the mahogany-haired beauty dressed like a wraith who had been sending him poisoned glances for the full duration of the first course.

He had been doing his utmost to charm her and had failed dismally. No more playing the gentleman now. He had her at his mercy. The servants had been dismissed and they were alone, the door to the dining room closed at his request.

Propriety could go hang.

He was going to win her over tonight if it was the last bloody thing he did. And since his would-be murderer was possibly still roaming London, plotting his next move, courting Virtue very well *could* be the last thing Trevor did.

Grim thought, that. He would do his utmost to protect her from the dangers facing him. Hell, he would save her with his own life if need be. He had known better than to ruin her with this terrible business hanging over his head, and yet he had been helpless to resist her. Now the responsibility for her safety was his, even more so than it had previously been.

He took a fortifying sip of his wine, turning his mind to happier thoughts. Such as Virtue in his bed, naked. Her soft thighs wrapped around his head as he licked her cunny until she spent. The perfect pink of her nipples and how deliciously sensitive they were. He wondered if she was wearing stays this evening and slanted a glance in the direction of her gorgeous breasts, hidden from view by her bodice and a godawful fichu.

"Will you please stop doing that?" she demanded, voice low and irritated.

Caught.

He lifted his gaze to hers, feigning innocence, and raised his glass in a toast. "Stop doing what, o future wife?"

She made a huff of annoyance, but her cheeks were flushed, and he didn't miss the little wriggle she made in her chair, telling him she was not as unmoved as she pretended. The attraction between them was palpable. His cock had been half-hard through the entirety of the first course.

"Pretending as if we are getting married, for one thing," she said. "We decidedly are not. And ogling me as if I am yet another dish on the menu, here for you to devour, for another."

Devouring her sounded utterly splendid. Nothing could be better.

He grinned, for she had led herself into an excellent trap. "But we *are* going to be married, and I *do* intend to devour you when you are my wife. Every day, if practicable. At least once, if not twice."

"Ridgely."

Was it wrong that her chastisement made his prick leap to attention? He suddenly wondered how far he could push

Virtue. Wouldn't it be amusing to try his best to scandalize her?

"Have I shocked you?" he asked, holding her stare as he toyed with the stem of his wine goblet. "Of course I haven't, have I? It isn't as if I told you I wanted to sweep away all these dishes, lift you onto the table before me, lift your skirts, and make a feast of you instead."

Her pupils had bloomed in her gold-brown eyes, the flush in her cheeks deepening to a fetching hue, and her lips had parted. "You are despicable."

"You have no idea how very despicable. I can show you now, if you ask nicely."

Her nostrils flared and her chin tipped up in defiance. "I'll not be asking you for anything."

God, he loved her rebellious spirit. The hurt in her eyes earlier, when he had told her that the sale of Greycote Abbey had been completed, had haunted him all day long. He'd never seen Virtue weep before, and the knowledge that he was the cause of her upset had been akin to a dagger between his rib blades.

Her fire was returning. He intended to keep it there, burning. Ready to scorch him.

"Don't be so certain, darling." He winked. "We both know you cannot resist me."

"Your arrogance never ceases to astound me."

And nettle her. Good. He wanted her to fight him. And then he wanted to win. To hear those soft, lush lips admit defeat.

"It is universally acknowledged that I am quite irresistible to the fairer sex," he said, goading her. "You are certainly not impervious. Do not dare to suggest otherwise."

The truth of it was that he didn't give a damn about the rest of the women in the world wanting him. All he desired was the one before him. Every wench in London could come crashing into the dining hall and fall at his feet, begging him to bed them, and he wouldn't be moved in the slightest. Nor tempted. No, for reasons he refused to contemplate and could not begin to understand, it had to be *her*, or no one else.

Lady Virtue Walcot had mesmerized him. Yet another sign she had been sent by Beelzebub himself to orchestrate Trevor's downfall. And yet, what better way to be led to his demise than in this woman's arms? He could think of no superior fashion.

"I am impervious now," she informed him coolly, "after what you've done to Greycote Abbey. Where are all the belongings I left behind?"

"Arrangements were made with the steward and domestics there and my man of business and the steward at Ridgely Hall. Anything belonging to you is awaiting you at my country seat. When we are married, you can attend to your belongings there at your leisure."

"How efficient you are." There was bitterness in her voice rather than praise. "You have managed to pack away my entire life and sell everything that was left, all without me ever knowing."

"You didn't ask," he pointed out, guilt slicing him like a knife. He hadn't wanted to carry out his obligations, to cause her pain, but the clause in Pemberton's will had left him without choice. He cleared his throat, tamping down emotion, and continued. "As I said, I thought you understood the terms of your father's will. The clause concerning unentailed property was quite clear on the matter. Greycote Abbey was a failing estate. You are fortunate to receive the tidy sum it brought rather than the headache and debts of its management. And you needn't fear I will seek to claim your inheritance. Your funds shall remain your own, even after we are wed. You have my vow."

"My funds will also remain mine if I don't marry you," she said tartly.

They could continue to speak in circles, or he could be blunt. Trevor opted for the latter.

"Not marrying me is no longer a choice for you now that my tongue has been inside you," he reminded her.

She looked away, giving him her profile. "Must you speak of it?"

"Yes. I must." He rose from his chair, quite abandoning the pretense of dining in favor of wooing his future bride. "Because it was glorious, and because I intend to do it again as often as you will allow it."

"You're scandalous." She pushed back her chair and rose as well, watching him with a wide-eyed stare as he circled the table with its untouched second course growing steadily colder. "What are you doing?"

"Showing you why you should marry me." To his relief, she didn't shrink away from him or attempt to retreat as he reached her. Instead, she remained where she was, allowing him to take her into his arms. God, she felt good there. Right there. *Perfect* there. "Showing you why you *must* marry me."

"Ridgely," she chastised, but there was a breathlessness in her voice that gave her away. "Trevor."

His given name on her lips pleased him. Her hands were on his chest now. Not pushing him away, but caressing. More pleasure unfurled, hot and thick in his veins. He loved when she touched him. Never wanted her to stop.

"Duchess," he said, testing the appellation and liking the way it sounded very much. Liking the implication, that she would be his, even more. "Virtue. There, we have both called each other by two different names."

Her gaze narrowed, but her hands continued their bold exploration of his body, traveling to his shoulders. "There are other names I might call you."

The minx.

"Such as?" His head lowered a fraction. Her intoxicating scent was driving him to distraction, and her lips were close enough to claim.

"Such as..." Her words trailed off and she frowned. "Inconsiderate lout."

"How can I be inconsiderate? You have been my sole consideration from the moment I became your guardian," he countered, and that much was true.

His every decision and each day had revolved around her and his obligations where she was concerned. He hadn't intended to hurt her by selling Greycote Abbey. But he also wasn't accustomed to dealing with wards or losing his bloody head over an innocent. No woman before her had ever held him in her thrall.

"Ha," she scoffed. "That is nonsense. If you were thinking of me, you should have told me my home was being sold and I would not have the opportunity to return."

It occurred to him that he owed her an apology. Even if he had only been carrying out Pemberton's will as was his duty under the law, he should have consulted her. Informed her of the process. Warned her, at least.

"I'm sorry," he said, finding the words were not as difficult as he might have supposed. He'd made a habit of living his life without apology. "I should have made certain you understood the clauses in the will, and I ought to have kept you informed. When I heard from my man of business, I should have come to you directly."

His contrition appeared to take her by surprise. For a long moment, she stared at him, her gaze searching, as if seeking some hidden mirth or a hint of insincerity. Very well. He deserved her doubt. She could look all she liked. She'd find nothing other than earnestness.

"Do you mean it?"

"Of course, I do." His hands were on her lower back, and he allowed them to move, smoothing over her, absorbing her heat, her curves, her strength. "I may be accustomed to everyone carrying out my wishes now that I am duke, but I can own when I am wrong. It was never my intent to hurt you, Virtue."

"Thank you for that. However, you did hurt me. I've told you how much Greycote Abbey means to me, how much I love its people. Did you not think I would want to say farewell?"

"I thought you had already done so," he answered honestly. "If I could undo what has been done, I would. However, even if I had wanted to keep the estate from being sold, I could not have. The clause in your father's will demanded it be done."

"Very well." She nodded. "I accept your apology, but not your proposal. I don't want to marry, as I've informed you on countless occasions."

"What of your love for the Viscount Mowbray?" he asked pointedly, understanding the games she had played far too well now. "I thought you were thoroughly besotted and wished to marry him."

She raised a brow. "Perhaps I shall yet. I am certain the viscount would not sell my beloved home away without at least informing me first."

A growl emerged from him at the notion of her marrying that fop. He couldn't control his response. Virtue was *his*. The sooner she realized it, the better.

"You're not marrying anyone except for me. Because you're mine. And I'm going to kiss you now."

He was giving her ample warning. She could step away, push him, hell, she could slap him if she liked. But if she hadn't any protest, not even the appearance of Prinny himself in the midst of the dining room was going to stop Trevor from having Virtue's lips beneath his.

"You are overbearing."

Trevor didn't argue. He was, and he knew it.

His head dipped.

"And infuriating," she added, apparently for good measure.

Yes, he reckoned he could be that as well.

Her breath was on his lips, laced with wine and hot and sweet. "And the man who is going to marry you," he said with finality.

Another scant inch, and their mouths met.

The man who loves you, he thought.

But he didn't say that aloud. Because he'd obviously consumed far too much wine during the first course, and all the blood had rushed to his achingly hard cock just now. Yes, that had to be the reason for such maudlin sentiment invading his mind.

Surely.

It had to be.

He couldn't have fallen in love with this maddening, bewitching, intelligent, stubborn, vexing, fiery, beautiful bane of his existence. Could he have?

Saint's teeth.

Logan Sutton had been right, damn his eyes. Trevor *was* in love with Lady Virtue Walcot, soon to be the Duchess of Ridgely.

His *wife*.

He deepened the kiss, too lost in her for further ruminations.

He was kissing her again. Trevor, Ridgely, *him*. The man she could not seem to resist regardless of how infuriated she was with him over his highhanded treatment of her.

He took your books, she reminded herself faintly as his tongue swept over the seam of her lips. *He barred you from the library. He sold Greycote Abbey.*

But he had apologized, she also thought in his defense as she opened for him, her arms twining around his neck of their own accord. He recited Shakespeare to her. He said silly things like *it is the east, and Virtue is the sun*. He kissed her and touched her as if he could not have enough of her.

And she knew the feeling.

Because she was nothing but a confused jumble of emotions, but when she was in his arms, she felt inexplicably as if all the jagged pieces inside herself had fit into place. And when his lips slanted over hers, she never wanted his mouth to leave hers. In him, she felt the same sense of belonging she'd felt at Greycote Abbey, a rightness to her very bones, to the marrow, to the deepest, darkest spaces inside her heart.

How could it be?

His lips dragged along her jaw, down her throat. "You're mine." He caught her fichu in his long fingers and tugged it away, tossing it over his shoulder where the garment landed with an indecorous plop in the *pois à la française*. "You know it, Virtue."

She did.

But curse him. He had to earn her. To make amends for his arrogance. To work harder for her hand, if she was to surrender it.

No, what was she thinking, surrendering? Agreeing to this madcap proposal of his? Binding herself to him forever?

"My fichu," she protested instead of giving him what he wanted.

Concentrating was increasingly difficult as his hot mouth

traveled down her throat. "Horrid little thing," he murmured against her skin. "Keeping me from what I wanted most."

"It landed in the..." He nipped the sensitive cord of her neck and she gasped. "Peas."

His hands settled on her waist, and then he was lifting her onto the long, elegant table, where no place settings had been laid. "I don't give a damn about the peas."

He was seducing her. That was what he was doing. And she was powerless to stop him. No, that wasn't right. Because she wasn't powerless. Trevor himself had shown her just how much power she had over him.

She just didn't *want* him to stop. That was the problem. Her body and her mind were at daggers drawn. One yearned for him with a desperation that set her teeth on edge and her body aflame. The other warned her to cling to her reservations and remember all the reasons why she must never agree to be this man's wife.

"Mine," he said into her ear before nipping her earlobe. "I've known it from the moment I first saw you, but I didn't want to believe that I could ever find myself so thoroughly at the mercy of any woman."

Her fingers found purchase in the knot of his cravat. "How do you suppose you're at my mercy when you are the one who has decided my future for me?"

"I haven't decided it." He kissed her cheek, the corner of her lips. His wicked hands had captured fistfuls of her gown and petticoats and he was steadily lifting her hems higher, fingertips grazing her knees. "Your future is yours to choose. But be warned, darling. I will make every attempt to persuade you until you capitulate and admit that you want me every bit as much as I desire you."

"Desire has never been in question." Her skirts pooled around her on the table, and he caressed the outsides of her thighs. She had to pause to gather up her thoughts, which had dispersed like a flock of startled birds the moment his touch reached her bare skin above the garters holding her stockings in place. Oh, what had she meant to say? Surely there had been more. A protest. Something coherent.

But then he kissed her again, stealing her breath and her ability to think both. His caresses swept up and down her thighs, gentle and slow and mesmerizing. The ache deep inside her intensified. Her legs parted, and he stepped into the vee she had created, and suddenly there was no barrier between them. He guided her thighs around his waist and pressed the thick ridge of his cock into her center. She hooked her ankles together and quite shamelessly writhed against him.

His lips left hers again to string a path of kisses along her jaw. "You desire me, then?" he asked.

How could he wonder? Perhaps he just wanted to hear her admission. His hand found her breast, his thumb stroking over her nipple. And oh, how good it felt, sending a bolt of pure need to her core. Her fault for not wearing stays again this evening, but she hadn't been in the mood, and this simple gown hadn't required them. Her fault for giving in to his kisses.

He knew how to make her melt with scarcely any effort.

He rolled her nipple between his thumb and forefinger when she didn't answer, then lightly pinched.

"Oh," she said involuntarily, liking it far too much. His breath fanned hot over her ear, and his tongue traced the rim, making her shiver. "You know I do, you ruthless rogue."

"I'm *your* ruthless rogue, darling," he murmured into her ear. "Say yes. Tell me you'll be my wife."

There were many reasons why she should not. Later, she would recall them, she was sure of it.

"Why?" she managed. "Why are you so determined to marry me?"

His fingers dug into her hips, pulling her even more snugly flush against him, so that her bottom was almost falling off the edge of the table. Only his body kept her from falling.

"Because." He tugged her earlobe with his teeth and then lightly nibbled on her jaw before lifting his head. His gaze was stormy and dark, almost obsidian in the flickering flow of the chandelier overhead. "I want to be inside you, buried deep in your sweet, wet cunny, and I cannot do that until we are wed."

His words sent a sizzle of pure, wicked fire through her. At the moment, all things seemed possible.

"You could do it now," she suggested, for yearning was eating her up from within. She wanted to be one with him more than she wanted her next breath. "We needn't be married first."

Or ever, for that matter. She may not be nearly as worldly as he was, but congress between a man and woman was far more grounded in the scientific than the spiritual. It was a matter of two bodies joining, nothing else required.

"O wicked ward, what have you been reading in all those books of yours?" He shook his head slowly, his expression oddly tender. "Marriage is most definitely needed. As your guardian, I am meant to protect you. As it turns out, the man you need protection from the most is myself, because I cannot resist you. You're wayward and wild and you rebel against me at every turn. You leave your books everywhere and drive me to distraction. You're intelligent and far too stubborn, and I find I cannot fathom my life without you in it." He paused, a rakish grin kicking up the corner of his lips. "And yes, I want to bed you more than I want to see tomorrow's sun rise. But that won't happen unless you are my duchess. Even I possess enough tattered shreds of honor to recognize that."

His words left her feeling…oh, she didn't know how to describe it. Strangely flushed. Vibrantly warm. Inside her brewed a curious mix of longing and emotion. Lust and fondness. Her anger with him was fading. How could he be so endearing when he was also so infuriating?

"I don't leave my books everywhere," she denied, rather than address the rest of what he'd said, for her whirling mind had yet to make sense of it all.

He raised a brow. "I found one on the library divan this morning, and another tucked into a pillow on the drawing room chaise longue."

She had been too distraught to read. If she hadn't been, surely she would have noticed their absences. Hmm, perhaps she *did* leave her books strewn about. She often had to recall where she'd last been reading and go on an impromptu investigation of Hunt House's many vast chambers.

"Are you holding them for ransom?" she asked rather than acknowledging that he knew her so well.

Apparently, better than she knew herself, in some instances. And that was a most vexing realization indeed.

"An excellent idea." He smiled again, and it was a different sort of smile, one that reached the depths of his eyes. "Thank you for the suggestion."

"I wasn't suggesting it, and you know it."

He kissed the tip of her nose. "I'll not blackmail you into marrying me. I hope to convince you in other ways."

"I know which ways you mean. I can feel one of them now." She flushed at her own boldness, her reference to the thick ridge of him pressed deliciously—and frustratingly—against where she longed for him most. Their scandalous embrace meant that she could feel all of him.

"Naughty minx." He kissed her slowly, deeply, ravenously, their tongues tangling.

Kissed her until her breathing was ragged and she was

grasping handfuls of his cravat and shirt and he was all she could think of. Kissed her and kissed her until he tore his mouth from hers, leaving her head spinning.

"You are the only woman I want to wed, Lady Virtue Walcot," he said. "I never thought I'd say those words to anyone, but here we are, life intervening in its own mysterious ways. Take pity on me and tell me you'll be my duchess. You belong at my side, in my bed. You know it as well as I."

The realization she had been avoiding ever since learning the fate of Greycote Abbey hit her then. All this time, she had been falling for Ridgely. Bit by bit. He had charmed her. Clashed with her. Infuriated her. And now, he wanted to marry her.

But did she dare accept? Did she dare to consign herself to the unknown with the Duke of Ridgely, a sinfully handsome, arrogant, maddening rake?

She could admit that her home was forever lost to her now. Perhaps remaining with the devil she knew—and the devil she couldn't stop kissing and wanting—was the best decision after all.

"*If* I agree to marry you, I have some stipulations," she said. "And you will note I have not yet said I will."

He grinned. "Of course you have stipulations."

"The first of which is no more denying me my books," she continued sternly.

"I'll buy you ten libraries," he said easily.

Too easily. But she believed him. The Duke of Ridgely was many things, but liar was not among them.

She cleared her throat. "The second stipulation is that I wish to ride in the morning."

He nodded. "Only with me at your side."

"The third is that you must be a faithful husband," she said, thinking this request, above the rest, was more likely to be the one he denied.

"I'll expect the same from you," he said solemnly. "No more protestations of love for Mowbury."

Her foolish heart gave a small leap, and she couldn't say why. "His name is Mowbray."

"A fop by any other name would still be a fop," he growled. "You'll be in no one's bed but mine, Virtue. That is *my* stipulation."

Not precisely a hardship.

She nodded, biting her lip as she attempted to think of more conditions. "I agree to that. I also request that my funds remain mine, to do with as I like just as you promised."

"It's done."

Virtue thought for a moment. "And I may have more stipulations. I reserve the right to add additional items to my list at any time."

His lips twitched. "I'll have my man of business draw up a contract. You can add more any time you wish."

He was being very agreeable. And almost—dare she think it—sweet. And she was wrapped around him like a vine as usual, with no intention of letting go, it would seem. What a pair they were.

"Very well," she relented. "I'll marry you."

His smile stole her breath as surely as his kisses did. "Excellent. I've already obtained a license. We'll wed tomorrow."

"Tomorrow?" That seemed impossibly soon. She'd only just relented to the notion of marriage, but to enter it within hours heightened her instincts to flee as fast as she could.

But where would she go? A return to Greycote Abbey was no longer achievable.

He kissed her again, smothering her protests and withdrawing slightly as his fingers stole beneath her gown and petticoats to find her where she was wet and wanting. He parted her folds and swirled a lazy caress over her pearl that made her moan helplessly into his mouth. Just when she thought he would bring her to her peak, however, his fingers retreated, leaving her throbbing and incomplete.

Trevor's lips left hers. "Tomorrow," he repeated. "And I'll make you come as many times as I can."

Tomorrow suddenly sounded quite fine to Virtue. Quite fine indeed.

CHAPTER 15

They were married by noon, their sole witnesses Pamela and the bodyguard called Beast, who was obliged to sign his given name—Theo St. George, apparently—on the register.

Virtue had been lovely in a pale gown, blue flowers threaded in her hair. Trevor had wondered at the touch. Had she thought of his dream when she had settled upon the flowers? Regardless, the way she looked as they spoke their vows would be indelibly imprinted upon his mind forever.

Not the wedding Trevor had intended for himself. But then, he hadn't intended to marry at all until Virtue had come crashing into his life, laying to waste all the carefully constructed lies he'd told himself in her wake. Pamela had been predictably horrified by the haste of the nuptials. She'd wanted to plan a massive affair at St George's. He'd informed her of his plans over breakfast, and within an hour, the entire concern had been finished.

Now, he was riding Rotten Row with his wife at his side, seated upon Hera, the very mare she'd stolen from his stables on more than one occasion. Hers, now. He had given her the mare as a wedding present, one of many. She still had yet to open his gift from the day before, but no matter. He was daft enough to keep showering her with them just the same.

The hour wasn't fashionable, a mist was drizzling from the gray sky, there was a chill in the air, and someone likely still wanted him dead, but Trevor had never been happier than he was in this moment. He was so proud of Virtue. Such a fine woman. Intelligent, bold, and brave and undeniably beautiful. Her true beauty was in her fire, her spirit and determination.

Look, he wanted to shout loud enough that all the corners of Hyde Park could hear him. *This magnificent woman is my duchess. Of all the men to be had in London, she chose me as her husband.*

But he wasn't a complete Bedlamite, so he slanted a glance in her direction instead, admiring how statuesque she looked on Hera, wearing a riding habit he intended to peel her out of when they returned to Hunt House. Preferably with his teeth. His instinctive reaction, upon the signing of their names on the register, had been to haul Virtue over his shoulder and carry her to his apartments, with the intent that there they could remain for at least the next week.

But he was not a complete barbarian, and so he had politely inquired what his new wife should like to do following the wedding breakfast. A ride, she had declared, and he had obliged. She was an excellent horsewoman, he acknowledged. But then, that was hardly surprising for a woman who had spent nearly all her life tucked away in the countryside.

He found himself angry anew at Pemberton for failing to appreciate Virtue as she deserved, for abandoning her to Nottinghamshire, and yet oddly grateful. Because now she was his, when otherwise, she might not have been. Their paths may never have crossed, and another man surely would have swept her up like the prize she was and made her his. And the notion of anyone else making her his was enough to make Trevor want to challenge that theoretical man to a bloody duel.

"Is something amiss?" Virtue asked him as they guided their mounts down the avenue.

"Not at all," he said smoothly. "Why do you ask?"

"Because you were scowling at me."

Had he been? *Christ*. What to say, that he was so besotted with her that he had been contemplating telling a nonexistent suitor of hers to name his seconds?

Saint's teeth, he was going mad.

"I was thinking of your father, if you must know," he said instead of making such a humiliating confession, for that was also true. "Thinking of the disservice he paid you in never getting to know you. It was his loss."

She cocked her head, considering him from beneath the brim of her jaunty blue military cap. "Thank you for saying that. It is kind of you."

"I always thought Pemberton a good man. But a good man wouldn't have abandoned his daughter."

"You were friends with him," Virtue observed.

It startled him to realize this was the first time they were discussing his friendship with her father and her relationship with him, in all the time since she'd come to live at Hunt House in the wake of her period of mourning.

"I was," he acknowledged. "I thought I knew him, but now I begin to wonder if I ever truly did."

Although Pemberton had been ten years his senior, Trevor and the marquess had bonded over their mutual love of horseflesh and women. What an odd thought it was, that one could know someone, consider him friend even, and yet never truly understand him. That there could be hidden depths and mysteries never broached.

"I used to despise him, you know," Virtue said, so softly that her voice could almost scarcely be heard above the din of their horses' clopping hooves. "When I was a girl, I wished for him to suddenly call me to wherever he was staying, London or Pemberton Hall, or anywhere in the world. I would imagine him telling me how wrong he'd been to keep me sent away, and all would be forgiven."

The thought of Virtue as a young girl pining for the love of her father was akin to a dagger in his chest. "My God, love. I'm sorry."

"You needn't pity me." She sent him a sad smile. "When I grew a bit older and realized my girlish fancies would never come to fruition, I lost myself in books. I found a vast world awaiting me."

It had never occurred to him that she had sought solace within the pages of the tomes she was forever carrying about. That reading distracted her from past pains. Knowing it now sent a new spear of guilt through him at his high-handedness in denying her books.

"I'm sorry," he offered grimly. "If I had known, I never would have taken your books from you."

"Yes, but if you had never taken my books from me, I never would have seen you without your shirt," she said with a minx's grin.

Once again, her resilience humbled him. And heightened his desire for her. He'd spent half the morning in a state of agony, counting down the hours until he could have her in his bed.

But this conversation between them was a different sort of intimacy, he realized. And he liked that, too. Very much. He suddenly wanted to know everything there was to learn about her.

"Tell me about Greycote Abbey," he said, taking a risk in mentioning her beloved home after it had nearly led to her refusing to marry him, and yet needing to better understand her. "What was it like for you there?"

"It was lovely," she said, a wistful smile curving the lips he longed to kiss. "I was not lonely there if that is what you are asking. I had a governess to look after me, and then when she was no longer needed, I had our housekeeper for companionship, along with some of the other domestics. They treated me as if I were a part of their family, and they were certainly mine."

"What of your cousins, your aunt and uncle?" he pressed. "Did they never call upon you?"

"Father was estranged from his brother, which I suppose is why he must have appointed you my guardian. I've never met my uncle, my aunt, nor any of my cousins. Father's family was small—just the two brothers—and my mother's family smaller still. She was the sole child in her family. You are fortunate indeed to have Lady Deering so close at hand. I always wished I had a sister."

Her tone was melancholy.

He wanted to take her in his arms, the need so sudden and strong that it took him by surprise. He wanted to reassure her she would never be alone again.

"You do have a sister now," he said instead. "Pamela is pleased to have a sister as well, having quite despaired of her brother."

Virtue smiled. "She was rather vexed with this morning's ceremony."

"I promised her a new wardrobe to blunt her affronted feelings," he said wryly.

Pamela dealt with her grief by losing herself in fripperies. He hadn't understood what drove his sister before. Not until he'd found these odd, overwhelming feelings inside himself for Virtue. He couldn't imagine what it would be like to lose her as Pamela had her husband. Couldn't bear to even think upon it.

"She certainly does love shopping," Virtue said wryly. "I vow, she quite wore me out with all our trips to Bond Street."

"And my coffers as well." He shook his head as they reached the end of the avenue and began directing their mounts back in the direction from whence they had come. "You are a part of a slightly larger family now. It is only my sister, my mother, and myself, along with a rather ragtag assortment of cousins, and some scattered aunts and an uncle."

"Lady Deering has spoken of your mother often, yet I notice you have not," Virtue said. "Are you not close to her?"

"My mother resents me because I took the place of her favorite sons," he answered honestly. "Bartholomew was meant to be duke, and Matthew before him, not I, and she's never allowed me to forget it."

"I'm sorry," Virtue said. "How terribly sad for you. I never knew my mother, and I've always wondered what she must have been like, whether or not we would have been close."

Virtue had essentially been an orphan, adrift without a mother and a father who hadn't been capable of showing her the love she deserved. His heart ached for her. It hardly seemed possible that such a vibrant, bold woman could have sprung from such dismal beginnings. But being Virtue, she had persevered, and was stronger for it.

He watched her as they rode on, toward Hunt House. "I am certain your mother would have loved you very much."

Because, he'd come to realize, to know Virtue was to love her.

The Duke of Ridgely was very charming when he chose to be.

And her new husband was apparently choosing to be very, very charming. *Husband.* Strange thought, strange word. Stranger still, the feeling accompanying it, her belly all quivery and light, yet the yearning deep inside her heavy and hot.

Virtue stared at the book he had given her the day before, but which she had not unwrapped until now, sitting on the writing desk of her new chamber. The brown paper and twine had come undone to reveal an incredibly rare book that must have cost him an immense price. And he had somehow secured it.

For *her*.

He had found the perfect gift, the only one she would want. Her eyes filled with tears, making her vision indistinct. No one had ever given her a gift before, and that it was from Trevor made it mean so much more.

She was afraid to touch the tome, to turn its pages, for it had been printed in the fifteenth century. Once she had made the discovery, the book had gone gently to the writing desk, where it now resided. A treasure from the past he had entrusted to her.

After returning from their ride in the park, they had adjourned to their separate rooms, changed, and joined Lady Deering for tea before Trevor had suggested Virtue might like some time to become acquainted with her new chamber.

Her new chamber which adjoined his.

Lady Deering had pinned her brother with a disapproving look, but had agreed, saying she had some calls to pay amongst friends in the hope she might blunt the sting of the gossip which would undoubtedly follow the news of Trevor and Virtue's hasty courtship and marriage. Virtue had already inspected the room, feeling quite as if she were an intruder within. The contents had been hastily unpacked that morning by the capable Hunt House domestics.

A knock sounded on the adjoining door, startling her from her thoughts.

Her heart leapt. Surely, it could only be her husband.

"Come," she called.

The door opened, and there he was, looking unfairly handsome in the buff trousers and crisp shirt and matching waistcoat he had worn for tea, but without the formality of his cravat and coat. He looked effortlessly elegant, as flawless as if he were in a ballroom, and yet there was an underlying air of potent sensuality he exuded that stole her breath.

"May I?" he asked, as if he required her permission to enter the room.

"Of course." She moved toward him, drawn as ever.

The attraction between them was magnetic. Undeniable. And they were married now. It had all happened as if a feverish dream, and part of Virtue felt as if she would wake any moment to realize none of it had been real.

He met her halfway across the room, and they stopped just short of each other. The desire to throw herself into his arms was strong, but she knew she could not allow him such power over her so quickly. Already, he had persuaded her to marry him when she had been most adamant that she would never wed at all. What else could he convince her to do with that wicked mouth and his knowing touch?

"Have you settled in?" he asked. "The furnishings and wall coverings and pictures are yours to change. You may choose what you prefer and see the chamber decorated as it pleases you." He cast a wry glance around the room. "Given all this gilt and pink, I can only suspect the previous duke allowed one of his mistresses *carte blanche*. My mother's tastes are far too austere for such a gawdy showing."

She had supposed the previous occupant had been the

dowager duchess; how odd and scandalous for his father to have kept a mistress at Hunt House, and to have allowed her free rein over the decoration of the duchess's apartments.

"Thank you for your generosity," she said, seeing the chamber through new eyes.

And seeing Trevor through new eyes as well. There was hurt lurking beneath his arrogant exterior. A fractured past not so different from her own. Like her, he had never been close to his father. And albeit in a different sense, he lacked a mother as well.

"You needn't thank me, darling. This is all quite pitiful on my behalf. If I had done this properly, the room would have been readied for you, and we would be on our way to our honeymoon by now." He paused, looking about the chamber once more before extending his hand. "Come with me if you please. This room is far too filled with ghosts for my liking."

She took his hand, and their fingers laced together. Virtue found herself enjoying the newfound luxury of easy touch. If there was anything to recommend marriage thus far, it was this quite pleasant relaxation of propriety between them. Not that they'd cared much for that before, either, she thought as he led her into the familiar confines of his chamber. Their lack of adherence to rules had, after all, led to their hasty marriage.

When they were ensconced in his room, the connecting door closed to ward off unwanted spirits of the past, he lifted her hand to his lips for a reverent kiss, his dark eyes burning hotly into hers.

"Alone at last, duchess mine."

Virtue almost looked about to find the duchess he was addressing.

Her.

They were married. Before her stood her husband. Ridgely. Trevor William—as she had discovered that morning his middle name was—Hunt. The guardian with whom she had clashed, and kissed, and more.

"I must thank you for the book as well," she said softly, reminded anew of the priceless gift. "I cannot imagine how dearly it must have cost you. Boccaccio's *Decameron*. It belongs in a museum, not in my unworthy hands."

"Your hands are most worthy." He kissed her palm, as if to prove his point, his tongue flicking out to trace the line running from her palm to between her thumb and forefinger. "And as for the cost, you needn't fret. I was able to purchase it for half the price the fellow before me had paid, and at the veritable bargain of less than one thousand pounds."

She shivered as he sucked on the surprisingly sensitive space between her fingers next. "Nonetheless, that is a small fortune."

"The previous owner overestimated his ability to build his libraries. Fortunately, I'll have no such problem with building yours."

"*My* library?"

"Yes." He nipped the tender flesh he'd just suckled with his teeth. "Your libraries, plural, darling. I promised them to you, did I not? Every library we own is utterly at your disposal. Just as I am."

Oh, she liked the sound of that far too much.

"You and your libraries both?"

He smiled against her palm, his gaze holding hers. "Both."

"Oh."

She had intended to say something far more intelligent, but in the end, she was too overwhelmed with a rush of sensation to manage anything else.

He pressed another lingering kiss to her hand and then rose to his full, towering height. "My God, you are so delicious. I could tear that gown off you, throw you over my shoulder, carry you to my bed, and fuck you for the rest of the afternoon. And all evening, too."

Wicked words. Sinful words. She was ablaze.

"Why don't you, then?" she dared.

"Because Pamela warned me against falling upon you like a starving lion being fed his first meal in a week," he said, grinning. "I am trying to be a gentleman, but it's damned difficult, when all I want to do is strip you bare and cover you in kisses from head to toe."

The most wanton part of her failed to see the problem with such a plan.

"Perhaps you should," she blurted.

His smile turned wicked. "I knew I married you for good reason."

Married. It still felt like a dream. As if she would wake in her bed at Greycote Abbey and realize her whirlwind time with the most seductive rogue in London had all been the wild imaginings of her slumbering mind. But no, this was all too real. She was the Duchess of Ridgely, standing alone with her new husband in his chamber. Longing for him.

She must guard her heart, she thought. Ridgely was a rake, after all. Even Lady Deering had warned her away from him. He had vowed he would be faithful to her, but promises could be so easily broken. Their relationship was grounded firmly in the carnal, and it must remain that way.

A pang of uncertainty hit her.

"You don't regret marrying me?" she asked.

He was still holding her hand, and he gave her fingers a gentle, reassuring squeeze. "No, darling. I don't regret it for a moment."

"It has only been hours. Of course you don't regret it now, but what if you do as time goes on? You are accustomed to having all the women in London at your feet."

"Yes, but all the women in London are not you." His

expression was laden with tenderness as he pulled her toward him, into the sturdy warmth of his chest. "And you are the only woman I want in all the bloody world."

"Since when?" Her hands settled on his shoulders. "Your reputation is quite wicked, you know."

"Reputations change," he said simply, cupping her nape. "So do people."

Here she was, complicating matters and thinking far too much when she'd intended to give herself over to sensation. But how could it be that this handsome, worldly duke who could have his pick of anyone would choose her, a bookish lady who had spent most of her life in the countryside, when her own father had not even wanted her?

She bit her lip, a new wave of uncertainty striking her. "In my experience, people don't change at all, regardless of how very much we want them to."

His thumb was stroking the patch of skin at her nape, his fingertips pressing into her with gentle insistence. "I'm not Pemberton. I'll not abandon you, and nor will I regret being your husband. I promise it, Virtue."

"I want to believe you." How she did.

"Then do." He kissed her brow, her cheek. "You can trust me. I am yours now, and you are mine. Forever."

The rasp of his whiskers on her cheek rescued her, bringing her back to life and plucking her from the abyss of doubt. His skin was hot, electrifying, their nearness making her body go heavy with need. The musky, citrus scent of him teased her. Here was something tangible, something she could cling to and forget the rest. He had shaved that morning, and already, the strong blade of his jaw was shadowed. She rubbed against him, seeking something she couldn't define. Not just comfort, but more.

She turned her head, and their lips met. He kissed her with such sweet reverence at first, his mouth soft and hot on hers. And then deeper, with need and fiery, claiming possession.

She gave herself over to the sensual spell he wove, her hairpins falling to the carpet in an echo of the lash of rains on the windowpanes. Her hair was coming undone, and so was she. His tongue swirled into her mouth, and she tasted the tea they'd shared earlier. He found the tapes on her gown and her bodice began to loosen.

Still kissing him, she trailed her hands down his chest, her fingers stopping at the buttons to his waistcoat, which she worked to free from their moorings. He was hers, just as he had said, and she wanted to touch him as she had before, bare skin on skin. They could take their time, savor each other without fear of interruption or scandal, and yet they were both equally frantic, not wanting to waste time.

He broke the kiss and sucked on her neck, helping her to divest him of the waistcoat. And then, he was stripping her out of her gown and petticoats, and he pulled his shirt over his head.

Her nipples protruded from her chemise, hard and aching. He took note, palming her breasts, rubbing over the stiff peaks until a noise of breathless need slipped from her. She touched him too then, her fingers glancing over the bands of muscle on his taut abdomen and chest, the effect of all his sessions at Angelo's.

He was so powerful, so broad and strong and alive. How could anyone wish to do this beautiful man harm? She wondered what, if anything, he had discovered about the intruder on the stairs, but then pushed the troubling thought from her mind. She would ask him later. For now, she would not allow anything or anyone else to interfere. He was here, he was hers, and there were guards in Hunt House to keep him safe.

"I have imagined this moment hundreds of times," he said, his voice low and quiet, steeped in reverence.

His words filled her with a renewed sense of urgency. Need was pulsing between her thighs, making her ache. She wanted him there. Yearned to be his in every way.

She fumbled with the fall of his trousers, her fingers clumsy with the pent-up need to touch and explore him. She grazed the thick ridge of his cock, pressing against the placket.

He groaned. "Saint's teeth, Virtue. I want you so badly."

She knew the feeling, because she felt the same way. Their bodies seemed to understand each other even if their minds were still growing accustomed to the newness of their circumstances. She grew bolder, cupping him for the first time, testing the length and firmness of him through his trousers in the same manner he fondled her breasts through her chemise.

He inhaled sharply at her touch, and she stilled, wondering if she had gone too far. But then he lightly pinched her nipples, his gaze hot and dark on hers. "Go on, darling. Do whatever you like to me. As I said, I'm yours."

Hers.

She managed to open his falls, and his cock surged forward, beautiful and thick and long, so much larger than she had imagined when she had only felt his manhood pressing against her. Instinct seized the reins as she took him in her hand, gently at first, not certain how she should touch him.

"Harder," he told her, releasing one of her breasts and wrapping his fingers around hers. He tightened her grip, then guided her hand to move up and down his shaft. "Yes, darling. Like that."

He was smooth and softer than velvet, yet firm. Such a

strange contrast, a bead of wetness seeping from the tip and slicking over her hand as she stroked together with Trevor. His head was bent, his lips parted, an expression of raw desire on his handsome countenance. The sight filled her with boldness and need. She thought of how he had used his mouth upon her in the library and wondered if she might do the same for him.

"I want to taste you," she said breathlessly. "Just as you did to me."

At her admission, his hips jerked, his cock going harder still. He lowered his forehead to hers. "Sweet Christ, Virtue. Are you trying to unman me?"

She kissed him, for she wasn't certain of the answer. All she knew was that she liked having him at her mercy. His pleasure stoked the fires of her own desire ever higher. Feeling unaccountably bold, she nipped his lip as she had done before. He deepened the kiss, until it became crushing, their teeth colliding in their eagerness. The slow, mutual seduction was no more as they disintegrated into a frenzy of need.

Their hands were everywhere, seeking, searching, scrabbling at fabric and seams. He tore her chemise over her head, and together, they removed his trousers.

"In the bed, darling," he told her breathlessly. "Now."

They moved as one onto the mattress, naked and desperate for each other, Virtue on her back, Trevor cradled between her thighs. His cock was heavy and hard against her belly, but he didn't push inside her yet as she had supposed he might. Instead, he caressed her curves, leveraging himself on his forearm as he lowered his head and took the tip of her breast in his mouth. He sucked hard, his cheeks hollowing out beneath their angular cheekbones, and then withdrew, using his tongue for slow, deliberate flicks over the sensitive bud.

Her back bowed from the bed. She was so eager for him,

desperate, it seemed, an ache dwelling inside her that only he could answer.

"I love the way your skin flushes when you want me." He kissed the curve of her breast, and then moved to the other, licking that tight peak as well. "I love your curves and softness, your body responding to mine. Your hungry nipples." Another kiss, and the hand traveling over her waist moved, caressing her hip, then her inner thigh, urging her legs apart. His fingers dipped into her folds, painting her own wetness over her. "Your cunny is dripping. God, I love that, too."

He played with the bud that was already pulsing, a light swirl of pressure that left her panting.

"Hurry," she said, wanting more.

"Patience, darling."

He kissed down her belly, settled his broad shoulders between her thighs, and replaced his fingers with his mouth. His tongue teased her pearl, and then he caught her between his teeth for a gentle bite that sent a rush of sensation shooting all the way to her toes.

She'd intended to pleasure him in this way, but now he was the one devouring her, and she was writhing on the bed, her body no longer hers to control but his. He sucked and licked, and then sank his tongue deep inside her, plunging hot and wet. It was agony and ecstasy, and it was too much and not enough all at once. One of his hands found her rump, fingers digging into her buttocks with delicious pressure, and he held her still as he fully made love to her with his mouth and tongue.

When he returned to her bud and gave her a lusty suck, his other fingers found her entrance, and she knew the pressure of a lone digit pushing inside her. Just a slow dip at first, nothing more than his fingertip swirling in her wetness. Then he probed deeper, to the knuckle, and he bit her again.

A stinging nip that made her jerk, bringing him all the way inside.

"Yes," he crooned against her folds as she whimpered and twisted beneath him. "Come for me."

In that moment, she would have done anything to please him, but even had she been otherwise inclined, she couldn't have stopped it. She felt that familiar tightness coiling inside her, and then his finger was moving, penetrating her then withdrawing, and his tongue was flicking over her bud with merciless precision as he renewed his attentions.

And good sweet heavens above, her heart was pounding, her breath seizing in her chest. She was going to die of delirious pleasure, and there could be no better way to meet her end, she was sure of it. Fingers clutching and twisting at the bedclothes, she arched her back and cried out her release as it pounded through her. She contracted on his finger, her hips twitching as he continued to paint his tongue over her in long, firm swipes until he caught her bud in his teeth and bit again. Pleasure shot from her center outward, and another small series of spasms shook through her as she spent again.

And then he rose, his body hot and unyielding over hers as he pressed her into the mattress, the blunt head of his cock slicking over her opening. He buried his face in her throat, kissing her there.

"This beauty mark," he murmured against her skin, "drives me mad."

She hadn't even known she possessed a mark there, where his lips grazed over her followed by his tongue. He kissed lower, to her shoulder, and he gently bit as his cock pressed deeper, sinking inside her as his finger had.

But this intrusion was different. Larger, so much larger. She gripped his shoulders with wonder at the newness of the sensation, her fingernails digging into his flesh as he eased into her body.

"Oh," she said, a soft exclamation of wonder, of joy.

This, she thought, was what she had been missing.

"How does it feel, darling?" he murmured into her ear, pausing, his shoulders tensing beneath her touch. "I don't want to cause you any pain."

"More," she demanded. "I want to feel you, all of you."

He thrust, his hardness going deeper, and she was stretched and full, and there was a stinging pinch as her body adjusted. Inside her, he felt suddenly massive, as if he might split her in two if he moved. And yet, her body needed him to move. Needed...

She didn't know.

But Trevor did. He took her mouth in a gentle kiss. Another angling of his hips, and the warm, wonderful weight of his muscled form pinned her to the bed. He slid the rest of the way inside her, with scarcely any objection from her body. How incredible it was, to be joined with him.

He broke the kiss. "I need to move."

"Yes," she hissed, because she needed that too. Needed friction. Needed motion. Needed his body possessing hers in the most primitive way.

He guided her legs around his hips, and then he almost withdrew from her entirely, the glide of his rigid cock through her slickness making sparks of desire shoot through her, supplanting any lingering discomfort. And then he filled her again, lodged so deep, finding an angle that created the perfect storm of pleasure bordering on pain.

This time, he didn't stop. He kept moving, in and out, the rhythm maddening. She felt herself spiraling, every part of her exquisitely sensitive. He kissed her cheek, her ear, her neck. Took her mouth again as he took her body, with fierce, voracious insistence. She understood then, how truly they were one, how wonderfully she had been made for this man, and he for her.

And just when she thought she could withstand no more pleasure, his fingers dipped between their joined bodies, stroking her pearl, moving with the firm pressure he'd learned she liked. Everything inside her seized, and she clamped down on him, throwing her head back into the pillow, tearing her lips from his to gasp with the delirious joy of her release.

He buried his face in her throat, his hand fisting in her hair, the pull at her roots not painful but just enough to heighten her climax and make her cry out as her pinnacle roared through her. He increased his pace, growing more frenzied, his hard cock stroking in and out faster until he groaned into her skin, and his powerful body tensed, and she felt the hot, wet spurt of his seed as he spent.

He collapsed, staying buried inside her, his cock pulsing as he kept her pinned under him. She held him to her, stroking his hair as she returned slowly to lucidity. It occurred to her then in one stunning rush as she lay beneath his warm, muscled weight, his body still within hers, that she had been wrong about the need to guard her heart against Trevor.

For it was too late.

She already loved him.

CHAPTER 16

He woke with a jolt, coming to in darkness, terror and dread filling his chest with a heavy tightness. His breaths were ragged and harsh, painful in his lungs. And the certainty was there. Someone was coming for him. Coming to kill him.

Trevor bolted upright, head swiveling as he tried to make sense of the shadows surrounding him and the morass in his mind. He grasped the bedclothes, swimming with delirium, thinking he was going to find the hilt of a knife. All he found was warm curves swathed in a counterpane instead.

"Trevor?"

A soft hand on his back, between his shoulder blades. He flinched, partially trapped in the dream he'd been suffering ever since the night of the intruder in his chamber as sanity rained down on him in slow drips.

The voice was Virtue's. So, too, the touch.

She was in his bed. In his chamber. Why? How?

More remembrance. The impromptu ceremony, Pamela and Beast as their witnesses in the drawing room. Signing their names to the register. The ride through Hyde Park, down Rotten Row at the unfashionable hour merely because she had requested it.

Saint's teeth, Virtue was his *wife*. He'd bedded her this afternoon like the barbarian he was, not even waiting for nightfall, and some time afterward, he had apparently fallen into a deep slumber.

"Are you well?" she asked, her voice concerned.

"Christ," he muttered, scrubbing at his forehead as if the action would rid his mind of the terrible thoughts dwelling within it. The feral dreams that haunted his sleep. The memory of the man who had intended to kill him.

The dream had returned each night since it had happened, without fail. And instead of fading, it seemed to become more vivid, more frightening.

He hadn't intended to sleep with Virtue in his bed. Not like this, not when the dreams continued to plague him. Not until he was assured he was safe. If he ever truly would be. That was the price of having led a dangerous life, was it not? He'd been a spy, a devil-may-care, living each day as if it could happily be his last because he hadn't given a damn about anyone else, and most especially not himself.

But that had changed now. He had a wife, a woman he, somehow, impossibly, *loved*. He had Virtue.

"You're shaking," she murmured, shifting nearer to him, pressing her naked curves against his back and side. Kissing his shoulder blade. "What is wrong? Won't you tell me?"

"It was a dream," he managed, his voice tight even to his own ears. God, he hated this weakness. He'd never been so vulnerable, not even in his days with the Guild. "Nothing is amiss."

A lie.

His gut clenched the moment he said the words, for he hadn't lied to Virtue, and he shouldn't begin. She deserved his honesty, even if it humiliated him.

"Not nothing," he amended quietly as her hand continued to caress up and down his spine in soothing motions. "I had a dream about…"

He paused, not wanting to ruin the sanctity of their intimacy by broaching the unfortunate subject of the person or people responsible for wanting to bring about his demise. *Bloody hell*, he'd had no business marrying her at all with this sordid nonsense underway. What had he been thinking, giving in to temptation and ruining her?

He'd been thinking, quite plainly, that he wanted her. That he had to have her in his life always. At his side. In his bed. That he had to make her his duchess and keep her forever.

"What was your dream about?" she asked, still gently stroking his back with a tenderness he hadn't known he craved until that moment. "The man who tried to kill you?"

"Yes." He waited for the accompanying pang of shame at the admission, the weakness. He'd faced down more villains than he could recall in his days with the Guild, and he'd never been haunted by it. But then, none of them had been trying to kill him. None of them had slipped into his chamber whilst he slept.

And yet somehow, miraculously, there was no shame he felt now. Not in the softness of the shadows, Virtue's soothing hand on his skin. He felt, instead, reassured. Comforted.

"Have you learned anything else?" she asked quietly, worry in her tone.

"Very little." He raked a hand through his hair. "Sutton and Tierney are investigating, as are the Bow Street Runners. Thus far, there is an indication the man may have been an actor who has gone missing."

Her hand hesitated in its ministrations, pausing between his shoulder blades. "An actor?"

He heard the true underlying question. Knew what she was likely suspecting. The carelessness of his past had never troubled him before, but it did now, rising like a hideous specter between them.

"I don't know the fellow, if that is what you are wondering," he said. "I haven't dallied with any actresses since long before you came to Hunt House."

He hadn't dallied with anyone at all since Virtue had come to stay with him in London. At first, he had imagined his disinterest in the opposite sex had been caused by the distraction of having a ward beneath his roof and all the associated responsibilities that came with it. Now, however, he could recognize the truth—he'd been drawn to Virtue from the first. And though she had been forbidden to him, his need for her had eclipsed all else. Even the need for having a warm, willing woman in his bed. Because the only one he'd wanted was her.

"You needn't explain yourself to me," Virtue said quietly, her hand resuming its course, traveling rhythmically up and down his spine. Soothing again. "I'm more than familiar with your reputation."

He wished he hadn't a reputation. Wished he'd taken greater care with the lovers he'd known in his past.

Trevor turned toward her, away from the shadows, longing to see her clearly. But they had been sleeping for only Christ knew how long. The day had been bleary, gray, and rainy, the sky leaden. He'd have to light a brace of candles, but doing so would mean moving away from her touch, her warmth, and he couldn't bear to do so yet.

"I cannot alter the man I was, before you," he told her. "I can only be the man I am now, your husband, your lover. And I can promise you this, I've never wanted a woman as I want you."

It was the nearest he could allow himself to come to

admitting his love. He wasn't certain why. The feelings were too new, he supposed. Too frightening. And there also remained the fear she would not return his emotions. She hadn't wanted to wed him, after all.

She kissed his shoulder again, a benediction he found himself reveling in. He wasn't accustomed to such caring with his lovers. Past occasions had been transactions of the flesh only. Two lovers slaking mutual needs. But what he shared with Virtue was different, somehow. Was it because they were married? Because he loved her? Perhaps a curious combination of both reasons.

"I don't want you to alter the man you were," she said, her breath hot and humid on his bare flesh, chasing the last vestiges of the dream from his skull.

Desire returned, feverish and heavy. He had made her his, and the glory of sinking deep inside her sweet cunny lingered in his veins, making him long to have her again, even as he reminded himself he must be gentle with her. She was inexperienced. He had tended to her in the aftermath of their lovemaking, but he knew she would likely be sore.

"You don't?" he asked her now, that unfamiliar vulnerability lingering behind his solar plexus.

"Of course not." Another kiss, and then her hand moved higher, caressing his nape. "I find myself rather fond of the man you have become. Why should I wish to change you?"

His stupid heart stuttered. He felt suddenly as if he were taller than the roof of Hunt House, presiding over Grosvenor Square like some manner of mythical god. How quickly and easily she could undo him, then build him back up again. He hadn't been wrong that day when he'd told her how much power she had over him. Within her short, feminine form was the ability to crush him without even raising a hand.

His head dipped, and he found her lips through the darkness, soft and warm. "Thank you," he murmured against her mouth. "I…this is new for me."

Loving a woman, he'd meant, but again, the words were trapped inside him, and he was too fearful to let them free. He rested his forehead against hers instead, breathing in her soft exhalations, feeling as at one with her as he had when he had been inside her.

"This is new for me as well," she said. "And it has its own merits, being married."

Her voice was low now, almost shy.

He kissed her again, because he could, and then couldn't resist stopping to prod her on. "Oh?"

He asked the question because he was greedy. He wanted to hear her tell him she'd been as moved by their lovemaking as he had been. He was no novice to bedding a woman, but what had happened between himself and Virtue had felt like a first experience, in its own way. He'd never made love to a woman he *loved* before Virtue, and that made all the difference. The connection was deeper, stronger. It went beyond mere pleasure.

"I do like being able to touch you whenever I wish," she confided, threading her fingers through his hair. Her lips landed on his jaw next. "And kiss you."

Ah, God. He reached for her, drawing her more firmly against him, until her breasts pressed into his chest, the hard points of her nipples prodding him with potent temptation. "I like it, too. No more haranguing from Pamela."

Virtue chuckled. "I suspect Lady Deering may find other reasons to harangue you."

"Yes," he agreed, kissing her cheek. "I am infinitely harangue-able."

"I am reasonably certain that isn't a word." She kissed his ear.

How he liked this easiness between them. He didn't know

if it was the calm of the darkness, the intimacies, or something else which had brought down her protective walls. Whatever the reason, he was grateful.

"Perhaps I shall invent it and lay claim to the definition," he said, smiling as he kissed the hair at her temple. "Harangue-able: needing correction by the willful females in one's life. The word is said to have originated with the sixth Duke of Ridgely, who was frequently harangued by his sister and wife."

She tugged at his hair. "I don't harangue you."

He raised a brow, even though she likely couldn't see his expression in the darkness. "No?"

"Well, not often," she amended, giving his hair another playful tug. He'd had it cut, but Virtue still managed to find enough to grasp. "Only when you steal my books and sell my home."

"I promise to never do either of those things again," he said wryly.

In fact, it had occurred to him that there could be a way to ameliorate at least some of his sins where Virtue was concerned. He had instructed his man of business to investigate whether or not the new owner of Greycote Abbey might be persuaded to sell the estate again. This time, to Trevor. He hadn't the slightest wish to attend a crumbling estate in Nottinghamshire, but he found himself astonishingly willing to do anything that would make his wife happy. He didn't wish to mention it now, however. Certainly not until he knew whether or not the new owner would be amenable to selling.

"Is the danger to you gone, then, if this man is gone as well?" she asked suddenly, tearing him from his thoughts. "Is there any proof the dead man is the same person who attacked you before?"

He sighed and buried his face in her throat, inhaling her

scent. "We can't be certain yet. I haven't an inkling why a man I've never met would be so determined to kill me."

"Not a jealous husband, surely?" she asked, but there was no censure in her voice. Only genuine concern.

"I suppose it is possible," he conceded. "Though again, I haven't been involved with anyone since before your arrival, and as far as I am aware, the missing actor was an unmarried gentleman."

Trevor and his last mistress, the widowed Countess of Carr, had parted ways just before Virtue's arrival in London. Adelina had been growing increasingly possessive and jealous, and he'd had neither the time nor the inclination to allay her unfounded worries. Her congé had been in the form of a diamond necklace for her and an untold amount of relief on his behalf. But Adelina had made it clear that she was aiming for a new husband rather than a protector, and a scarcely known actor would not possess wealth or clout enough to suit her aspirations.

"It frightens me," Virtue said, "the thought that someone could still be out there who wants to harm you."

He didn't want to dwell on his mortality any more than he wanted to return to the dreams that had been plaguing him since that night. He found her nose and kissed the bridge, then the corners of her lips. "Take care, darling, or else I shall grow even more conceited than I already am, thinking you are concerned for my welfare."

It was easier to tease. To make light of desperate situations. To laugh instead of allow himself to grow mired in the darkness. It always had been.

"Why do you insist upon making jests when the circumstances are so serious?"

He heard a frown in her voice, and he could picture how it would look, turning down the corners of her lips, crinkling her brow. He cupped her cheek, his thumb traveling over her silken skin, absorbing her heat, her vibrancy. How impossible it seemed that this fiery woman should have become the center of his world. And yet, she had.

"I suppose for me, it's easier to face seriousness with laughter. To battle darkness with light." Trevor thought for a moment. "I am pleased you care enough to worry, though not to be the cause of your apprehension."

"Of course I care." She turned her head and kissed the pad of his thumb. "I wouldn't have agreed to marry you if I did not."

That, too, was gratifying.

He smiled. "I thought it was because I promised you ten libraries."

She sighed. "Oh, Trevor."

He kissed her again before she could take him to task. "You see? Harangue-able."

She gave a small chuckle he suspected was inadvertent and then she was kissing him. "Please stay safe. That is all I ask."

He could have told her that it would require an army of would-be assassins to keep him from her side, from her bed. But he wasn't prepared for such weighty admissions just yet.

"I shall," he said instead. "I promise. Now, then. As much as I love having you naked in my bed, I fear we ought to at least emerge for dinner, lest Pamela send one of the servants to find us. Besides, you must be quite hungry."

Lord knew he was, but not necessarily for dinner. Plenty of time for that later, however. They had the rest of their lives.

Or for as long as his life would last.

The thought was a rather somber one, most unwelcome. He banished it and tamped down the accompanying burst of dread.

He kissed her once more for good measure, unable to resist. "Come, darling. We should dress."

∼

VIRTUE HAD CHOSEN the wrong room in which to read her husband's most recent gift, which had been waiting for her when they had returned from their customary morning ride in Hyde Park. A copy of *The Tale of Love*, the book he had forbidden her from reading in the library what seemed like a lifetime ago now. A note had accompanied its presence, carefully tucked into the frontispiece so that only a small sliver of it was visible.

For her eyes alone.

Darling,
I thought perhaps you might enjoy this forbidden fruit at last. I recommend in particular, and, quite wholeheartedly, the epistle from Lady X to her friend.
Yours,
Trevor

The day was rainy again, dull and gray. It was also a Wednesday, which meant Trevor was spending his afternoon at Angelo's fencing. Virtue was alone on the Grecian divan in the library, a cheerful fire crackling in the grate. No husband to assuage the aches wrought by the deliciously wicked letter he had recommended she read first.

She snapped the book closed with a sigh and clamped her thighs together, feeling achy and flushed. If only she were in the privacy of her chamber, she would have removed her afternoon gown and slippers, then slid beneath the cool, soft comfort of her sheets to rid herself of this gnawing, horrid need.

The notion held appeal. Her mind was filled with the naughty imagery spun by the account in *The Tale of Love*. Lady X's groom had caught her watching him bathe, and although Lady X's intent had not been to spy, the groom had taken her to task for her daring. And Lady X had quite liked it.

Virtue found herself strangely roused by the notion. Not of the groom and Lady X herself, but the forbidden nature of such a coupling. Two people utterly lost to their body's desires, transcending societal roles. When the lusty groom had tied Lady X to a bench using her own garters...

Good heavens.

She hadn't known she would find such a thing appealing. But she did. And she decided that perhaps retiring to her chamber to tend to herself wouldn't be such a bad idea. No one would guess at the reason, surely. It wasn't as if her wickedness was written on her face. Was it? Of course not.

Virtue made haste in departing the library, her naughty book held firmly to her bodice lest anyone spy the cover and discern what she had been reading and why she was in such a rush to seclude herself in the privacy of her chamber. Oh, why did Hunt House have to be so frightfully large? Its size certainly rendered navigation most distressing when one was in need of swiftness and privacy. She passed two chamber maids and Mrs. Bell on her way and prayed she was not blushing furiously.

At last, she was within the haven of her own apartments, the door firmly closed at her back. She returned *The Tale of Love* to its place on her writing desk, thinking she would further investigate more of its contents later. Deciding against ringing for her new lady's maid Abigail, she undid the tapes on her gown and had herself down to nothing more than stockings, chemise, and garters in no time.

That was when a familiar knock came on the door

adjoining her room to Trevor's. Two knocks, in quick succession. Strange to think that even his knocking had become something she recognized, along with his scent, the sound of his breathing when he slept, the beat of his heart beneath her ear when she laid her head on his chest.

"V, is that you?" he called, using his newest pet name for her, which he had adopted following their wedding. "I thought I heard your door."

It pleased her greatly to have a name that only Trevor called her, for it felt as if it were a secret between the two of them. Something that was theirs alone, just like their kisses and their lovemaking.

"It is," she called, realizing that a smile already curved her lips without her even being aware of it, for now she would not need to tend to herself after all. "Come."

Their marriage had fallen into a surprisingly lovely routine over the last few days. Being a wife was still new, but it was not nearly as daunting as she had previously supposed. She genuinely enjoyed the time she spent with Trevor, whether in the privacy of their chambers or when they were accompanied by Lady Deering in the dining room or drawing room.

He crossed the threshold, wearing a blue silk banyan that fluttered about his bare feet and muscular calves and hugged his broad shoulders. His dark hair was damp, as if he had just bathed. The thought of him naked in his bath, warm water sluicing over the beauty of his masculine body, was enough to make her wish she had fled the library earlier. She might have caught him performing his ablutions and offered assistance.

"Have I interrupted something?" he asked, sauntering toward her in that bold way he possessed, as if he owned all the world and not just the impressive edifice in which they were currently housed.

Belatedly, she recalled her state of dress. "No, you haven't. I was intending to…indulge in a nap."

Not just a nap, but perhaps a lovely one could have followed her other intentions. She wasn't certain how to make such a revelation, however. Would he be affronted that she had planned to tend to herself in his absence? She didn't think so. However, she'd never engaged in such a sensitive conversation before.

"A nap?" He quirked a brow, coming to a halt before her. "Have I kept you from your sleep?"

The wicked grin on his lips was unrepentant, and she knew he was referring to the hours she had spent in his bed the night before, blissfully at the mercy of his knowing mouth and tongue. Her nipples, already tightened with awareness, gave a dull ache.

"You know that you did, but that I have no objections in that regard," she said primly, fighting another answering smile of her own as he took her hands in his and lifted them for a kiss on each of her knuckles.

His mouth was like hot silk grazing over her, and her entire body awakened to the promise in his eyes. Why tend to herself alone when she could have the attentions of the handsome man before her instead?

He kissed her inner wrist next. "Do you wish to rest? I can take my leave. I just finished bathing when I heard you enter, and I wanted to see you."

She searched his gaze. "Was there something you wished to discuss?"

"I…missed you." His countenance was suddenly sheepish.

"It's only been hours since we last saw each other," she reminded him, though his admission sent a rush of soul-deep gratification through her.

"It may as well have been an eternity." He kissed her other wrist lingeringly. "It felt as if it were. Did you find my gift?"

Ah, the book.

"I did," she said softly, cupping his angular jaw, delighted by the light prickle of whiskers kissing her palm. "I was reading in the library just now and grew so overheated that I decided to retire to my chamber."

There, she'd made the concession, albeit indirectly.

"Oh?" He released her, his hands taking her waist instead, pulling her into his strong, unyielding form. "Which story were you reading?"

His cock was already thick and firm, rising between them. Why had she fretted her husband would be displeased by the knowledge the book had roused wicked feelings within her and that she had intended to placate them herself? How foolish. Trevor had taught her to revel in her body and all its varied responses, had shown her how to appreciate pleasure being given and received.

"I read Lady X's letter to her dear friend," she said, voice husky as she wrapped her arms around his neck. "In particular, when her groom found her watching him bathe."

"I seem to recall the groom taking her to task for spying." His dark eyes were hot on hers. "Which part of the story did you like most?"

She licked her lips, which had suddenly gone dry, summoning her daring. "When the groom used her garters to tie her to a bench as punishment."

Trevor's hands were moving up and down her back, gliding deliciously over her with nothing but the linen of her chemise in the way. "What did you like about it?"

"I..." Her face went hot. No one had ever asked her about what made her blood quicken and her body ache before. "I liked that she was at his mercy. That she was helpless to do anything but accept the pleasure he gave her, pleasure she secretly wanted."

He pressed his face into her throat, his mouth finding

eager bare flesh and skimming over it. "Did it make you wet, darling, reading that naughty book?"

He raked his whiskers along her neck, over her jaw.

Her head fell back, giving him greater access. Anything he wanted. "Yes."

"And you came up here to pleasure yourself, didn't you?" he asked softly in her ear.

How well he knew her.

"I did. I'm quite wicked, aren't I?"

"Very wicked indeed." He kissed the hollow behind her ear, then nuzzled into her upswept hair with his nose, inhaling deeply. "Perhaps I should punish you, just as Lady X's groom punished her."

Virtue's knees threatened to give out. Her body's reaction to his suggestion was instant.

"Mmm," she managed. Not a coherent response, but all she could find the wits to say at the moment, so strong was the need he had brought to life.

"Perhaps I'll strip you out of your chemise and stockings," he murmured into her ear, his breath hot. "I'll use your garters to tie you to the bed. And then I'll see just how soaked your cunny is from the filthy book you've been reading. Would you like that?"

"Y-yes." The lone word escaped her as half sigh, half stutter.

"How shall I investigate, do you suppose? With my fingers?" He licked her. "With my tongue?" He kissed down her throat. "My cock?"

Oh heavens, he was melting her. She would be a puddle at his feet. She would combust from his words alone.

"However you like."

He made a low sound of approval as his mouth investigated her clavicle. "Perhaps I shall be your groom, and you shall be Lady X. I'll make you pay for watching me bathe. I'll spank your rump, and then I'll lick your pretty cunny until you come."

He intended for them to don the roles of the characters. It was sinful and alluring, to pretend to be someone else. To place herself in the role of Lady X. She was breathless now, the ache between her legs stronger than ever.

"Would you like that, darling?" Trevor nipped her shoulder.

"Yes," she gasped, wanting everything he had said and more. Wanting it so much, she could scarcely think straight. "Do anything, everything. Whatever you want, I want it, too."

He kissed her then, and the last of her embarrassment fell away as she surrendered to the man, the moment, and the needs of her own body.

CHAPTER 17

By the time Trevor had his wife naked on her bed, he was half-wild with the need to be inside her. She matched him in every way, from her carnal appetites to her willingness to embrace her sensuality. He had known that she would be a force when her husband awoke her to the pleasures of her body. He had simply never dreamed that man would be him.

But *saint's teeth*, he was thankful it was.

His hands shook with reverence as he caressed her curves, tracing over her hips and waist, the role he was playing momentarily forgotten as a blazing rush of feeling overwhelmed him. Each day that passed buttressed his love for Virtue, until he had to clench his jaw to keep from announcing the words to the world, to her.

I love you.

He thought them now, as he took in her glorious body, flushed and ready for him. But as always, he couldn't shake the feeling that it was too soon. That he might frighten her with the intensity of his feelings for her, and so he tamped them down. Kept them locked inside the heart he'd sworn he hadn't possessed. The heart that was hers now.

"You had the pleasure of watching me at my bath," he said, his voice husky with suppressed desire as he recalled the role he played. "Now you're going to have to be punished for your wanton ways."

"How will you punish me, sir?" she asked, her voice sultry and low.

God, she was everything he could have ever wanted in a woman, in a wife. Trevor had told her before they began this little game of theirs in truth that she only needed to tell him if he went too far. The pace would be set by her. So, too, the boundaries. He was more than aware that she was very much a neophyte to lovemaking, even if her carnal abandonment suggested otherwise.

He straddled her hips, keenly aware of the heat of her sex through the silk of his banyan. "I'm going to have to tie you up and have you at my mercy, just as I was at yours whilst you watched me when I was naked."

"It was very wrong of me to watch you, wasn't it?" she asked breathlessly. "But how I loved watching the water trickle down over your chest, dripping over your cock. I loved seeing how hard you were."

At the last, she reached between their bodies, cupping his rigid length and giving him a delicious squeeze. He wasn't prepared for his reaction to her saying such filthy things to him. He was harder than stone.

"Fuuuuck," he groaned, hips arching into her knowing touch.

He had unleashed a monster. As always when he was with Virtue, Trevor was no longer certain which of them seduced the other. They were equal partners in their hunger for each other, in their desire to bring one another pleasure.

But then he remembered he was meant to play the part of the groom, making her do penance for her sins.

He gently took her hand in his and brought it to his lips. "Is my lady so hungry for my cock?"

"Yes."

She needn't have made the admission. He could smell the sweet musk of her desire, see the heat in her gold-flecked eyes. He knew she wanted him. But hearing her say it was its own aphrodisiac, potent and pleasing.

"Then I'm going to have to make you wait for it," he growled. "As part of my lady's punishment."

"How cruel you are to deny me what I want." She pouted.

Damn it, those lips of hers. He was imagining them opening to take his cock, whilst her hands were bound over her head. If he wasn't careful, he was going to spend before he was inside her. He was more desperate than he'd ever been, his restraint utterly laid to waste.

"Crueler still of you to watch me at my bath without me knowing," he countered, the game they played making him think of more they could try. There was room aplenty in the tub for the two of them, he was certain. Yes indeed, the notion held infinite appeal. But now, he had other matters to attend to first. "Give me your wrists. Time for your punishment to begin."

She surrendered her wrists without hesitation, offering them to him. Trevor gathered up one of the pretty ribbon garters which had been holding her stockings in place. And as providence would have it, they were the same pink garters he'd admired in the library when she had been on the ladder and first spied *The Book of Love*.

Trying to fight back his desire, he wrapped the ribbon around both her wrists, gently enough that she would have the sensation of being bound, yet loosely enough that she could easily pull free if she wished it. He looped the garter into a bow and dipped to whisper in her ear.

"If the game becomes too much for you, say the word."

She rubbed her cheek against his, as sinuous as a cat, and he swore she purred. "It won't."

This woman. God, he loved her. Perhaps this would be the day he told her after all. Later. When their bed sport was done.

He kissed her temple and then resumed his role, stretching her arms over her head and pinning her bound wrists to the pillow. "Hold on to the pillow. If you release your hold, you'll receive another punishment."

"Yes, sir," she said, grasping the pillow as he'd instructed.

He took a moment to admire the positioning of her body and the way it thrust her breasts forward for his delectation. The sight of her wrists bound with the pink ribbon, high above her head, was every bit as enthralling. His cock was leaking, and he hadn't even licked her yet.

"You are perfection," he said, bending to catch one of her nipples in his mouth and suck hard as he knew she liked.

He was rewarded by a soft moan and the arch of her back. Trevor caught the stiff peak in his teeth and tugged, and she moaned louder, shifting restlessly beneath him, as if she sought friction to ease the ache between her thighs. But he was in no hurry. He intended to prolong this seduction, to wring every last drop of pleasure from her beautiful body. To that end, he moved to her other breast, taking his time to lave and suck and nip until her breathing was ragged.

Next, he pressed his lips to the smooth, flat skin between her breasts, over her breastbone. Leveraging himself on his elbows and knees, he cupped her breasts, kneading them, their full softness spilling through his fingers. She was so very warm and soft, sweetly responsive, and he knew he would never have enough of her.

"You are still wearing your banyan," she protested. "I want you naked."

Yes, there would be skin on skin soon enough, but first he wanted to worship hers without the temptation to sink inside her. He glanced up, his lips still grazing her silken flesh, following the rise and fall of her breasts in his hands, past the creamy column of her throat, where a necklace he had given her was still clasped, to her parted lips and the honey-brown mysteries of her eyes.

"But you are being punished, my lady, not pleasured," he said, keeping his voice low, enjoying this forbidden game more than he had supposed he would when the notion had occurred to him as she'd shyly confessed which parts of the book had moved her and why.

She sighed restlessly, and he licked a lazy circle around her nipple, then blew on the puckered bud. "Forgive me, sir. I am merely impatient."

Yes, he knew that about her. Trevor smiled against the warmth of her stomach as he kissed lower, to the dip of her navel.

"Patience, my lady," he cautioned, before swirling his tongue into the sensitive hollow.

"Oh," she said, jolting beneath him.

But she was doing as he had asked, fingers clasping the pillow over her head, wrists still wrapped in pretty pink garter ribbon. She was glorious. Magnificent. *His*.

Trevor kissed the gentle roundness of her belly, finding his way to her hip bone. Here, he took a moment to bring her sweet feminine scent into his lungs, to savor her body's need for him as he stroked her hips and kissed the vee between where her thigh ended and her mound began.

"Open for me," he urged, and she did, spreading her thighs wide.

Exposing herself to him. The pink of her cunny matched

her garters. He'd never seen a more decadent sight than Virtue beneath him, naked save that ribbon, her hair a wild halo spilling over the pillow.

He settled himself between her limbs and lowered his mouth to her. She was slick and hot and sweet on his tongue. He traced her seam, then parted her folds with his thumb, his mouth closing over the swollen bud and sucking as he had her nipple. Her response was another low moan, and he lapped at her, licking and sucking, savoring the taste of her, the feeling of her, needy and writhing and wet.

As always, he lost himself in the act of giving her pleasure, her every sigh and hitch of breath, each moan and jolt of her hips like music he would never grow tired of hearing. She was all he could see and feel as he lavished her cunny with light flicks of his tongue and gentle nibbles, then hard sucks on her pearl that had her whimpering and her fingers sinking into his hair to tug.

A dim part of his mind that wasn't entirely swamped by pure, animal lust realized she'd broken the rule. He dragged himself from between her thighs and caught her bound wrists, pinning them above her head, their faces close.

"Naughty," he said, licking his lips to savor the wetness of her dew, coating them. "I warned you there would be punishment if you didn't remain as you were told."

"Oh," she said, eyes wide in feigned astonishment. "What shall you do?"

He descended her body slowly, stopping to lightly bite her shoulder, her nipple, to kiss down the very center of her, stopping when he reached the beckoning heat of her cunny. Instead of bringing his mouth to her once more, however, he flattened his hand and gave her a quick, gentle spank on her lips and clitoris.

She moaned, thighs trembling, hips bucking. She had liked it. *Good.* Just as he'd thought she would. He gave her a soothing caress and then resumed, devoting himself to pleasuring her with his mouth until she was quaking beneath him. But her touch returned, sifting through his hair. Intentional this time, he knew. She was testing him. Giving him permission.

He lifted his head and repeated his motions, securing her hands above her head on the pillow.

She was breathing heavy, her pupils wide, skin flushed, arms taut against a bed of mahogany waves. *Beautiful*, he thought. *A goddess. My goddess.*

"You've been bad, my lady," he told her with mock severity, leaning close so that her hard nipples prodded the silk of his banyan and the lush handfuls of her breasts strained into his chest. He rocked his hips, letting her feel his hard cock and how badly he wanted her. "Do you know what I think? I think you disobeyed me intentionally so I would spank your sweet cunny again. I think you liked the way it felt."

"Mmm," she murmured, writhing beneath him, making his cock brush over her folds in a way that would cause him to lose control if she continued for too long. "I did like the way it felt. I'm wicked, and you should punish me for it."

He bit the inside of his cheek to keep from coming right then and there, the bruising pressure enough to ward off a sharp wave of desire threatening to undo all his careful work. His heart was pounding, his cock so hard. God. He was going to die of pleasure. The murderer after him would be disappointed to find his quarry had fucked himself to perdition. No better way to go, Trevor was sure of it. He'd die just to sink his cock inside her perfect, sleek cunny. It would be worth it.

But he wasn't dead, not yet. So he gave her what she wanted. One last drag of his cock over her swollen folds, and then he returned to his position between her spread thighs. There was a spot on the bedclothes, steadily growing, from her wetness, and it filled his head with fire to see the evidence of her desire, to know he was responsible. That he had made her mindless and aching with want.

He planted a palm on her inner thigh and pushed, spreading her open as she moaned and thrust her hips, so free in her sensuality, seeking to alleviate the need within. He caressed her smooth, soft skin, reveling in the shape of her curves, the lush femininity of her form. And then he flattened his hand and delivered another firm spank to her quim.

"Oh," she cried out in ecstasy, head rolling back on the pillow, eyes closing. "Yes, please. More."

He gave her another because she'd asked for it. And then even he had reached the limits of his control. His restraint snapped, and he buried his head between those beautiful legs, deep into her pulsing, dripping flesh, and sucked and licked until she bucked and twisted against his lips, against his teeth as he lightly abraded her clitoris.

Only then, did he give her what he knew she wanted, sinking two fingers deep inside her. The grip of her cunny around him made his ballocks draw tight and his cock even more rigid. But he wanted her to come like this, on his tongue and fingers. To keep her position until she was utterly spent. His fingers moved quickly through her slick channel, probing deep, curling as he found the place inside her that never failed to make her splinter apart.

And she came with a cry that he knew the servants would hear. But he didn't give a bloody damn. In the frenzy of his desire, he wanted her to cry out so all London could hear how well he had pleasured her. He stayed with her as she spasmed around his fingers and beneath his lips. Licked and sucked and fucked until she was panting and spent, and then he rose to his knees, clawing at his banyan, more eager than he'd ever been, his cock aching to be inside her where it belonged.

The banyan fell away, and with it went the game. No more pretense now, no more roles. They were only Trevor and Virtue, husband and wife.

"I want you," she murmured, seeming to sense the shift without him needing to say it. "I want you to make love to me, Trevor."

No surprise, for they were attuned to each other in a way he'd never experienced.

"Yes," he managed, reaching for her wrists, feeling clumsy as he untied the ribbon and freed her. "Touch me now, darling. I need your hands on me. My God, V, I want you so much it hurts."

She obliged him, caressing him everywhere. His chest, his shoulders. Down his arms, passing over the muscles he had earned from fencing, to his flanks, her fingers finally sinking into the flesh of his arse and pulling him against her. He didn't know how he'd managed to deserve her. Likely, he *didn't* deserve her. But she was his. And he would love her forever. Love her as best as he could. In every way.

He guided his cock to her cunny and thrust, filling her in one roll of his hips. For a moment, he lowered his body to hers, reveling in her walls pulsing around him, tightening on him in delicious welcome, so wet and hot. His face dropped to her neck, lost in her, in the swells of her breasts pressed to his chest, the supple give of her hips. Her legs locked around his waist, and he slid even deeper.

With a sigh from her, he moved, finding a punishing rhythm, chasing the need to lose himself inside her. Their bodies moved together. He'd always prided himself on his skill as a lover. But he abandoned all finesse now, the slippery sounds of their fucking and the clench of her cunny on his cock driving him to the edge of madness.

She held him tightly, meeting him thrust for thrust, and he reveled in the scrape of her nails on his back, up and down. He hoped she'd draw blood. Hoped that later he could look in the mirror and see the marks she'd left, a reminder of how well he'd loved her. He hoped he fucked her so well that she fell in love with him, that she forgave him for being such a fool and selling her beloved home when he should have married her from the first and preserved it for her.

There was the exquisite, sharp sting of her teeth on his shoulder, and *fuck*. That was almost all he could bear. He moved faster, remembering her needs belatedly and reaching between them to find her pearl and rub it furiously, coaxing another spend from her. Her gasp in his ear told him she was close. He gave her more, and when she reached her next orgasm, she tightened on him, the steady pulses of her release milking his cock.

No more holding back.

With a guttural groan, he sank deep, burying his cock as he filled her with his seed, coming so hard that dark stars speckled his vision as he emptied himself inside her. He thought of his seed taking hold, of his babe one day growing inside her, her belly round with child. How badly he wanted that, wanted her. The rush was almost overwhelming, the pleasure excruciatingly good. So good that he collapsed atop her, panting, body damp with perspiration, blood pumping with the after effects of the strongest orgasm he'd ever had.

I love you.

The words were there. His shattered mind couldn't seem to form them on his tongue. She turned her head, her lips finding his, and held him tightly to her, their bodies still one.

CHAPTER 18

The chandeliers in the ballroom were ablaze. With the number of revelers in attendance at the ball being held by Viscount Torrington and his new viscountess, the heat was nearly enough to make Virtue dizzy. She would have thought, given the similarly abrupt nature of Lord and Lady Torrington's nuptials, that Virtue's would not have been as remarked upon. But in truth, the source of her discomfiture had also been the curious glances cast her way, the raised eyebrows, and the less-than-subtle whispers abounding after she had been announced as the Duchess of Ridgely that evening. The ball was her debut in polite society as a married woman.

A scandalous married woman, who had wed her husband the duke with enough haste that tongues were indeed wagging, despite the intense efforts Lady Deering made on their behalf to suppress even the slightest hint of gossip. It seemed that everywhere she looked, someone was watching her with ill-concealed disapproval. She, a veritable country booby who had been abandoned by her own father, had managed to snare the most handsome duke in London as her husband.

And although she most certainly had not set out with such an end in mind, it was where she had found herself. She was the Duchess of Ridgely, impossible as it seemed.

"Do you think we might leave after I share my dance with Ridgely?" Virtue asked her sister-in-law, who was a dutiful presence at her side whilst her husband spoke with their host beyond earshot.

She was already weary, and the effect of so many stares upon her had been most taxing. For someone who had never cared for balls, the spectacle was more than a trifle overwhelming, and more so because of the unwanted attention she was receiving.

"We have not yet gone to supper," Lady Deering said. "I expect that if we take our leave early, gossip shall swirl."

The night loomed before them, endless and interminable. She far preferred the quiet manner in which she had spent much of her marriage thus far—alone with Trevor. Usually, in his chamber. Or the music room. Or any chamber that suited them. Just the other day, he had caught her on the ladder in the library and pleasured her as she clung to the rungs and did her utmost to keep from toppling off.

Yes, she rather enjoyed the quiet moments she'd had with her husband. Enjoyed them far too much. Each day, she fell a bit more in love with him as he showed her new facets, teased and kissed her, bathed with her, read books with her, and squired her about Rotten Row at the hour she preferred. And good heavens, that night when they had acted out the scene in *The Tale of Love*. It would be emblazoned upon her mind forever.

No doubt about it, the Duke of Ridgely was unfailingly charming, wickedly sensual, and he could reduce her to a puddle of lust with a mere look.

Virtue fanned herself, overheated now from more than the candles overhead and the hundreds of revelers about. "If you think it prudent to remain, I suppose we must. However, I find that I need some air. It is dreadfully warm in here, do you not think?"

"It is rather stifling, I must agree." Lady Deering fluttered her own fan, the scene which had been painted on it looking almost as if it were coming to life, so swift were her movements and so intricate was the scene.

The action captured Virtue's interest suddenly, for she had accompanied her sister-in-law on a visit to Bellingham and Co. earlier that day when Lady Deering had admired the frippery. She hadn't, however, purchased it.

"The marvelous fan you were so favoring today," she said. "When did you return to Bellingham and Co. for it?"

There scarcely seemed to have been time or opportunity.

A curious flush stole over her sister-in-law's cheekbones, her pale skin and golden hair in stark contrast. "Perhaps a brief respite on the terrace will prove restorative!" she suddenly exclaimed instead of answering Virtue's question, her tone overly cheerful and bright.

Lady Deering's customary self-possession was so very infrequently out of place. Why, the last time Virtue had seen her sister-in-law looking similarly flustered, it had been the day she had spied her kissing the bodyguard, Mr. St. George. That had been the day Trevor had compromised her in the music room, and her life had become such a whirlwind since then, Virtue had never pursued the subject. Nor was she certain how she would do so, should she dare. It was hardly any of her concern whether or not her sister-in-law chose to have a dalliance with the man. She was a widow, after all.

Still, her reaction to Virtue's question was interesting indeed, she thought as Lady Deering led the way through the throng to the doors that opened to a narrow terrace. Unlike so many of the recent days, it wasn't raining this evening, which meant that the blessedly cool evening air welcomed them as they escaped from the din of the ballroom.

"There we are," Pamela said, fanning herself a bit more discreetly. "Some fresh evening air to fortify our spirits. Precisely the thing! I don't know why I didn't suggest it sooner."

She walked ahead of Virtue, her shoulders a tense, if elegant, line beneath her pink, Grecian evening gown, the fan flapping away as if she intended to take flight.

"Is something amiss?" she dared to ask her sister-in-law, trailing after. "You seemed suddenly nervous at my mentioning of the fan. I hope I didn't overset you. It's a truly lovely piece."

Pamela issued a laugh that was unnaturally high, bordering on shrill. Also most unlike her—her voice was ordinarily carefully modulated. "Of course you haven't overset me, dearest. Why should I be overset by something so insignificant as a fan?"

Why indeed?

"If there is anything you wish to tell me, I am always eager and ready to listen," she told her sister-in-law, increasing her pace to fall into step at her side. "You will find me an excellent confidante."

She had always longed for a sister, and now that she had one in Lady Deering, it was true that she would be more than happy to play that role. She had also come to care for Pamela, who had always been unfailingly kind to her despite her eccentricities. It was the nearest she would come to blurting out what she'd witnessed that day.

"Thank you, my dear." Pamela closed her fan and flashed Virtue a grateful smile. "I am so pleased to have you as my sister now. I must say that Ridgely has never seemed so happy as he has since you wed. I scarcely recognize him these days."

Virtue answered with a smile of her own, for her days as a married woman had been surprisingly and unexpectedly fulfilling thus far. There were untold depths to Trevor, and she was enjoying learning them all.

"And now, it would seem that I must thank you in kind. It contents me to know that you think I may have, in some small way, made him happier." For Trevor William Hunt, Duke of Ridgely, deserved happiness. Like Virtue, much of his life had been laden with disappointments. Troubled relations with his parents, the loss of his brothers, his days as a spy, the unexpected inheritance of a title he'd never been meant to bear.

It had startled her to realize just how much she and her husband had in common.

Pamela was about to respond when the sudden arrival of another guest on the terrace gave her pause. Her spine stiffened even more, chin going up, and her countenance may as well have been hewn of ice.

"Come, dearest," she told Virtue, *sotto voce*, "I do believe we've managed to take just enough air. Ridgely is likely wondering where we have disappeared to."

Curious, Virtue turned to find the source of her sister-in-law's sudden displeasure. A dark-haired woman in a stunning gown of white muslin and crimson velvet approached. She was, even in the flickering torchlight on the terrace, undeniably beautiful, her hair contained in a braided chignon, a matching crimson ribbon wrapped around, her bodice shockingly low, the better to put her ample breasts on display.

"Lady Deering," the woman called. "How delightful to find you and your companion enjoying the air."

Pamela was even more rigid at Virtue's side, but her face was a polite mask.

"Lady Carr," she acknowledged. "We were just about to return to the ball. If you will excuse us?"

"Pray, do not rush away from the terrace so quickly," Lady Carr said, her tone oddly smug. "Indeed, I confess I saw you leaving the crush and made haste to join you outside so that I might be introduced."

"Of course," Pamela said stiffly. "Her Grace, the Duchess of Ridgely, I present to you the Countess of Carr."

The countess's smile was insincere. "How lovely to make the acquaintance of the lady who has at last ensnared Ridgely."

Virtue frowned, studying the woman before her, who watched her with a strange intensity. Her eyes appeared opaque in the torch light, almost obsidian.

"Ensnaring sounds rather reminiscent of a hunt," she returned calmly, thinking she did not like Lady Carr. Not at all. "I shouldn't like to think of a marriage in such terms."

"Indeed, I suppose you might not." Another small smile, this one condescending. "His Grace is the sort of gentleman, however, who I should think required a great deal of *encouragement* toward that institution. He was, after all, a dedicated bachelor, by his own insistence to all who know him well."

An eerie sense of trepidation unfurled down Virtue's spine. There was a thinly veiled innuendo in the countess's words, the suggestion that *she* was someone who knew Trevor well.

"We truly must return to the ballroom," Pamela said coldly. "Pray excuse us, Lady Carr."

"But we have only just begun our little tête-à-tête," the countess protested, resembling nothing so much as a bird of prey descending upon her next meal. "Surely there is no need to make as much haste as was required for the duke and duchess's nuptials."

"Lady Carr, you are beyond the bounds of propriety," Pamela snapped. "This introduction was solely to spare you the humiliation of a cut, and yet you are intent upon trampling upon the tattered remnants of my patience for you."

Lady Carr pressed a gloved hand over her heart. "Good heavens, Lady Deering. You must forgive me my missteps. I merely wished to meet Ridgely's bride." She cast a dismissive glance in Virtue's direction. "She has youth to recommend her, if nothing else. I simply could not fathom why Ridgely would bind himself in such a dreadful mesalliance."

Virtue stepped forward, anger rising within her, making her stays go tight and her hands tremble. "Who do you think you are, madam, to speak as if I am not standing before you?"

"You don't know, do you?" The countess gave her a condescending smirk. "Oh, my dear. You will learn soon enough. Ridgely has never wanted for female companionship, and I don't doubt, having seen what a little mouse he has wed, that it won't be long until he returns to me." She paused, dipping into a mocking curtsy. "Good evening, my lady, Your Grace."

With a flash of white and crimson, the countess turned on her heel, leaving Virtue and Pamela alone once again on the terrace. The altercation had left her shaken and startled. It was more than apparent that the Countess of Carr was one of her husband's former lovers. And Lady Carr was not happy he had married Virtue. But her daring in calling Virtue a mouse and her suggestion that Trevor would return to her…

The twin affronts stung. Badly.

"Are you well?" Pamela asked softly at her side, touching her arm with a gloved hand, jolting her from her whirling thoughts.

"I am...yes," she managed. "I think so."

"I am so very sorry, Virtue. It was unconscionable of her to approach and ask for an introduction. I should have given her the cut, but I had hoped she possessed the manners and refinement to behave herself. Clearly, I was wrong."

"She is very beautiful," Virtue said, thinking again of the striking picture the countess had presented. She was a lovely woman, and she knew how to take full advantage of her every asset. Undoubtedly, she and Trevor had made a striking pair together, both unfailingly gorgeous.

"She is perfectly hideous where it matters most," Pamela countered quietly, "on the inside. I should have been a better protector to you. I apologize again for that unfortunate showing. She is only bitter because she threw her cap at Ridgely, and in the end, he would not have her."

"Lady Carr wanted to marry him?" she probed, needing to know more about this unpleasant mystery from her husband's past and yet feeling vaguely ill at the notion of the details she may face.

Details she could not unknow, after learning them.

"Very much so. She has been a widow for more than five years now, and rumor has it that her widow's portion has been stretched thin by her love of gambling. She was aiming to become a duchess." Pamela gave her arm a gentle squeeze. "You needn't concern yourself with such a dreadful woman. The past is where it belongs, and you are Ridgely's future."

But how could the past be where it belonged when it had just approached her on the terrace and insulted her with the suggestion her husband would return to her. Return to her how? To her bed? Trevor's reputation was well-known to Virtue. It ought not to have been a tremendous surprise to meet one of his former lovers.

And yet, the antagonism fairly dripping from Lady Carr's pores... Virtue had not anticipated such a public clash.

"Was she his mistress, then?" she found herself asking.

Pamela's face was pale in the torch light, her lips unsmiling. An altogether grim picture, when ordinarily she was so vibrant. "It is not for me to discuss."

That was her answer, then.

Yes.

The Venus-like Countess of Carr had once been Trevor's lover. And, it would seem, she intended to return to that position soon.

~

SOMETHING WAS AMISS WITH VIRTUE. Trevor took note the moment he saw her returning with Pamela at her side. He had been conversing with his host, Viscount Torrington, idly keeping an eye on her as he chatted. He'd seen her accompany Pamela onto the terrace, presumably to escape the devilish crush of the ballroom, and he couldn't blame them. He was sweating into his cravat beneath the blaze of these bloody chandeliers and the heat from at least two hundred guests all swarming within the confined space, rather like bees in a hive.

He watched her now as she moved through the revelers, his gut clenching. She looked pale, the set of her jaw telling him something had given her cause for distress.

Trevor turned back to Torrington. "If you will excuse me, Torrie, I do believe the next waltz belongs to my wife."

The viscount inclined his head. "By all means. I should seek out Lady Torrington as well. She's been twirling about on the dance floor without me for long enough."

With a few more polite words, he and his host parted ways, Trevor moving in the direction of his own wife. He hadn't missed the possessive edge in his host's words. The viscount's sudden wedding had been something of a scandal as well. He'd married a governess after having spirited her away in his carriage by mistake, thinking he'd been carrying off his latest mistress. The flurry of resulting gossip had set London on its ear. But it would seem the viscount had developed a *tendre* for his new viscountess despite the scandalous circumstances which had precipitated their union.

He knew the feeling all too well.

Hell, he'd been half in love with Virtue from the moment he'd first set eyes on her. She'd descended from the carriage he'd sent to fetch her, carrying an armful of books. She'd been wearing a carmine pelisse trimmed with ermine and a matching hussar cap, and he'd known in that instant that her personality was as bold as her dress. Oh yes, he'd known that she would be trouble as he'd watched her descent from the vantage point of his study window.

Trouble of the most delicious sort.

Trouble who reached him now as the faint strains of a waltz began. He bowed to his sister and his wife.

"I do believe this dance is mine," he told Virtue, wondering what had caused the pinched expression she now wore, and intending to find out with all haste.

He'd find the person responsible and verbally disembowel them.

"Yes, of course," Virtue said, her voice almost wooden, lacking its usual fire.

Pamela cast him a glance that was laden with worry, which only served to tighten the knot of apprehension in his gut. "Enjoy your waltz. I do believe I'll enjoy some ratafia and gossip with the dowagers."

His sister wandered off in the direction of a gaggle of tittering widows in turbans, and Trevor offered his arm to Virtue. "She would have everyone think she is a shriveled husk, pining away as she has for Deering. He wasn't worthy of her in life, and now that he's gone, she may as well continue with hers."

He was careful to keep his voice from carrying, more than aware of the curious stares upon them, the lords and ladies sidling nearer in the hopes of overhearing a new *on dit*.

"She loved her husband," Virtue said quietly, a hint of reproach in her dulcet voice. "However, perhaps she is struggling between loyalty and duty and what she wants."

"Hmm," he said, considering Virtue's words. To him, Pamela remained very much a mystery who buried her sorrows in endless trips to Bond Street and the like. "And what is it you think she wants?"

"I'm not certain she knows," Virtue said softly.

They took up their position on the dance floor, offering each other a customary curtsy and bow, and then she was in his embrace, their hands linked, and he wondered if they were merely discussing Pamela or if his wife was talking about herself, as well.

"Are you speaking of yourself as well as my sister?" he asked, concerned.

"Oh." She offered him a smile, but there was sadness in it. "Of course not. I already know what I want."

The waltz was underway, and they began the steps, moving as fluidly together in the ballroom as they did in the bedroom. "And what is that?"

They spun about, and he admired the way the glow of the candles overhead brought out the burnished-gold flecks in her vivid eyes.

"You, of course," she said, then paused, her smile fading. "For as long as you want me."

What the devil was this?

"I want you forever," he said firmly. "You're my wife."

She gave a soft sigh. "But you are accustomed to being a

rake, having your choice of ladies. I can hardly compare to the beautiful women you've known."

He nearly stumbled and tripped over his own feet, but recovered at the last moment, quite thankfully keeping both of them upright. "You are the most beautiful woman I've known. The most beautiful woman I shall ever know, inside and out."

Her physical loveliness aside, it was her fierce spirit and keen, intelligent mind that drew him to her most, along with her innate sensuality. How could she doubt her own magnificence? He wanted to kick himself in the arse for not praising her enough, for failing to show her just how incomparable she was.

"What of Lady Carr?" she asked, so quietly he almost failed to hear her above the din of the orchestra.

Adelina. *Christ*. He had known his former mistress was in attendance this evening; he'd seen her glaring daggers at him from across the ballroom and had promptly ignored her.

He tensed, wondering if the countess he had once parted ways with had somehow caused Virtue upset. "What of her?" he asked, twirling them effortlessly through the next set of steps.

"She demanded an introduction this evening," Virtue said, confirming his suspicion. "She seemed convinced you would be returning to her soon, now that she has seen what a little mouse you have wed."

A little mouse.

Trevor ground his molars as fury rolled over him. "How dare she pay you such insult? I'll see to it that she is removed from the invitations of every notable social engagement in Town."

It was only by sheer force of will that he carried on with the waltz, not wanting to cause Virtue further upset by making a scene. He hated that his past had hurt her, particularly when he hadn't been there to offer his protection as he should have done. The fault was clearly Trevor's for being foolish enough to dally with a viper. He had known Adelina was possessive and jealous, but he had never imagined she would dare to confront his duchess. Particularly not with the malicious inference that he would be returning to her bed. Virtue's and Pamela's strained countenances upon their return from the terrace made perfect, sickening sense now.

"You needn't have her name withdrawn from guest lists on my account," Virtue said stoically, her chin going up in that stubborn fashion that never failed to make him want to kiss her senseless.

"She has upset you and insulted you," he countered grimly, a protective surge making his grip on her gloved fingers and waist tighten. "She is fortunate that I do not denounce her to the ballroom right now."

"You are angry," she said, her brow furrowed. "Please do not be so. I shouldn't have mentioned such unpleasantness to you."

"The hell you shouldn't have," he growled, keeping his voice low so that it wouldn't carry to the dancers around them. "No one hurts the woman I love without consequence. I'd happily fight to the death to protect you from harm."

Her lips fell open, and she missed a step. Trevor had to spin them both to avoid faltering. And that was when he realized what he'd said.

The woman I love.

Saint's teeth, he hadn't meant to tell her at a time like this, when they were surrounded by the *ton*, and his former mistress had just insinuated—entirely incorrectly—that he would return to her bed.

"You…" Virtue's lips parted and her words trailed away as she seemed to struggle to comprehend what he'd just revealed.

She was in fine company. He was still trying to understand it himself, these vast emotions inside himself, bigger than anything he'd ever known. Eclipsing him. The way he loved her frightened him.

"I love you," he said, repeating the words in a different way. The *right* way. Merely the wrong place and time.

He would make that up to her later. She deserved to know. By God, he wouldn't have her thinking he didn't worship every bit of her, from her glorious mahogany hair all the way down to her dainty, slippered feet. Wouldn't have her wrongly concerned that he would ever choose another over her. She was the only woman for him, the other half of his very soul. Strike that. She *was* his soul. The very best part of him.

"You love me," she breathed, gazing up at him with wonder, the chandeliers catching in her glistening eyes and sparkling from the diamonds at her throat.

"I love you," he said it again, and how good it felt, that weight off his chest.

He felt as if he had run a great distance, and the exertion had left him clear-headed and so very alive. Suddenly, he wanted to declare his love for her to the entire ballroom. Louder than the waltz. To let everyone know just how much the woman in his arms meant to him.

He tamped down the urge with great effort. No scandal like declaring his love for Virtue in the midst of the Torrington ball, bellowing over the pianoforte and violin. It was his intent to make amends to her, to ease her entrée into society as his duchess. Not to heighten the whispers already swirling around them. Half the *ton* would think him a Bedlamite, if they didn't already.

"Trevor, do you mean it?" she asked, interrupting his mad thoughts.

And it occurred to him that the shimmer in her

extraordinary eyes was not from the chandeliers after all. Rather, it was the sheen of unshed tears.

His own throat went thick, and he had to swallow hard against a rush of new emotion. Good Christ, he could not weep in the midst of a ball. He did yet possess some pride. He was reasonably sure of it.

"Of course I mean it," he said, guiding them through another turn and deftly keeping them from colliding with another couple. "Never doubt it. I love you, V. I think I always have, from the moment I saw you arrive at Hunt House."

"You saw me arrive?" There was wonder in her voice, awe in her expression.

He nodded, for he had been too nettled by the responsibility of a ward to greet her himself. Instead, he had remained in his study, watching.

Falling.

"You were wearing a red pelisse trimmed with fur and a matching jaunty hussar cap, and you had two books tucked under your arm," he said.

"Oh," she said, and then a single tear, which had caught on the spikes of her lashes fell, gliding down her cheek. "You did see me. I'd quite forgotten what I was wearing, but that pelisse is one of my favorites."

"I have always seen you," he told her, the words rife with meaning. "Always."

"Trevor," she said, her voice hushed, a wealth of emotion in her voice. "I love you, too."

His breath caught. "You do?"

A nod. A shy smile. Another tear coasting down her silken cheek. Emotion, so much of it, burning in the depths of her gaze.

"I do," she confirmed. "Very much."

The explosion of joy inside him was deeper and stronger

than even the physical connection they shared when they made love. This transcended everything. His knees threatened to give out beneath the force of it. Virtue loved him.

What had he done to deserve her love? He couldn't say. But he damned well wasn't going to question the gift. He was unworthy and greedy, and he was going to keep those words tucked inside his heart forever. She couldn't have them back.

He swirled them about, trying to keep them from crashing into their fellow couples yet again. But dancing was the least of his concerns just now. All he cared about was the woman in his arms. The woman who loved him. He was grinning like a fool, and he didn't care who saw. Let the tongues wag and say what they would.

The Duke of Ridgely was hopelessly besotted with his duchess, and he wanted everyone in London to know.

One person in particular.

He would deal with her later.

༄

Trevor found the Countess of Carr when the Torrington ball was nearly drawing to a close. She was wearing a gown that had been designed to put her ample assets on display, and when she saw him, a smug feline smile curved her lips. The effect was lost upon him; he felt nothing save anger when he looked upon her.

"Lady Carr," he greeted her, unsmiling.

"Your Grace," she returned, dipping into a curtsy as she cast him a sultry look from beneath lowered lashes. "You've come to me at last."

Had it been her intention to lure him to her by insulting Virtue? If so, she would quickly discover her tactic had been disastrously wrongheaded.

"I've come to you to tell you to keep your distance from

Her Grace, the Duchess of Ridgely," he said, taking care to keep his voice *sotto voce*.

They were on the periphery of the festivities, but he was ever aware of the guests surrounding them. He'd never fretted over scandal so much in his life. But then, he'd never had to care. Nor had he ever taken such great pleasure in his title. When he could call Virtue his duchess, however, and upbraid someone who had dared to pay her insult, he most assuredly reveled in it.

Lady Carr raised a dark brow. "Oh? And why should I do that? Pray do not tell me you have come rushing to me merely to play the role of gallant knight defending her honor. I did nothing wrong."

"You should not have approached her," he bit out, "nor asked Lady Deering to perform an introduction. It was beyond the pale, and you know it."

It simply wasn't done to beg an introduction with a former lover's new spouse. Adelina knew that. Even had she not been cutting and cruel to Virtue, calling her a little mouse, and insinuating Trevor would betray her, the forced introduction alone was affront enough to warrant his outrage.

"Why was it beyond the pale?" the countess asked, dragging her fan over her decolletage. "Because you've been in my bed? Or because you want to return there?"

Damn her. She was pushing him dangerously close to the end of his patience, and he was doing his utmost to maintain his self-control. For his wife's sake, not for Adelina's.

"We parted ways civilly," he said coldly. "You were rewarded handsomely, as I recall. I had no intention of returning to your bed then, and I most certainly have no intention of returning to it now. Nor ever."

"Don't deny it. I can see the fire in your eyes, see how very much you want me."

She swayed nearer to him, and Trevor took a step in retreat.

"Any fire you see in my eyes is born of fury, madam. You were discourteous to my wife, and I want it understood that you are never to speak either to her, or about her, again."

Lady Carr gave an elegant shrug. "Good heavens, Ridgely. I was hardly discourteous. Is that what she told you? If so, she was lying. Likely to gain your sympathy. I merely pointed out that she is young and plain. I dare say she does not have an inkling of what to do with a man like you."

A man like him? He was not the man he'd been when the Countess of Carr had known him, that much was certain. He would never resemble that aimless devil-may-care again, and he was deuced glad for it.

And his entire being vibrated with anger at her daring to call Virtue a liar.

Trevor's jaw clenched. "If you were a man, I would tell you to name your second and demand you meet me for pistols at dawn."

She flapped her fan in annoyance. "You needn't be so defensive. I am only saying what everyone else whispers behind your back as they laugh. All London is talking about how she entrapped you. It's common knowledge. A hideous little country booby catching the interest of the Duke of Ridgely? Why, she must have thrown herself at you, forcing herself to be compromised. Why else would there be a need for such a hasty wedding?"

By God, he had never been more livid in his life than he was now.

His hands had balled into impotent fists at his sides. "Listen to me carefully, Lady Carr. I was endeavoring to be politic about this matter, but you've driven me beyond reason. So I will tell you this now, and I will tell you quite plainly, so that there be no misunderstandings between us. If you dare to say one unkind word about my wife again, or if you dare to approach her in any fashion, I will see to it that you are given the cut by every goddamn person I know. Every lord and lady, every shop, every milliner or modiste. I won't stop until even the horse dung in the street reviles you and you've no choice but to flee London in abject misery."

At the conclusion of his speech, he offered a courtly bow and a smile that even felt wolfish on his lips. "I strongly caution you not to try my patience. Good evening and goodbye, Lady Carr."

With that, he left her where he had discovered her, determined that it would be the very last time she would cause any harm to Virtue or his marriage. The past was now where it belonged.

Forever.

CHAPTER 19

"The horse dung in the street?" Virtue laughed delightedly. "Did you truly say all that to Lady Carr?"

"Yes, I did." Trevor's voice was a deep, beloved rumble at her back.

They were seated together in the tub, where they had been soaking away the strains of the night in the pleasant warmth of heated water. She was nestled between his long legs, surrounded by his strength, her head resting comfortably against his shoulder. He still sounded outraged on her behalf, as if he were about to leap from the tub to hunt down the countess and deliver another biting set down.

"In the midst of a ballroom, no less," she added as her mirth faded.

The silliness of his threat aside, the way he had defended her left Virtue humbled and awed. Thankful, too. So much had happened over the course of the Torrington ball, and she was still awash in confusing emotion.

"I could have said and done far worse," Trevor said wryly, dipping his fingers into the water and then removing them to leave a trail of droplets on her forearm where it rested on the lip of the tub. "She is bloody fortunate I didn't throw her into a pile of it after the way she treated you."

Another chuckle escaped her at his protectiveness toward her. She had been shaken by Lady Carr's cruel words, yes. But it had been the countess's suggestion that Trevor would return to her that had been the most distressing. Comparing herself to the beautiful widow had left Virtue feeling vulnerable and uncertain. But her husband's unexpected declaration during their waltz had cast any lingering doubts to the ether. Precisely where they belonged.

"It wasn't as terrible as that," she reassured him. "Besides, I hardly think Lord and Lady Torrington would have been impressed had you carted one of their guests off to the mews for an impromptu bath in dung."

He kissed her crown. "Don't think I won't toss her into the nearest heap of manure, head first, if she ever dares to insult you again."

Oh, her heart. Give her an arrogant duke who gifted her books, spouted incorrect Shakespeare, and threatened to throw awful women into horse manure on her behalf, and she could not help but to fall in love. Trevor was so much more than she had first realized on the day she had come to Hunt House, overwhelmed by its size and the strangers to whom she would be commending herself.

Little had she known he had been watching from his study window. That he had committed that day to his memory—his initial sighting of her—as if it were a precious treasure in need of preservation.

"You are quiet," he observed, nuzzling her ear. "What are you thinking?"

"I am thinking that I was wrong about you when I arrived," she said, watching as his long fingers dripped more water over her forearm. "I spent the entirety of my journey to London thinking you some ancient ogre intent upon robbing me of my future. But then I met you."

"And what did you think then?"

She smiled, recalling their first meeting in his study, how elegantly he had been dressed, his cravat impeccably tied, his buff trousers fitted to his muscular thighs, his boots gleaming. But it had been his face which had been most intimidating and arresting, such masculine beauty the likes of which she'd never seen.

"I thought you were a young, handsome ogre intent upon robbing me of my future," she said.

"Not fair," he said lightly against her ear, his lips grazing it as he spoke. "My sole intent was to give you a future."

"By marrying me off," she said archly.

"Because I couldn't resist you." As if to prove his point, he cupped her breast, catching her nipple between his thumb and forefinger and tugging gently, creating an answering ache in her sex. "I knew if I didn't take care, I'd want to keep you for myself."

"And why shouldn't you keep me for yourself?" Feeling bold, she caught his hand in hers and guided it beneath the water, between her legs.

He groaned, his fingers gliding expertly through her folds, finding her pearl and stroking. "I was afraid to be vulnerable. To give someone else so much power over me, the power to crush me with but a word. I've spent my life avoiding attachments. Imagine my horror at forming the greatest one of all."

"Love," she said, sighing as he swirled over her swollen bud, the hot water and his touch making her restless. But this was an important conversation. She wanted to know more about this enigmatic man who was her husband. Wanted to know everything. "You were afraid you would fall in love, do you mean? With me?"

"God, yes." He kissed her throat. "You terrified me from the moment you swept into my study. I knew I couldn't have you, and yet I had never wanted anyone more."

Knowing he had felt the same attraction as she had, an invisible pull between them, from that very first meeting, pleased her.

"But now you have me." She turned her face toward his, caught in his dark-brown eyes, smoldering with love and desire. For her. All for her. "And I have you."

"We have each other." He kissed her, lips moving tenderly over hers, chastely at first and then deepening as he gave her his tongue.

His caresses gathered intent and pressure, moving faster over her hungry flesh, just as he knew she liked. Soon, she was gasping into his mouth, her tongue tangling with his.

"I want to fuck you," he murmured against her lips. "But not in this bloody tub."

His wicked words sent an answering rush to her core. "Yes."

Together, they rose from the tub, water running down their bodies. Trevor stepped out first and then extended a hand to her, helping her over the high lip of the tub. They didn't bother to dry off in their eagerness, making their way to Trevor's bed instead.

Their damp bodies clung like their mouths as they lay on the bedclothes. They were on their sides, and the position brought to mind something Virtue had been longing for. She urged Trevor to his back, and then she strung a path of kisses along his jaw, to his ear.

"Thank you for championing me tonight," she murmured. "For loving me."

Her heart was full, so full. She wanted to show him how much he meant to her. To worship his body in the way he did hers. Since they had married, she had slowly come to realize that whilst Greycote Abbey would forever hold a place in her heart, her new home was with Trevor. In his bed, in his arms. He was her home now.

His hands coasted along her sides, molding her curves. "Thank you for loving me, ogre that I am."

She smiled against his skin, working her way down his neck. "Perhaps not so much an ogre after all."

"I'm relieved you've altered your opinion of me." His voice was husky, laced with amusement.

Virtue kissed the protrusion of his clavicle and then nipped his shoulder as she knew drove him to distraction. "Quite altered. Let me show you just how much."

He stiffened, his cock growing harder against her. "V, you needn't…"

His protest faded as she peppered his chest with kisses, following the dark trail of hair that led lower. Oh yes, she did need. She needed to taste him. To take him in her mouth. She longed for it, so badly that it was a steady throb pulsing in her pearl. So much that she was wet from the thought, and not from her bath.

"I *want* to," she said, shifting her body so that she was settled between his legs, his cock standing to attention, ruddy and thick, mere inches from her.

She had read a most enlightening passage in *The Tale of Love*, and she allowed that edification to guide her now as she grasped the base of his manhood and brought the glistening head to her lips. She flicked her tongue over him, the drop of mettle seeping from his slit coating her tongue with the taste of him. Trevor, man, slightly salty.

Perfect.

"My God, V," he rasped. "You'll undo me."

She hoped she would.

"Lady X wrote that she tried to take as much of her groom's cock into her throat as possible," she said, glancing up at him over the glorious planes of his lean body. "Would you like that?"

He groaned, reached down to caress her hair, her cheek. "I would."

Taking her time, Virtue applied her tongue to him some more, holding him firmly and pumping slightly with her hand. Teasing and tormenting him just as he so often did to her. Listening for cues; the sharp inhalation of his breath, the twitch of his hips, the hardening and lengthening of his beautiful cock.

When she had him restless beneath her, she took him into her mouth, just the head at first, and then more. He was smooth and hot and firm, and long. She inhaled and brought him to the back of her throat.

"Ah, God."

His moan from the head of the bed was a spur. She worked at her task, taking him deep and then withdrawing, then deep again. She was one with his body, hand on his hip, the other on his cock, pleasuring him until his hips were moving in quick, mindless thrusts beneath her and her own sex was wet and aching.

His fingers caught in her hair, slowing her motions. "Wait. Stop. I want to lick you."

His cock slipped from her lips, and the world slowly returned in the form of flickering shadows in the soft glow of candlelight, bouncing off the ormolu accents in the room. His big body was flushed and hard, his need evident in the harsh angles of his face. She had done this to him, she thought proudly, reduced him to this. But she wanted him to lose control fully. Wanted him as wild as she was when he brought her to spend.

"I want you to come in my mouth," she told him, surprising even herself with her raw candor.

But it was true. The mere thought of this powerful man

losing himself in her mouth filled her with almost unbearable desire.

"Yes," he said, extending his hand to her. "I want that, too. There's a way for us both to receive pleasure. To spend together. Come, let me show you."

She took his hand and allowed him to guide her into a new position. A strange position at first, but when he turned her around so that she faced his feet and guided her hips toward his face, she understood the freedom it would allow them both.

"Closer, darling," he urged, his voice low and laden with the promise of something wicked.

His hands on her hips pulled her backward, closer to his waiting mouth.

"Now bend forward and spread your legs a bit wider."

She did, her hands planted on the bedclothes, his cock straining toward her, glistening with a mixture of her own saliva and him. Cool air swept over her hot flesh as she exposed herself to Trevor, and then he brought her to his lips, and he gave her a kiss, open mouthed and lusty, directly on her cunny.

A sigh fled her lips as he licked into her, and she remained there for a moment, loving the newness of the angle, the vulnerability inherent in it. His tongue sank deep, gliding in and out of her wetness, and he moaned, his grip on her sliding to the cheeks of her bottom, his fingers digging into her flesh with just the right amount of delicious pressure.

His cock hardened as she watched, the act of pleasuring her having an effect upon him that finally urged her into motion. She gripped his cock and took him in her mouth, one deep plunge that brought the head of him into her throat. He fucked her harder with his tongue and rubbed his face against her sensitive folds, his whiskers abrading her in a way that sent acute sparks of bliss shivering through her.

Concentrating on her task grew more difficult when he sucked on her pearl and his fingers sank inside her. First one, then another. Slow, decadent thrusts that matched the draw of his lips on her bud. Little pinpricks of light edged her vision as she moaned around his cock, taking him farther down her throat.

"Yes, my love," he growled his approval into her aching quim. "Take more of me. Faster, harder. Whatever you like. Just take me."

Take him.

Oh, she liked that. Liked the notion of making him hers in every way. Claiming him. Loving him. *Yes.*

She did as he asked, devoting herself to making him come undone, her breathing ragged, her moans in time to the thrust of his fingers and the sinful lash of his tongue. The pleasure built until it was excruciating, until it overtook her entire being, and she quaked and cried out, riding his face and fingers as the frenzy of her release washed over her. But he remained with her, holding her tight, keeping her spread over him, his lips and tongue and teeth working another series of spasms from her as his fingers fucked her so deep she was nearly delirious with it. Drunk on him and the pleasure he gave her.

"Ah, God. V, I need to be inside you when I come."

His low words reached her dimly, through the mists of lust which had fogged her mind. His cock had nearly slipped free of her lips as she had surrendered to the orgasms rocking through her, but she reapplied herself now, taking him down her throat and sucking hard one last time before releasing him.

"Fuck," he groaned, and then his capable hands were on her, helping to rearrange her so that she was astride him. "Ride me, love."

He gripped his straining cock and guided himself effortlessly inside her. She was incredibly wet after all Trevor's delicious ministrations, the glide of him slick and easy. He filled her to the hilt, the new angle bringing him deep. She was already sensitive, and she knew it wouldn't take long for her to splinter apart again as she began moving, finding a rhythm that had them both groaning and breathless. He caught one of her nipples in his wicked mouth and sucked, and she rode him relentlessly faster and harder, seeking the next release.

When it claimed her, she tightened on his cock so hard that she nearly forced him from her cunny. He gripped her hips, bringing her back down on him, pumping into her again and again until his body stiffened. Another thrust, and he found his own pinnacle, the warmth of his seed filling her. And it was good, so good. She collapsed atop him, heart galloping in her breast, her breathing as ragged as if she had run up and down the grand staircase of Hunt House at least half a dozen times.

Utterly spent, she laid her head on his chest, his hammering heart keeping rhythm to her own against her ear. He pulled the counterpane around them, cocooning them in warmth, and wrapped his arms around her, kissing the top of her head.

"I love you," he murmured. "Never doubt that."

And she knew then that she never could.

"I love you, too," she returned, feeling suddenly tired after the upheaval of the ball, the late hour, and all their lovemaking.

Exhausted but sated in the best possible way. She fell asleep in her husband's embrace to the certain knowledge that whatever confronted them in the unknown future, they would face it together. No one and nothing could tear them apart.

CHAPTER 20

Trevor led Logan Sutton and Archer Tierney to a table at The Velvet Slipper. The club was still and quiet around them, for it was closed this morning, no other patrons about. All the better for privacy and a frank discussion. After the evening he'd had with his wife, Trevor had arrived late to the requested meeting destination, finding Sutton and Tierney finishing an interview with Theodosia Woodward, the club's proprietress.

Since he had married Virtue, he had not stepped foot inside these walls save to speak with Theodosia to inquire about any potential problems at the club which could have provoked the attacks on him. She had known of none, leaving the mystery of who had wanted him dead and why yet unsolved.

And now that he was a happily married man, the club no longer held the allure it once had to the reckless youth he'd been. He was selling it to Theodosia, the contract being drawn up by his man of business, along with the purchase of Greycote Abbey from its new owner at a much higher price, a separate matter he hoped to surprise his wife with soon.

Much had changed for him over the last few months, and before that as well. He'd left his spying days entirely behind him, become a duke, gained a ward, and now had a wife he loved more than life itself. Life, he'd discovered, could be an unexpected whirlwind of the very best sort.

"Would you care for a drink?" he asked his guests. "There is likely to be some excellent wine about somewhere."

He wouldn't ask Theodosia to fetch it for them; she had arrived at his behest and was likely still as exhausted as he was after spending the night watching over wayward patrons. Moreover, she had never been a servant at The Velvet Slipper, always a trusted partner. He couldn't have run the club without her. Over the years, the Guild had used the Slipper for any number of purposes. It had suited all their needs well enough. With the Guild disbanded and Trevor wed, its need was no longer.

"No wine," Tierney said as they sat at an empty table. "I prefer gin, but I never drink in the morning."

"Nor myself, thank you," Sutton offered. "We've called you here with news."

His spine went stiff, apprehension curdling the pleasant glow which had been suffusing him ever since Virtue had told him she loved him. "Oh?"

"We were waiting until we had sufficient evidence to prove our theory," Tierney added. "Our interview with Mrs. Woodward this morning confirmed everything we've learned and begun to suspect about the person who hired John Davenham."

"The actor," Trevor said, recalling the name. "You're certain now that he and the dead man are the same?"

Sutton nodded. "His brother has finally claimed him. Apparently, he was warned against speaking and paid handsomely for his silence."

Tierney smiled grimly. "A visit from a few of my men altered his opinion on the matter."

"You had the brother beaten?" he asked, knowing from the time he had spent in the Guild that the man could be capable of anything, particularly when he was determined to right a wrong.

"Eh, beaten is a strong word," Tierney said, strumming his fingers idly on the polished surface of the table. "I prefer to think of it as *persuasion*."

The man's heart was dark as Hades.

"And after this *persuasion* of yours, the brother admitted the dead man was Mr. Davenham?" he guessed, frowning as his sluggish mind whirled to understand.

The life of a duke had made him soft; Christ, and to think he had once been as cunning and hard as Tierney.

"He did," Sutton answered. "Just yesterday. We searched Davenham's rooms and discovered a calling card for the Countess of Carr. His brother admitted that Davenham had been sharing the lady's bed. He told us that Lady Carr had paid his brother a handsome sum to attack the Duke of Ridgely. When that initial attack failed at killing you, she forced him to make a second attempt."

Saint's teeth. Trevor felt as if all the air had been knocked from his lungs.

"John Davenham was never seen again," Tierney added. "The sketch Bow Street created of your dead housebreaker matches. The brother confirmed it, and also admitted he had been paid a visit by Lady Carr herself following John Davenham's death, and that she had both threatened him with repercussions and paid him for his silence."

"We needed to be certain John Davenham's brother's word is reliable, however," Sutton said. "That is why we aimed to meet Mrs. Woodward here. She confirmed that Lady Carr and a man matching John Davenham's description have been guests at the establishment, though not recently, and they were in each other's presence. Although Lady Carr was masked, Mrs. Woodward recognized the countess from her days as your mistress."

"God." Trevor bit out the lone word, bile scrabbling up his throat. "Are you telling me that the Countess of Carr paid John Davenham to murder me?"

"We are," Tierney confirmed. "All the evidence leads to only one conclusion."

Suddenly, her angry tirade when he had broken off their arrangement returned, words he had mistaken for fury rather than true threats. *If I cannot have you, then no one can.*

He stood, reeling, all the pieces falling together in his head and making sense. In his time with the Guild, not one of the villains he had faced, fought, or captured had ever been a woman. It was so obvious now that he could scarcely credit the possibility had never occurred to him.

His ugly confrontation with Adelina the evening before rose, and a fresh wave of sickness hit him with the force of a fist. His legs were moving, striding, steps ahead of his mind.

"Where the devil are you going, Ridgely?" Sutton demanded.

"To Hunt House," he said, lips numb. "Lady Carr confronted my wife last night, and I defended her. I'm afraid I may have unintentionally made Virtue the target of her vitriol. My God, if she is that unhinged…"

He allowed his words to trail off, refusing to complete the thought. To comprehend it. There was no telling what the Countess of Carr was capable of. Already, she had paid a man to murder him, twice over.

Sutton and Tierney were on their feet, as grim as he'd ever seen them.

"We need to get to Hunt House at once," Tierney agreed.

VIRTUE WAS READING in the drawing room, enjoying the pleasant languor of the day and the memories of making love with Trevor the night before when the butler appeared at the threshold, looking uncertain.

"Forgive the interruption, Your Grace," Ames said. "There is a lady caller who refuses to be turned away. What would you have me do?"

A caller who refused to be turned away? Her brow furrowed.

"Has she left a card?" she asked, snapping her book closed and belatedly straightening herself on the settee she had been draped across, engrossed in yet another letter in *The Tale of Love*.

The butler entered with a bow and proffered the silver salver in his gloved hands. "She did, Your Grace."

Virtue retrieved the calling card, recognizing the flowery script of the visitor in question immediately.

Countess of Carr.

Something inside her froze, her instinctive reaction to deny her ladyship. It would not be the first time in her tenure as duchess where she had pleaded *not at home*. However, doing so, refusing a call from the woman after the valiant defense Trevor had given on Virtue's behalf at the Torrington Ball, seemed akin to admitting fear.

And she had nothing to fear from Lady Carr. Trevor loved Virtue. She loved him. They were married. The countess was a bitter remnant of his former life, and Virtue had not been a part of that.

Clutching the card, she raised her chin, forcing a smile to her lips. "You may see her in, Ames."

"Of course, Your Grace." With another bow, the butler took his leave.

She had a few moments to rise and prepare herself for the unwanted arrival of her caller, taking care to hide the book beneath a pillow, lest Lady Carr spy the title and spread idle gossip.

Lady Carr appeared, looking elegant and lovely as she had the evening before, if a trifle pale. She was still wearing her pelisse, which was a rare shade of not quite blue, yet not truly green, that matched her eyes. A reticule hung from her gloved wrist, catching Virtue's attention for a moment as the other woman swirled into the drawing room.

"Your Grace," the countess greeted, dipping into a mocking curtsy. "You have my gratitude for seeing me this morning."

It was a most unusual hour for calling, but Virtue did not remark upon it.

She remained unsmiling. "My lady, I decided to give you the dignity of an audience, however I cannot think we have anything to say to each other after last evening."

"Indeed?" A small, odd smile pulled up the corners of Lady Carr's lips. "I can think of a great many things."

With that pronouncement, she slowly and methodically pulled at the drawstring of her reticule, reaching inside. When her gloved hand extracted a small pistol, Virtue could not suppress her gasp. Her first reaction was to flee, but Lady Carr was prepared.

She raised her pistol, training the barrel upon Virtue with eerie calm. "Do not move, whore."

The drawing room door was yet open, but Hunt House was frightfully vast. Virtue's heart pounded as she wondered if anyone would hear her scream. Would Lady Carr shoot? Where were the bodyguards who had been stationed about? But then, she supposed none of them would have anticipated a countess, the widow of a peer of the realm, paying a call to also be carrying a weapon.

"What do you want from me?" she asked, taking care to remain still as she sought to make a plan for her escape.

Surely someone would come looking for her, perhaps even a maid passing in the hall, and alert others? Oh, if only Trevor had not left for an early-morning appointment with his old friends Mr. Tierney and Mr. Sutton. He would know what to do in a time of crisis such as this, she felt certain.

"I want you to pay for marrying him," Lady Carr snarled. "What did you do to force his hand? Tell me now, or I'll shoot."

The countess's hand trembled, the only outward show of emotion, save rage.

Virtue swallowed hard. "I did nothing to force his hand, nor to take him away from you. Ridgely parted with you before I arrived in London."

"You have bewitched him," the countess accused, seeming not to have heard Virtue's denial. "That is the only explanation. He would never leave me for you. Look at you, a plain, ugly crow when he could have a swan instead. Yes, you are evil, and you deserve to be punished."

"Punished how?" Virtue cast a longing glance toward the door, knowing that extending the conversation between herself and the mad countess was her only chance to survive.

"Killed." Lady Carr sneered. "I'll kill you first, and then I'll kill him, too. Where is he? He's mine and no one else can have him. I warned him when he left me that if I couldn't have him, no one could. He would have been dead before he married you if that fool hadn't broken his own neck."

Good God, the woman was a Bedlamite. She had been behind the attempts on Trevor's life.

"H-he is not at home," Virtue managed, grateful that Trevor's life could be spared, even if hers could not.

"Don't lie," Lady Carr snapped, the pistol wavering in her

grip. "I know he is here. Where else should he go at this hour of the morning?"

The timing of Lady Carr's call made sense now as well. She had planned this. Had planned to kill them both.

"He isn't here," she repeated, trying to keep her voice calm, soothing. "Please, Lady Carr. Calm yourself. I understand that you are overset—"

"Overset," the other woman screeched, interrupting her attempt. "I am furious, you stupid slut. Enough talking. Take me to him. If you say a word to any of the servants, I'll shoot you. Do you understand?"

Fear held her immobile, before she nodded. "Yes, I understand."

Before Lady Carr could move, there was a commotion at the threshold. The report of a pistol rang through the drawing room. Everything seemed to unfold at once. Virtue screamed, Lady Carr cried out, eyes going wide as the hand holding her pistol went limp, and the weapon clattered to the floor. Blood ran down her white kid glove, soaking it.

"You've shot me," the countess said, her voice quiet, laced with shock, and then she swooned, crumpling to the floor.

"V!" Trevor was upon her in an instant, taking her into the haven of his powerful arms, cradling her against his chest. "Thank God. You aren't hurt, are you?"

"N-no," she managed, clutching the lapels of his coat tightly, burrowing into his reassuring warmth and breathing in his familiar scent. "Is this real? Are you here?"

"Yes, my love." He kissed her crown, her temple. "I'm here. I'm here, and I'm sorry."

Her mind flew to Lady Carr and a renewed surge of terror clawed at her throat. "B-but Lady Carr. She wants to kill us both, Trevor."

"Hush," he said. "I know. Sutton and Tierney are with me.

They'll see to her. After this, I've no doubt she'll be sent to an asylum."

"We'll see that the Runners are called for," Mr. Tierney said from somewhere across the room, echoing Trevor's sentiment. Everything had unfolded so quickly that she hadn't realized Trevor wasn't alone. "The countess will never hurt anyone again."

Thank heavens.

There was a further flurry of activity as guards and Pamela came rushing into the drawing room, but Virtue couldn't bear to look.

She was snuggled against her husband's chest, tears coming now, scalding hot. "She's mad. The th-things she said…"

"It's over now," Trevor reassured her. "I have you, love, and you're safe."

She slid her arms around his waist, holding him with all her strength. "And you're safe too."

At last.

"I love you," he whispered against her hair. "Forgive me for putting you in danger."

She shook her head. "You couldn't have known."

"I should have. This never should have happened," he argued, still holding her as if he expected her to disappear from his arms.

Virtue tipped her head back, meeting his beloved dark gaze. "I love you, Trevor. Nothing else matters."

He closed his eyes and took a shuddering breath. "My God, I don't deserve you."

"Yes, my darling, you do."

She rose on her toes and pressed her mouth to his, the salt from their mingled tears lacing the kiss.

EPILOGUE

"*I* cannot countenance that the new owner of Greycote Abbey has invited us for an extended visit," Virtue was saying excitedly as their carriage at long last pulled onto the approach that would lead them to her old home.

Hers again, now.

Hers, just like his mare.

Just like his heart.

But unlike the latter two gifts Trevor had bestowed upon his wife, Greycote Abbey remained a carefully guarded secret. In the wake of the horrible day he had almost lost her forever, Trevor had been newly determined to give his wife everything she deserved. To make her happy. To restore to her the home she still spoke of with wistful fondness, even if she'd forgiven him for the original sale.

When he had told her that the current owner had invited them to stay for as long as they wished, she had been elated at the prospect. He had been waiting, as eager as a lad, to tell her the full truth. That the new owners were people with whom she was decidedly familiar.

That Greycote Abbey had been restored to her.

"I knew you would be pleased," he said, smiling fondly at her as she dipped her head and nearly pressed her nose to the carriage window in her eagerness to catch a glimpse of the old stone estate. "I hadn't realized just *how* pleased you would be, however."

Smiling, she cast a glance in his direction. "I am so grateful you corresponded with them. I simply cannot wait to show you every corner of the abbey. I hope little has changed. It hasn't been that long, after all."

"Nothing has changed," he reassured her, because he had demanded it be so, in return for the veritable king's ransom he had paid to bring Greycote Abbey back to Virtue.

He had also arranged for the return of her belongings, previously stored in Hunt Hall. The servants at Greycote Abbey had been happy to restore Virtue's possessions.

"I hope you are right," she said, nibbling on the fullness of her lush lower lip and almost eliciting a groan from him.

They'd been trapped inside the confines of this carriage, swaying over pitted roads and making their beds at travel inns, for far too long. He was looking forward to making love to his wife here, in a proper bed, along with revealing his surprise to her.

"I am right," he said gently. "I know it."

Out the window, Greycote Abbey's centuries' old walls were growing larger as they neared it.

"But how can you know?" she wondered. "Have you asked them?"

Time to tell her now, he reasoned. He'd kept the secret long enough—coincidentally, the *only* secret he kept from his beloved wife.

"I know because I arranged for it to be so," he revealed. "And for your belongings to be removed from storage at Ridgely Hall and returned here."

She cocked her head, her honey-brown gaze searching. "Why should you do that?"

He smiled. "Because I arranged for my man of business to secure Greycote Abbey for you. The new owner was willing to resell the estate to us for the correct price. It is ours now. Yours, truly. Just as it always should have been."

Virtue pressed a hand to her lips, smothering a shocked gasp as tears shimmered in her eyes. "You bought Greycote Abbey?"

Trevor nodded. "We bought it, love."

"Oh, my darling man," she said, her hand lowering to her lap, disbelief and awe warring on her lovely countenance. "What of Mrs. Williams, Mr. Smith, Miss Jones, and all the rest? Have they stayed on?"

"They have," he confirmed, drinking in the sight of her, so thrilled, the love for the domestics who had been the only family she'd once known so beautiful and readily apparent.

She was laughing, tears of joy streaming down her cheeks, as she threw herself into his lap. He caught her with a grunt, holding her tightly to keep her from injuring herself with her antics.

"I cannot fathom you did this for me." She rained kisses on his face. "I love you so much."

"It is the least I can do, to pay penance for my many sins," he drawled. "And I love you too, V."

He'd never grow tired of saying those words. Could never possibly say them enough. He would never quite forgive Pemberton for abandoning Virtue for all her life, but he was damned thankful his old friend had left her in his care. There she would remain, forever.

"Do you think I might have my confinement here?" she asked excitedly, in between kisses sprinkled over his cheeks, jaw, and nose.

He froze, his head jolting back against the silk tabberett

squabs to study his wife's face more thoroughly. "Your confinement?"

Had she just said what he thought she'd said? Hope, foolish and pure and uncontrollable, rose within him.

"Yes." Her smile grew. "I didn't want to tell you before our journey began, because I so desperately wanted to see Greycote Abbey, and I was afraid you would not want me to travel if you knew."

"Damned right I wouldn't have," he growled, feeling instantly protective of the new life beginning within her womb. "Traveling to Nottinghamshire from London is not fit for a lady in a delicate condition."

She kissed him again. "But we are here now."

"Yes, we are." He couldn't keep himself from smiling back at her. His heart was full enough he was reasonably certain it might burst and go flitting about the wilds of Nottinghamshire.

"And you are happy?"

A question this time, her look turning shy.

"Happier than I ever dreamed possible," he told her honestly, his voice breaking beneath the weight of his emotion. "No more secrets between us, however, V."

"You also kept Greycote Abbey a secret from me," she pointed out wryly.

She had him there. "So I did." He kissed her swiftly. "No more secrets from this moment on, then. How is that?"

"Perfect." She kissed him again. "Thank you, thank you, thank you. You are a wonderful husband, and I know you will make the very best papa in all England."

Her praise had his chest swelling, and other parts of him, too. But the carriage swayed to a halt before the front steps of Greycote Abbey just then, and all the servants Virtue had so desperately missed were assembled and awaiting her. With another hasty kiss, she flew off his lap and out the door, leaping to the cobblestones without help and before the blasted step was down.

"V," he called grimly after her. "A lady in a delicate condition ought not to jump and..." She caught her travel pelisse in her hands and shot across the drive. "Run," he concluded lamely.

For, as was often the case, his beloved firebrand was defying him. But as he watched her throw herself into the housekeeper's arms, Trevor William Hunt, sixth Duke of Ridgely, Marquess of Northrop, Baron Grantworth, proud husband of the Duchess of Ridgely and elated future father, knew he wouldn't have it any other way.

∽

THANK you for reading Virtue and Trevor's story! I hope you adored these two and had as much fun reading their delicious happily ever after as I did writing it. If you're wondering what happens next for Pamela and the handsome bodyguard she's been sneaking about with, don't miss *Her Dangerous Beast*, the next book in the Rogue's Guild series, to see these two get their own chance at forever. Read on for an excerpt from their story or get it here now. Stay in touch! The only way to be sure you'll know what's next from me is to sign up for my newsletter here: http://eepurl.com/dyJSar.

I also had fun connecting the Rogue's Guild world to my other series. You may have recognized *Tales About Town* as Lady Octavia's gossip journal from *Sutton's Spinster*. *The Tale of Love* first appeared in The Wicked Winters series. The Duke and Duchess of Montrose find their happiness in *Duke of Debauchery*. The Marquess and Marchioness of Searle appear in *Marquess of Mayhem*. Viscount Torrington and his new viscountess find their own HEA in *Viscount of Villainy*. And last but not least, you may remember

Bellingham and Co. as the shop owned by Tarquin Bellingham in *Sutton's Scandal*. Until next time, happy reading, and don't forget to read the sneak peek of *Her Dangerous Beast*!

Her Dangerous Beast
Rogue's Guild Book 2

Exiled from his country long ago, Theo St. George forged a new life in London's dark and seedy underworld. As a cold-hearted mercenary, he's willing to do anything for a price. But when he accepts a position as bodyguard to a duke in danger, he finds his true opponent in the nobleman's prim and icy sister.

Pamela, Lady Deering, has been forced to accept her brother's generosity after the death of her wastrel husband. One of society's irreproachable pillars, the last thing she needs is to dally with a sinfully handsome bodyguard called Beast. Neither her battered heart nor her good reputation can survive yet another rogue. So why can't she resist him?

Living beneath the same roof, Theo and Pamela are destined to clash. And kiss. And clash some more. But surrendering to their fiery passion has greater consequences than either of them realize. Because when desire turns to love, two hearts and a kingdom are at risk…

Chapter One

Through the crack in the door, he saw toes.

Bare, without the veil of stockings or slippers, illuminated by the warm glow of flickering candles. Against his will, the lack of decorum intrigued him. He took a silent step closer and was rewarded by the sight of trim, well-turned ankles, crossed and peeping from beneath the hem of a white dressing gown. Reminding him he was a man for the first time in...

As long as he could recall.

He should turn around. Leave those beautiful ankles and toes to their solitude. Instead, Theo hovered at the threshold of the Duke of Ridgely's salon, as if his boots were cemented to the hallway Axminster at his feet. The door had been left slightly ajar, and he knew why it had not been firmly closed. The hinges needed oiling. On his earlier midnight pass, he had noted the squeak, a small detail which would have been beneath his notice in his former life, but one he noticed now. The chamber had been empty then, claimed by darkness.

If he didn't know better, he would have sworn he'd conjured this nighttime visitor. But then he heard her talking to herself, mumbling something unintelligible, and he knew she was real.

Who was she?

Who would dare to wander about in her bare feet, inhabiting the duke's divan, lighting his candles? It hardly seemed likely to be a servant, and yet there were only two other females in residence aside from the domestics. One was the duke's ward, and the other his sister. Neither were women Theo ought to linger about, admiring. He was being paid handsomely to guard the duke's London town house. Not to dally with his women.

Theo cleared his throat, making his presence known.

A feminine gasp sounded from within, and the toes and ankles disappeared.

Pity.

He'd rather been enjoying the view.

"Who is there?" demanded the owner of the ankles and toes.

The sharp, crisp, perfect elocution, even tinged with an edge of trepidation, was as pleasant as a warm caress. He had spent most of the years since his exile in London, and he had come to appreciate the English language in all its peculiar accents, so different from his native tongue. There was something about this voice, however, the odd mix of starch and huskiness it possessed, which settled over him. That voice was like sinking into a hot bath after a punishing day on horseback.

"One of the guards, madam," he said, tamping down his unwanted reaction.

Theo flattened his palm on the paneled door and pushed, allowing himself one step over the threshold. Enough to cast his own features into illumination, so that the room's occupant might not be frightened. He was ever mindful of the reason for his presence here at Hunt House—an assassin had attempted to murder the duke in his sleep.

Through the dancing candlelight, he saw her then, standing by the divan she had so recently been occupying, holding a leather-bound folio before her as if it were a shield. She possessed a classical beauty reminiscent of the ancient goddesses captured in the marble sculptures of his homeland. Her unbound, golden hair was bright, even in the shadows, the same color as the rolling wheat fields he remembered from his youth in Boritania.

"A guard?" she repeated, eyes wide, tone wary as her gaze darted about.

With some amusement, he wondered if she was searching for an object which might be used as a weapon against him. Some candlestick with which to bludgeon him.

"One of the guards hired by His Grace," he added, for he did not know how much the duke had revealed to his womenfolk of the danger surrounding him.

Apparently not the necessity for hired protection, judging from her confusion.

Belatedly, Theo offered as elegant a bow as he could

muster, given that it was the darkest depths of the night and he was carrying a pistol, two knives, and ligatures. Reminders this was no social call; his days as a courtier had long since ended. He was a mercenary now, happy to live unfettered by the twin crushing weights of duty and obligation.

His own man.

"Why should Ridgely have hired guards?" she asked. "And why would I not have been informed? I was told of no such amendment to the household, and I am His Grace's sister."

Ah, he had his answer about the mystery goddess's identity. Not the duke's ward, then. But the widowed marchioness, Lady Deering.

"I'm given to understand it's a precaution," Theo said. "As for the rest, I couldn't say, my lady."

Her eyes narrowed on him, and he felt the intensity of her stare to his marrow. They were blue, he realized. The deep, dark blue of the moonlit sea.

"What is your name, sir?" she asked next.

He remained as he was, grave and unsmiling. "They call me Beast."

It was a name he'd earned. A name that was his alone, unlike Theodoric Augustus St. George, the hated appellation of his birth.

"Beast," she repeated, her tone steeped in disbelief.

He inclined his head. "Aye, my lady. Beast."

"I cannot fathom what Ridgely could have been thinking, inviting such a rogue into Hunt House." Her voice possessed the chill of winter ice.

"It would not be for me to guess at His Grace's thoughts," he said simply, humbly, mindful of the man he was now.

Even if there was something about Lady Deering's hauteur that made him wish, for the briefest of fleeting moments, that he could tell her who he truly was. Or rather, who he had been, what seemed as far away as a lifetime ago now. But then he recalled all the reasons why he had left that world behind him, and the instinct faded quickly.

"Why are you wandering about in the night?" asked Lady Deering.

Her suspicions almost amused him. But neither Beast nor Theo had ever had much use for levity.

"I was tasked with protecting Hunt House and its occupants," he answered simply. "I cannot do so if I am sleeping."

She was frowning now, brow furrowed. "Where are you from, sir?"

He kept his expression carefully blank. "London."

Her chin went up. "Before London. Your accent is unfamiliar to me."

No one had remarked upon his accent in years. He'd thought he had lost all traces of his native language, for he had been raised to speak both English and Boritanian. That this woman detected suggestions of his past gave him pause.

"London," he repeated anyway, undeterred.

She tilted her head, considering him in a way he did not like, a way that made him feel as if she saw *into* him, plumbing his very soul for all his secrets. "Why do you lie?"

Because he had to. Because lying about who he was had become as instinctive as breathing. But he wouldn't—couldn't—tell her any of that.

Theo bowed again instead of answering her question. "I dare not linger any longer. If you will excuse me, my lady, I must continue with my task. I bid you good evening."

"You haven't answered me," she pointed out.

He had already pivoted and was making his retreat, holding his tongue. The truth would serve neither of them.

"Wait," she called after him. "Don't go just yet."

And, fool that he was, he paused, casting a glance at her over his shoulder. The candlelight caught in her hair, granting her an ethereal glow, and he had never seen a woman more lovely or tempting than the Marchioness of Deering, barefoot in her dressing gown at half past two in the morning. Theo had a sinking feeling within that, of all the perils he would face in his role as Hunt House bodyguard, none would compare to the maddening heat unfurling within him now, the undeniable danger of desiring a woman who was forbidden to him.

Want more? Get *Her Dangerous Beast* now here!

DON'T MISS SCARLETT'S OTHER ROMANCES!

Complete Book List
HISTORICAL ROMANCE

Heart's Temptation
A Mad Passion (Book One)
Rebel Love (Book Two)
Reckless Need (Book Three)
Sweet Scandal (Book Four)
Restless Rake (Book Five)
Darling Duke (Book Six)
The Night Before Scandal (Book Seven)

Wicked Husbands
Her Errant Earl (Book One)
Her Lovestruck Lord (Book Two)
Her Reformed Rake (Book Three)
Her Deceptive Duke (Book Four)
Her Missing Marquess (Book Five)
Her Virtuous Viscount (Book Six)

DON'T MISS SCARLETT'S OTHER ROMANCES!

League of Dukes
Nobody's Duke (Book One)
Heartless Duke (Book Two)
Dangerous Duke (Book Three)
Shameless Duke (Book Four)
Scandalous Duke (Book Five)
Fearless Duke (Book Six)

Notorious Ladies of London
Lady Ruthless (Book One)
Lady Wallflower (Book Two)
Lady Reckless (Book Three)
Lady Wicked (Book Four)
Lady Lawless (Book Five)
Lady Brazen (Book 6)

Unexpected Lords
The Detective Duke (Book One)
The Playboy Peer (Book Two)
The Millionaire Marquess (Book Three)
The Goodbye Governess (Book Four)

The Wicked Winters
Wicked in Winter (Book One)
Wedded in Winter (Book Two)
Wanton in Winter (Book Three)
Wishes in Winter (Book 3.5)
Willful in Winter (Book Four)
Wagered in Winter (Book Five)
Wild in Winter (Book Six)
Wooed in Winter (Book Seven)
Winter's Wallflower (Book Eight)
Winter's Woman (Book Nine)
Winter's Whispers (Book Ten)

DON'T MISS SCARLETT'S OTHER ROMANCES!

Winter's Waltz (Book Eleven)
Winter's Widow (Book Twelve)
Winter's Warrior (Book Thirteen)
A Merry Wicked Winter (Book Fourteen)

The Sinful Suttons
Sutton's Spinster (Book One)
Sutton's Sins (Book Two)
Sutton's Surrender (Book Three)
Sutton's Seduction (Book Four)
Sutton's Scoundrel (Book Five)
Sutton's Scandal (Book Six)
Sutton's Secrets (Book Seven)

Rogue's Guild
Her Ruthless Duke (Book One)
Her Dangerous Beast (Book Two)

Sins and Scoundrels
Duke of Depravity
Prince of Persuasion
Marquess of Mayhem
Sarah
Earl of Every Sin
Duke of Debauchery
Viscount of Villainy

The Wicked Winters Box Set Collections
Collection 1
Collection 2
Collection 3
Collection 4

Stand-alone Novella

DON'T MISS SCARLETT'S OTHER ROMANCES!

Lord of Pirates

CONTEMPORARY ROMANCE
Love's Second Chance
Reprieve (Book One)
Perfect Persuasion (Book Two)
Win My Love (Book Three)

Coastal Heat
Loved Up (Book One)

ABOUT THE AUTHOR

USA Today and Amazon bestselling author Scarlett Scott writes steamy Victorian and Regency romance with strong, intelligent heroines and sexy alpha heroes. She lives in Pennsylvania and Maryland with her Canadian husband, adorable identical twins, and two dogs.

A self-professed literary junkie and nerd, she loves reading anything, but especially romance novels, poetry, and Middle English verse. Catch up with her on her website https://scarlettscottauthor.com. Hearing from readers never fails to make her day.

Scarlett's complete book list and information about upcoming releases can be found at https://scarlettscottauthor.com.

Connect with Scarlett! You can find her here:
    Join Scarlett Scott's reader group on Facebook for early excerpts, giveaways, and a whole lot of fun!
    Sign up for her newsletter here
    https://www.tiktok.com/@authorscarlettscott

facebook.com/AuthorScarlettScott
twitter.com/scarscoromance
instagram.com/scarlettscottauthor
bookbub.com/authors/scarlett-scott
amazon.com/Scarlett-Scott/e/B004NW8N2I
pinterest.com/scarlettscott

Printed in Great Britain
by Amazon